HAUNTING THE DEEP

ALSO BY ADRIANA MATHER

How to Hang a Witch

HAUNTING THE DEEP

ADRIANA MATHER

ALFRED A. KNOPF
NEW YORK

THIS IS A BORZOI BOOK PUBLISHED BY ALFRED A. KNOPF

Visit us on the Web! randomhouseteens.com

Educators and librarians, for a variety of teaching tools, visit us at RHTeachersLibrarians.com

Library of Congress Cataloging-in-Publication Data
Names: Mather, Adriana, author.
Title: Haunting the deep / Adriana Mather.
Description: First edition. | New York : Alfred A. Knopf, [2017] | Summary: Samantha Mather, fifteen, is having recurring dreams of the Titanic and, while awake, receives strange missives and visions of those who went down with the ship.
Identifiers: LCCN 2017028256 (print) | LCCN 2016056936 (ebook) | ISBN 978-0-553-53951-6 (trade) | ISBN 978-0-553-53952-3 (lib. bdg.) | ISBN 978-0-553-53953-0 (ebook)
Subjects: | CYAC: Supernatural—Fiction. | Ghosts—Fiction. | Magic—Fiction. | Titanic (Steamship)—Fiction. | Ocean liners—Fiction. | Shipwrecks—Fiction. | Family life—Massachusetts—Salem—Fiction. | Salem (Mass.)—Fiction.
Classification: LCC PZ7.1.M3765 (print) | LCC PZ7.1.M3765 Hau 2017 (ebook) | DDC [Fic]—dc23

Printed in the United States of America
October 2017
10 9 8 7 6 5 4 3 2 1

First Edition

For my amazing family,

who have empowered me to dream and

encouraged me to always have a sense of humor.

You all are my heroes.

CHAPTER ONE

Ready to Run

I sip my hot cocoa, not the powdered kind that comes out of a packet, but the shaved-chocolate kind made from scratch. Mrs. Meriwether places a plate of steaming croissants in the middle of my dining room table. They smell like warm butter.

Jaxon grins, poised to take a bite of French toast. "You've got that morning punk-rock thing going on again."

I touch my hair and discover that I do in fact have a cowlick. I smile. "At least I don't have toothpaste on my face."

Jaxon makes no attempt to check if I'm right; he just chews away.

"Sam and Jax—Monday-morning match: round one," my dad says, pouring a second cup of coffee into his #1 DAD mug and looking at Mrs. Meriwether. "I think there's a frightening possibility that our children take after us, Mae. Neighbors, best friends, surly dispositions."

Mrs. Meriwether pats the corners of her mouth with a

white cloth napkin. "The way I remember it, I was mostly an angel. It was *your* mother who had to threaten you with weeding the garden for a month just to keep your slingshot on your lap and off her table," she says.

My dad smiles at her, and I stop chewing. His time in a coma felt like an endless walk down a dark tunnel. I'm sure I'll eventually get used to him just sitting here drinking coffee and smiling. But for these past six months, every minute I've spent with him still feels like borrowed time.

My dad's eyes twinkle with mischief. "Now, we all know it was your slingshot. You're too young for your memory to be slipping. Maybe you should do more crossword puzzles."

Mrs. Meriwether raises her eyebrows. "Be very careful, Charlie, or I'll tell them about the time you tried to prank Ms. Walters. Emphasis on the word 'tried.'" She looks at me and Jaxon. "I believe you know her as Mrs. Hoxley."

"Wait, you pranked my homeroom teacher?" I ask. No wonder she's always eyeing me like I'm about to do something wrong.

My dad shakes his head. He's got that dignified and refined thing about him—gray at his temples, big brown eyes, confident. When he wants to, he can shut the world out behind his stoicism and clean button-downs. But right now he's bright and alive, enjoying himself.

"I definitely want to hear this story," Jaxon says.

My dad checks his watch. "Don't you two need to get ready for school?"

"That bad, huh?" I say, and pick up a forkful of blueberries and whipped cream.

"Why are you wearing boys' clothes?" asks a little girl's voice just behind me. My fork drops with a clang, and a blueberry goes flying, hitting Jaxon smack in the face. I whip around in my chair.

A girl about ten years old stands a couple of feet away from me in an old-fashioned pink dress. Her brown hair is braided and tied with ribbons. She giggles, scrunching her dark eyes and small nose together as the blueberry sticks to Jaxon's cheek. No one else is laughing but her.

Jaxon wipes his face and stares at me without looking in the girl's direction. My skin goes cold. *He doesn't see her.* I shut my eyes for a long second and take a breath, turning back to the table and away from the girl.

Jaxon, Mrs. Meriwether, and my dad all watch me with matching worried expressions.

"Is everything okay?" Mrs. Meriwether asks.

My hands shake, and I put them under the table. "Um, yeah."

"Are you sure, Sam? You look spooked," my dad says, all his good humor replaced with concern.

I glance behind me; the girl's gone. My shoulders drop an inch. "I thought I heard something."

My dad frowns. "What?" We've only talked once about what happened while he was in a coma. And I only told him selective pieces. How Vivian sold our New York City apartment and lied about his medical bills. How when I found out she was lying, she threatened my friends to manipulate me. How when she realized I wouldn't do what she wanted, she tried to kill us with spells. And how those spells backfired on her. Mostly, he just listened with his eyebrows pushed forcefully together. When I finished, he had tears in his eyes. He told me to get some sleep, and he kissed me on the forehead. He doesn't know how many people she killed. And I left out all the magical elements I could. Every time I said "spell," he flinched like someone had burned him. There was so much guilt on his face that I hated telling him even the pared-down version. He hasn't brought it up since. And I'm grateful, because I can't stand being reminded that I lied to him. That was the first time I ever did.

"Just a noise," I say, and look down at my plate. A second lie.

"A ghost noise or a people noise?" Mrs. Meriwether asks.

My dad stiffens at the word "ghost." Mrs. Meriwether and Jaxon know I saw Elijah, but he's one of those details I never mentioned to my dad. How would I even start? *Hey, Dad. I fell in love with this dead guy from the sixteen hundreds who was stubborn and beautiful. And then he disappeared and I had a crap time getting over him.*

"I don't know," I say. "Maybe I imagined it."

Mrs. Meriwether turns to my dad. "I really think she needs some training, Charlie. Otherwise, it's just a loosey-goosey free-for-all. What happens when she learns to drive? What if a ghost appears in the seat next to her?"

I sit straight up, every muscle in my body ready to run away from this conversation. Did Mrs. Meriwether tell my dad about me seeing Elijah? Or did he hear the rumors in town? How could I be so stupid to think this would all just go away?

My dad stares at me with such seriousness that everyone gets quiet, waiting on his reaction. "Sam, did you see something just now?"

"No," I say, doing my best to keep my anxiety out of my voice.

My dad's home from the hospital, the kids in school don't hate me, and with Vivian gone, my bad luck has basically vanished. *Vivian.* My stomach tenses. All I want is for things to stay normal; I'm happy for the first time in a long time.

My dad looks from Mrs. Meriwether to me. "Then why is Mae worried about a ghost appearing in your passenger seat?"

I push my plate away, avoiding the matching sympathetic

looks from the Meriwethers. The words don't want to leave my mouth. "I saw a spirit during the whole thing that happened last fall." My cheeks redden. "But I haven't seen one since." *I'm not seeing spirits again. I won't. Elijah was different. He . . . he was just different.*

The corners of my dad's eyes wrinkle as he narrows them.

"Be sure to let us know if you do," Mrs. Meriwether says. "The last time you saw a ghost, a whole set of unfortunate circumstances followed."

My eyes meet hers. Is she saying that seeing a spirit is a bad omen?

"No more talk of . . . no more talk of training, Mae. She's fine," my dad says with such finality that Mrs. Meriwether raises a questioning eyebrow.

"I'm gonna go get dressed," Jaxon says, sounding almost as uncomfortable as I feel and sliding his chair away from the table.

"Me too," I say with a grumble.

My dad leans back in his chair, and the tension rolls off him. "Aaah. Now, there's the cranky morning Sam I know and love."

I pause, soaking up his dad humor. He's said some version of this to me since I was little. "Don't do that. I can't make anyone believe I'm angsty if I'm smiling."

We share a smile, and I can tell he's relieved to have changed the subject.

I push back my chair, but what I really want to push away is Mrs. Meriwether's comment about the last time a spirit showed up.

CHAPTER TWO

———

After the Hanging

I'm the last one into homeroom. I slide into my desk beside Susannah just as the bell rings. Susannah, Mary, and Alice sit in a row, all wearing their trademark gothic-chic clothes. I wear black, too, but more torn and casual than their high fashion. Plus, they have that whole powerful, mysterious vibe that makes you want to compulsively steal glances at them. Maybe it's because they're descended from the accused Salem witches and I'm descended from the stodgy Puritan minister, Cotton Mather, who hanged them.

Susannah flashes me a smile and places her slender, black-nail-polished fingers over mine. When she pulls her hand away, there's a small note tucked under my palm. I don't know where this girl gets her stealth, but I'm definitely jealous.

Mrs. Hoxley clears her throat. "Quiet for the morning announcement, please." She pauses until everyone settles. "It's April fourth and two weeks until the Spring Fling. The student council has tallied the votes for this year's theme and is ready to officially announce it." She squints at one of the well-manicured girls in the back of the room. "Blair, if you'll do the honors."

Excited whispers fill the room. I've never seen people campaign as viciously as they did for the themes of this dance. For the past week the Borgias Masquerade Ball and the Enchanted Forest supporters have been practically fist-fighting in the halls. But then again, costume parties are to Salem what Christmas is to the North Pole. I'm desperately hoping the Enchanted Forest doesn't win, though. The attention I got right after the whole hanging-in-the-woods ordeal was overwhelming. I'm pretty sure a forest theme would only bring up the topic again.

The Descendants haven't really said anything specific about what happened, claiming shock and confusion. But the basic details about a mysterious woman trying to kill us all spread through the town faster than I could have imagined. And the only thing that doesn't seem to die in Salem is gossip. The police are still searching for her; little do they know the crow woman was my stepmother, and she's dead.

Everyone turns to look at Blair, who's taking her sweet time sauntering to the front of the class. She leaves a scent trail of vanilla and hair spray, and her outfit suggests she just stepped out of the pages of a Ralph Lauren catalog.

"I'm thrilled to share this with you all." Blair flicks her blown-out waves over her shoulder and scans the room. "While there were *very* strong themes this year, one stood out above the rest and got an almost unanimous vote."

"It was yours, wasn't it?" Alice says. "The idea that won."

Blair's smile grows and she looks coy. "We're not supposed to reveal who came up with what theme, Alice. Buuut, I wasn't *opposed* to the idea."

"Uh-huh," Alice says. "Well, good thing you're so subtle, then."

I cough out a laugh, and Mrs. Hoxley gives Alice a warning look. Now that I'm not fighting with the Descendants, I can appreciate Alice's dry humor. No one's exempt from her scorn.

"Let's just say I'm excited to announce that the theme of this year's dance will be . . ." Blair pauses for dramatic effect. "The *Titanic!*"

The room explodes with objections. Everyone starts yelling at once. The tension leaves my shoulders. *Phew.*

"You're joking," Mary says. "The *Titanic* wasn't even in the running."

"Democracy's dead," Alice says. "The dictatorship of Blair and the fluff-ettes is now a disturbing reality."

"Shush," Mrs. Hoxley says to the class. "We'll have none of that. Absolutely none."

Blair doesn't react. In fact, she looks increasingly smug. "There's more. Since the dance committee supervisor is also the head of the history department, the other history teachers have agreed to rearrange their lesson plans and teach a *Titanic* curriculum for the next two weeks. Plus, the dresses are gonna be *amazing.*"

Blair squeals with excitement and heads toward her desk. She stops dramatically in front of Matt, Salem High's new British exchange student, who's leaning into the aisle going through his backpack and blocking her way.

"Um . . . *hellooo?*" Blair says.

He makes no effort to move. "You know you can fit past me, right? Or were you just sayin' 'ello?" Matt says in his Cockney accent.

Blair's jaw tenses. "So much for being a dance committee member, Matt. You're not even paying attention!"

He pulls out the pen he was looking for from his backpack and peers up at her. "Sorry, what'd ya say?"

"Ugh. Forget it." Blair walks past him, and he smiles to himself.

I smile, too. I have to admit, I've enjoyed watching the drama between him, Blair, and Niki these past few months. Not only because the rumors that Niki mail-ordered herself a boyfriend have taken attention away from my situation, but because Matt's living with Blair, and their bizarre trio has spawned soap-opera-style fights in the middle of the hallway. I've never seen anything like it. He looks up and catches me staring at him, and I immediately turn back to the front of the class.

"Okay, enough. The theme is the *Titanic* and that's it. Stop chattering and get to work," Mrs. Hoxley says.

I open Susannah's note under my desk and discover it isn't from Susannah at all.

> *Meet us by the bleachers after school.*
> *We need to talk. Don't even think about*
> *saying no.*
> *Alice*

I knew they would want to talk at some point; I just wasn't expecting it to be today. I haven't spent time with the Descendants since everything happened. I was in bed for a few weeks recovering. After that, my dad was my priority. But to be honest, I'm not ready to talk about the woods. I actually hope to *never* discuss what happened. Thinking about Vivian hurts in ways I haven't sorted out yet.

I look past Susannah to Alice, and her black-outlined blue eyes challenge me. Sometimes I wonder if they're made of ice instead of normal eyeball material. I lean toward her. And as I do, the young girl from this morning appears in front of me. My face almost collides with her dress.

"What the . . . ?" I jerk backward, and my reaction is so sudden that I half slide off my seat and have to grab my desk to keep from landing on the floor. She disappears.

I pull myself back into my chair. The entire class, including Mrs. Hoxley, watches me. *It doesn't mean anything. Nothing. Nada. It's a fluke.*

"Spider," I say, and Mrs. Hoxley's face wrinkles up. "A big hairy one," I add.

Mary looks suspiciously at the ground. "So *not* a spider fan."

The other students look, too, lifting their feet and backpacks. Everyone except Susannah, who stares pointedly at me. I avoid her eyes.

The bell rings.

"I can't meet today," I say to the Descendants.

Susannah frowns. "Can't or won't?" She pulls on a black Victorian jacket over her floor-length black dress.

"I have to go home after school."

"Then we'll walk you to your house," says Alice, pushing her straight blond hair away from her face like it was intentionally bothering her.

I press my lips together and exhale. "Fine, I'll meet you. But I can't talk for more than ten minutes."

Mary stands up. "Are you mad at us?"

"No. Not at all." I stand up, too. "I'm just, well . . . I don't want to talk about what happened."

"Well, good, 'cause neither do I," Alice says. "These two won't shut up about it, and I need a break."

"I can't help it that I get nightmares," says Mary, and crosses her arms. Her dark curls bounce lightly with the motion.

"Oh." Maybe this isn't about the woods after all? "What's this about, then?"

"Just . . . trust us," Susannah says. She looks at the straggler students who haven't made their way out of the classroom. They grab their bags and head for the door.

"How much do you want to bet the history department finagled the dance theme decision?" Mary says to Alice as they exit.

I pick up my black bag and shove my notebook in it. Something shiny inside reflects the overhead light. In the bottom of my bag is a strange metal rod with a hooked end, like some kind of old-fashioned crochet needle. I've never seen it before. I scan the room. Nothing's amiss. *Maybe it belongs to Mrs. Meriwether? Could I have accidentally put it in here when I packed my books up this morning?*

I slap my bag closed and head into the hallway. I'm still amazed that people aren't recoiling from me. They're not exactly talking to me, either, but it's a definite improvement.

A shoulder collides with mine. I jump.

Jaxon laughs and hooks his callused thumb under his backpack strap. His sandy hair is slightly messy, and his demeanor exudes its usual enviable confidence. His blue eyes dance with mischief. "Daydreaming about me?"

I laugh, too. "You wish."

He opens the door to Mr. Wardwell's AP History class for me. "I do wish."

I look at him for a second. Was he joking or flirting? These past six months Jaxon and I have just been friends— best friends, really. He gave me my space when I asked for it after the woods and after Elijah left. He even accepted my story that Vivian was after my dad's money and that's why she ran off when my dad woke up from his coma.

I take my usual seat next to him in the back. "Truth? I was just thinking about how glad I am that I'm no longer the cursed girl. Now I'm just the weirdo everyone thinks sees dead people. Yay, me."

"For Salem you're actually doing some fast social climbing. I'm pretty sure clairvoyant is only a couple of positions below mayor."

I smile. "Oh yeah? Well then, give me a few years and I'll be running this town."

"You're telling me. I've already started making my list of requests for when you take office." He pauses. "Speaking of weirdness, what was that this morning at breakfast, anyway?"

I shrug like it was nothing, trying to convince myself as much as him. "Is it cool if we don't talk about it? People only recently stopped staring at me with that concerned look."

Jaxon hesitates like he wants to say something, then shakes his head and smiles instead. "As long as you don't start flying around on a broom, I'm good."

Mr. Wardwell lays a few papers on my desk. He's sporting one of his usual tweed blazers. "Some of your makeup work. I still have a few items to grade, and then we can decide what to do about those two missed exams."

I nod.

The bell rings.

Mr. Wardwell makes his way to his desk and turns toward the class. "Monday really is the best day, isn't it? A full week of history to explore before the weekend."

There are a few grumbles. I look at Lizzie's empty seat and sigh. I can't help but feel partly responsible that she's gone. She was the fourth Descendant, and she had a harder time dealing with what happened than any of us did. She left right after the hanging, and I heard she goes to a boarding school in upstate New York now.

"As you all learned in homeroom this morning, we history teachers are making room in our lesson plans to include the *Titanic*. As head of the history department, I'm also working with the dance committee and the faculty to make the next two weeks immersive and fun. You're all in for a real treat. It's a fascinating moment in history, ladies and gents. One where approximately fifteen hundred women, children, and men died in an avoidable tragedy." He talks about mass death the same way some people say they won the lotto.

"When the *Titanic* set sail from England on her maiden voyage in April of 1912, she was the biggest and the most opulent passenger steamship in the world. She was eight hundred eighty-three feet long and was described as a floating city of lights. From the first heated swimming pool to the inlaid mother-of-pearl paneling, the *Titanic* offered passengers every luxury they could dream of . . . except enough lifeboats to save them."

CHAPTER THREE

We All Have Nightmares

I click my locker shut and check my phone. I already have a text from Jaxon.

Jaxon: *With Dillon. Be there in a min.*

Me: *I've actually got some things to take care of. Don't wait for me to drive home.*

I shove my phone into my pocket and head down the hall toward the sports fields. I push the back door of the school open and almost walk into Niki.

"Hey, Sam." She readjusts her navy purse on her cashmere-covered shoulder.

I stop short. She never talks to me.

"Sorry I almost hit you with the door," I say.

Niki waves off my apology. "Actually, I wanted to ask you something. . . . Do you know if Jaxon is dating anyone?"

I blink at her. "'Scuse me?"

"It's just you're *always* with him," she says, like it's a bad thing. "I figured you would know."

I honestly have no idea how to respond to her. Is she asking me to not hang out with my best friend so she can flirt with him or something? I decide to shift the focus back to her. "What about you and Matt?"

"Over it." Niki twirls a gold bracelet around her wrist. "So if you could just—"

"Piss off, Niki," Alice says from behind me. "Sam isn't going to do jack for you."

Niki narrows her eyes.

Alice grabs my arm and pulls me into the field. The chilly breeze carries the scent of freshly cut grass and the promise of spring.

I look at Alice as we walk. "So you and Niki are close, huh?"

Alice shrugs. "Yeah, we have that thing going where we spend so much time together that we've started to look alike."

I laugh.

Susannah and Mary stand behind the bleachers, black gothic silhouettes against the tree line. Susannah smiles, and her delicate face lights up.

"So what's all the mystery about?" I ask as we approach them. My words sound disjointed. The only times we've spoken, we've had the type of conversation where one person starts to talk, then realizes they don't know what to say, and the whole conversation dissolves.

For a second everyone is still; even the breeze stops blowing.

Mary breaks the silence. "We need you to talk to the dead."

I frown.

"Mary!" Susannah says, and Alice gives Mary the stink-eye. "We're not asking you to come see if our attic is haunted. Mary spoke too soon. The thing is, Alice read her bones yesterday for the first time since V—"

I put my hand up before she can finish Vivian's name. "Don't. You said you wouldn't. And truthfully, I just want to forget all about magic."

"Well, tough," Alice says. "Because you were in my reading, and so you're part of the message I got, whether you like it or not. Chin up, chest out. It's time."

Is she criticizing me for not bouncing back fast enough from almost being *hanged* by my stepmother? "It's not time. I'm absolutely fine living the rest of my life never being in a situation like that again." I back away from them by two steps.

"So you're saying you won't listen to what we have to say, even if we need you to help prevent something bad from happening?" Alice asks.

I hesitate for a half second and then shake my head.

"Wait, Samantha," Susannah says. "We know this is hard for you, but none of us are having an easy time recovering from what your stepmother did. We were right there with you through that whole awful thing, and we almost died, too."

There it is. The truth. "You said we weren't going to talk about V . . ." Her name sticks in my throat.

Mary tugs at her curls. "Guys, she's not ready yet."

"Seriously, Mare?" Alice says, like she can't believe Mary is still talking.

Susannah closes the space between us with a few graceful steps, blocking my view of Mary and Alice. She's so gentle and confident that it makes it impossible to brush her off without feeling guilty.

Susannah looks at me now like she just wants me to understand her. "There isn't a morning I wake up and look in the mirror that I don't still see the faint red mark from the rope on my neck. We all think about it. We *all* have nightmares." Her voice is calm. "We don't need to talk about that night specifically. But we need to talk to you about this because it's important. You trusted me once; trust me again."

I want to walk away, but I can't seem to break eye contact with her. I exhale audibly. *Please don't let me regret this.* "Okay, Alice. I'm listening."

Alice gestures toward the woods. "After you."

We walk through the trees until we're hidden from any stragglers hanging out in the back fields. Mary pulls out a black wool blanket and spreads it on the ground.

I reluctantly sit down next to them. The blanket looks like the same one we used when I did the clarity spell with them.

Alice pulls her hair into a ponytail. "Despite what you may think, Sam, none of us are ready to deal with the outside world right now. Personally, I'd like to spend the rest of the year with nothing more serious to think about than what I'm going to wear to the Spring Fling. And if I never hear the dopes in our school gossiping about the shreds of misinformation they have from that night, it will be too soon." She twirls a leaf between her fingers. "We haven't even attempted magic. The *only* reason I read my bones yesterday was to convince Mary that all threats had passed. You have no idea how many times in a row she can ask the same damn question."

Mary rests her head theatrically on Alice's shoulder. "You would be lost without me and you know it."

"Anyway," Alice says, pushing Mary off her shoulder. "My reading told me exactly nothing about our previous situation. Instead, I—"

"Found out something bizarre," Mary says. Susannah and Alice both look at her. "What? We don't know for sure that it's something *bad.*"

"The bones said you need to join our circle," Alice says. "And don't get your back up thinking we're just using you to be the fourth person for a spell or something. I can see the wheels turning in that brain of yours."

An image of Lizzie's empty chair flashes through my thoughts. Nothing good comes from magic.

"Alice's reading also said that someone's coming." Susannah makes eye contact with me, gauging my response as she speaks. "And we got the message that if we don't work together, we'll be like the wanderer. Darkness will be over us, and our rest will be a stone."

Alice tosses the leaf. "No more information than that. No matter how many times I cast them, they came up with the same riddle."

I press my fingers into my forehead. "Please tell me that means we'll be traveling and not that one of us is going to die. 'Rest will be a stone' sounds morbid as hell."

Susannah tightens her lips. "We don't know. As Alice said, we haven't done a reading since the fall. We don't know what we may have missed." She pauses. "Have you seen anything odd, anything at all?"

I make eye contact with her. "Like what?"

"Like spirits," she says, and I look away. Damn Susannah's ability to read people.

I stand up. I can't do this. I've only recently started sleeping well again. "I'm sorry, but I can't be part of your circle. If you want to go to the movies or something, cool. But if it's about magic, just . . . no."

I walk away before they can respond.

—————

CHAPTER FOUR

About That Night
That Everything Happened

I trip walking up my uneven brick driveway. *Awesome.*

"Samantha!" Mrs. Meriwether says, loading a stack of beautifully tied pastry boxes into her truck bed. She waves me over. "How was school? No more weird noises today, I hope."

"Nope."

She searches my face. She looks like she wants to say something more, but decides against it.

I take a step toward my door and stop. "Just curious, but does my dad ever ask you about that night that everything happened?"

She tilts her head, considering my question. "Your dad has always been the silent, stoic type, even when we were kids. One summer he fell out of a tree and broke his finger. The thing swelled up to the size of a plantain, but he refused to admit that it hurt. In fact, he climbed right back up that tree and jumped out, just to prove it couldn't get the best of him."

She raises a knowing eyebrow at me. "Now, I have to get to the bakery with these new recipes I was experimenting with. But anytime you feel like chatting, you just come on over."

I open the side door to my house. "I will." But I probably won't.

The house is quiet. "Dad!"

"In the ballroom!" His voice comes from down the hall to the right of the stairs. I close the door and speed-walk in the direction of the sound. We're calling the room with the piano and the uncomfortable-looking old furniture the ballroom?

I step through the door, and I instantly relax at the sight of him, alive and healthy.

I avoid looking at the painting of Abigail that hangs at the other end of the room. In fact, I haven't come in here since Elijah left. All I see when I look at Abigail is eyes just like his, eyes that I miss. And I don't want to miss them. No magic. No thinking about Elijah.

My dad stands by a set of white silk couches and looks up at the high ceiling.

"What are you doing?"

"Just looking around this old place," he says, and smiles. "You know this room was never quiet when your grandmother was alive." He gestures toward an antique record player. "There was always music and hordes of ladies having tea and playing bridge."

I smile, too. "The way you used to describe her, I thought that Grandma didn't have many friends."

"Not when she got older, no. But when I was young and my father was still alive . . ." His voice trails off without completing his sentence. "You would think this place would be too big for just the three of us, but Mom always filled it somehow. She would be severely disappointed if she saw how we never use this room now."

I watch him as he sits down on the couch near the fireplace. He hasn't talked about Grandma since our conversation about what happened in the woods. Does this mean he's going to want to talk about that now, too? He pats the cushion next to him, and I choose the side that keeps my back to the painting.

He watches me. "What would you think about moving back to New York?"

What? "Leave Salem? Is this because of my sleep? I was having a hard time right after . . . but it's way better, I swear. I'm sleeping through the night now." My words come out faster than I intended.

His forehead knits in concern. "I'm not saying we should go. I'm just checking on you. I want to make sure you're happy. I know you have friends here."

"At least one."

He smiles. "The way Jaxon tells it, the whole school's fascinated with you."

"Don't believe him. He's an optimist. It's more like they don't clear out when I enter the hall." I look up at my dad. "But seriously, I really like it here."

"I just want to make sure it's the right choice. If this place is unhealthy for you, then we'll go."

"Funny enough, I feel more myself here than I ever have. And one friend is more than none."

He nods. "I can do my business from Salem almost as well as I could from New York. I don't plan on traveling for a while longer anyway."

He puts his arm around me, and I lean my cheek into his shoulder, breathing in his familiar musky aftershave.

He chuckles to himself.

"What?"

"I was just thinking how much your mother hated those parties your grandmother threw."

"She came to them?"

"Her mother made her. And my mom had a strict dress code, as you might imagine by the decor in this house, and both of our mothers made her conform to it. I used to watch your mom stomp around the lunching ladies and purposefully pull curly strands out of her own braid. By the time the parties were over, her hair would be sticking out every which way, and there would be at least four holes in her tights. Once, she even spilled a cup of tea on herself in order to go home, only to find out my mother had a spare dress her size."

It's weird how much I don't know about my mom. "Were you guys dating then?"

"Nooo." He laughs again. "It took me all of our teenage years to persuade her to go out with me. And a whole year in a relationship for her to stop calling me 'Charles the fancy.'"

"It's been forever since we talked about Mom."

He stares at the fireplace. "This place brings up a lot of old memories."

"Is that why you always stayed away? Because of Mom's memory?" I hesitate. "All those times I bugged you to visit Salem . . ."

He nods against my head. "At first, yes. But then it was because your grandmother was convinced that your mother's death was part of a curse. She wouldn't let it go. It became an unpleasant topic. We started fighting and drifting. I didn't want her spreading her ideas to you. I was trying to protect you." He stiffens slightly. "Meanwhile, I was the one who put you in danger by marrying—" He stops just before he says Vivian's name.

I pull back and look at him. "Dad, don't do that. Please don't blame yourself." This is why I can't ever tell him the full extent of what she did. It's bad enough that he knows she tried to hang me and put him in that spell-induced coma. If he knew he'd gone straight into the arms of the very person who killed my mother and my grandmother, I don't know what he'd do.

He ruffles my hair. "Don't worry about me. You've got enough going on right now." He stands up. "You hungry? Mae brought over a box of her spring pastries. They're little flowerpots made out of chocolate, mousse, and meringue."

I stand up. "I definitely need to eat that."

"I thought you might."

We make our way into the hallway, and the old floorboards creak. The familiar faces of our ancestors look out from the portraits lining the walls. I wish my grandmother was still alive to tell me their stories. I find her handwritten note cards describing family furniture all over the house and shoved in the back of drawers with old diaries, but it's not the same.

I scan each portrait as we pass, some beautiful, some old and serious-looking. Wait.

I stop abruptly. This can't be right. "Dad?"

He stops, too. "Yes, sweetie?"

"This painting." I point at the woman in a formal gown. A chill runs down my arm, raising all the hairs as it goes. "There was a man in it."

My dad's eyebrows push together. "I don't understand."

There was a man in it, I'm sure of it. She was standing and he was sitting. And now she's still standing but he's gone. "Don't you remember a man being in it?" My voice rises.

He frowns. "This painting's new. Well, not new, but I don't remember seeing it displayed when I lived here. Mom must've brought it down from the attic at some point."

"Oh." I pull my hair over my shoulder. "You know what? I could be wrong. There are so many paintings in this place, and I haven't really been down this hallway in a while. I may have gotten it confused." More than anything, I want that concerned look to disappear from my dad's face. "Whoever she is, she's beautiful."

He nods. "By her clothes, I'd bet she lived in the early nineteen hundreds or so."

I study her big hat and proud expression. "Do you know who she is?"

"If I had to guess, I'd say she might be one of our extended relatives. I seem to remember Mom saying they were from New York. I think some of them survived the *Titanic*. But I really don't know much more than that."

Titanic? "That's interesting."

CHAPTER FIVE

They Were Warnings

The hum of the ocean at night relaxes me. I grip the banister and look fifty feet below at the white foam kicked up from the bow. Brightly lit portholes extend down the length of the large ship, twinkling like Christmas lights on the endless water.

I scan the deck behind me. A beautifully dressed young couple chat quietly a ways down the railing. And three men in suits and top hats walk toward a door, smoking cigars and talking loudly. A butler opens it for them. I follow, but the door closes just as I reach it.

I peer in the window and my mouth drops. The walls are adorned with elaborate molding, and chandeliers dot the ceiling. Men and women play cards and drink out of crystal glasses. The women's dresses remind me of the lady in the painting I was looking at with my dad.

I take a quick step away from the door. There's something I don't like about this place, something I want to remember but can't. It's like trying to stick a pin in a drop of mercury. Everything's foggy.

I walk toward the railing. In my path, on the deck, lies the painting from my hallway. Next to it is a green silk evening gown and a silver book the size of a playing card. These definitely weren't here a second ago. I step around them and move toward the water. The wind whips my hair. I have this strong urge to leave. I lift my leg to climb up the railing, but my ankle feels like it's tethered by a fifty-pound weight.

My eyes open, and I'm gripping the air in front of me. My right leg's raised high, straining against my thick blankets.

Someone laughs, and I sit bolt upright, blinking at the bright light streaming through my window.

Jaxon stands just inside my door, wearing blue plaid pajama pants and a navy-blue hoodie. "Sorry, I did knock before I came in." He laughs again. "I didn't know you slept with all your arms and legs in the air like that."

"Jaxon?" I take a deep breath. *I'm back in my bedroom.*

"Yes, Sam?"

I throw back my covers. "What time is it?"

"Late. Breakfast's ready. The parents sent me up to get you."

"Your house or mine?"

"Yours." He hesitates. "You okay? You look a little, I don't know, upset?"

"Yeah." I rub the corners of my eyes. "Bad dream."

He nods. "Want me to stay? I'll tell you funny stories and make you forget about it."

I look at Jaxon, with his messy hair and inviting smile. I shake my head. "Thanks, though. I'll be down in a minute."

Jaxon lingers for a second and walks out of my room.

I slide out of bed and slip my feet into black fuzzy slippers. My *Titanic* history homework sits on my vanity, where I left it last night. I freeze. *The luxurious ship, the old-fashioned people.* I grab my phone and type "Titanic lounge" into the search bar.

One of the first pictures to pop up is an exact match for

the room I saw through the window. But I've never seen this room before. How could I get it right in my dream if I didn't know what it looked like? I flip through my *Titanic* homework just to be sure. There's no lounge picture. Dreaming about it makes sense, but exactly replicating it is just . . . strange. *Unless . . .*

I throw my phone onto my bed and backstep. *Unless, it's like those other dreams, the ones I had of Cotton. Only those weren't really dreams at all; they were warnings that started right after I saw Elijah for the first time and everything spiraled out of control.* I push my palms against my eyebrows.

And it was only yesterday that I saw that spirit girl. Could Mrs. Meriwether have been right? Was seeing a spirit a sign of bad things to come?

"No. And no. And also no."

CHAPTER SIX

I Just Need It to Stop

M̲y literature teacher, Mrs. Powell, passes out copies of Archibald Gracie's book *The Truth About the Titanic.* Her box braids are swept up into an elegant high bun, and her suspenders and white blouse are way more fashionable than most teachers' pantsuits. She's by far my favorite teacher. She doesn't put up with nonsense from anyone, but she's always fair. And she was one of the few who didn't reflexively turn on me after John died and Lizzie blamed me for it in front of the whole school.

"Colonel Archibald Gracie was cutting the last collapsible boat free from its ropes when the waterlogged *Titanic* lifted into the air," Mrs. Powell says as she makes her way down the rows of desks. "He was pulled down by the suction created from the weight of the ship as it sank, and he was lucky enough to free himself and emerge not far from that same collapsible boat. Unfortunately, it was overturned and covered with men. He and the others hung on all night until one of the lifeboats eventually found them. They were in the Labrador Current at the time, and the water was no more than twenty-eight degrees."

Mrs. Powell plops a copy of the book onto my desk. The black-and-white photo of the large ship on the cover reminds me of my dream. I immediately turn it over. The upper left corner is frayed, and I run my thumb over the worn bit.

"This book is not without its faults. You'll find that the third-class passengers are often neglected and that their nationalities are generalized. Keep in mind that this is a first-person telling of what happened. The colonel died in December of 1912 from health complications related to the exposure and hypothermia he suffered in the water. He didn't live to see this book published."

The bell rings.

"Remember, if you keep a journal about your reading progress, you get thirty points extra credit. Some of you are in desperate need of those points," Mrs. Powell says as everyone stands up.

I shove the book into my bag and head into the hall. There's no way I'm reading this thing. From now on I'm steering clear of all things *Titanic,* avoiding the painting in the hall, and definitely not going to the dance. *Done and done.*

I twist my combination lock and open my locker. Blair passes with a group of girls.

"Hey, Sam," Blair says, and stops.

"Hey?" First Niki talked to me, and now Blair?

"Sooo, I wanted to ask you about something."

Oh man, not this. Her long lead-in is a dead giveaway. "Is it about someone in your family who died?"

Blair's face lights up. "How did you know that? That's crazy. The thing is, my dog died a few years ago. And ever since then my mom keeps finding these unexplainable holes in her garden. You know, almost like someone or something was digging, and she *swears*—"

"I'm sorry, but I can't."

"You haven't even heard the question yet."

Damn that school assembly where I announced that I could see spirits. Anywhere else, people would think I was off my gourd, but here they all think I should come check out their attics and basements for dead grandparents and stray cats. "I know. I'm sorry, but I just can't."

Blair crosses her arms, and for a second we just stand there in awkward silence. "Any new leads on who attacked you in the woods?"

I turn away from her and take my lunch bag out of my locker. *Please just let this whole topic go.* "Not that I've heard of."

Blair plays with her hair. "I can't believe you guys got hanged and this mystery woman is just gone. It's so wrong. And my dad was saying that the police aren't even looking anymore. Like it's okay to just leave that psycho out there."

"So wrong," the group parrots.

People talk about the worst thing that's ever happened to me like it's nothing more than entertaining gossip. I slam my locker shut.

I turn away from them and head down the hall.

Blair snickers behind me. "Wow, someone's in a mood."

I pick up my pace and make a fast left around a corner, walking smack into someone wearing an old-fashioned suit and a hat. *The butler from my dream.* I scream and stumble backward.

He lifts his head and his hat, revealing a grinning Dillon. "Whoa, sorry, Sam."

I exhale.

"Dude, you look like you saw a ghost. Oops. You do see

ghosts. I guess that actually makes sense." Dillon laughs at his own joke.

My chest drops a little farther from my chin and I take a breath. "Nah, I just wasn't looking where I was going. What's with the suit anyway?"

"Trying out costume options for the dance." A piece of his red lacrosse jacket peeks out from under his suit jacket.

I manage a smile. "That doesn't sound like you."

He briefly breaks eye contact. "Girlfriend. She thought my last costume choice was total shit. 'Scuse me . . . was 'not up to standard.'" He uses his fingers to make quotation marks.

"Aaah. Well, this one works. Very authentic."

"Really?" He's all smiles.

"Dillon!" Blair squeals from down the hall. "I *looove* it!"

Oh, you've got to be kidding me. He's dating *her*? So disappointing. And it's weird that Jaxon didn't tell me.

"See ya," I say, but his attention has already shifted.

I push open the side door and follow the walkway toward the bench that's my current favorite lunch spot.

I glide for a split second on wet grass cuttings. The concrete squares ahead of me have a trail of watery footprints. And at the end of them is a guy in an old suit, not unlike the one Dillon was wearing. He sits on my usual lunch bench with his head tilted down, a hat covering his face.

"Let me guess, you're friends with Blair and Niki."

No answer. He doesn't even look up.

"Seriously, the dance isn't for another two weeks. You guys can chill out with the costumes." Plus, this is my lunch spot. I feel strangely territorial over it.

He stands up, his hat shadowing his eyes. There's thick stubble on his chin. He's older, I realize, maybe early twenties. I take a quick step backward. The wooden bench where he was sitting is wet. He's dripping water. *Salt water.* I can smell the brine on the breeze. It feels like the temperature dropped twenty degrees.

Behind him Niki and Matt head down the path toward us. They seem to be arguing about something. Niki walks right through the drenched man's body. Dread coils around me like a boa constrictor.

Matt and Niki take note of my expression. Matt looks confused.

I sprint toward the school.

"Sam?" Niki says, but I don't turn around.

I run through the hallways toward the one place I know is full of people.

I burst through the double doors and into the crowded lunchroom. There's an explosion of chatter. I skid to a stop. Across the room, at a round table near the window, sit the Descendants. People turn and watch as I walk toward them. Blair takes one look at my heavy breathing and starts whispering to her friends. It's like being in an aquarium tank with people oohing and aahing and tapping on the glass.

I drop my bag and pull out a chair at the Descendants' table. "I need to make spirits leave me alone. How do I do that?"

"Well, hello to you, too," Alice says.

"What do you mean, leave you alone?" Mary asks, scanning the nearby area. Her face mirrors my anxiety. She lowers her voice to a whisper. "Are they here now?"

"No, but . . ." I stop, considering how to phrase it. Oh, screw it. There's no sugarcoating this. "I just saw a man in an old-fashioned suit dripping salt water in front of school. Like he walked right out of the ocean after he drowned in it."

Mary's eyes widen. Susannah looks at the nearby tables.

"Okay, get up," says Alice.

"There is no scenario where I'm going back outside right now."

Alice stands, and Mary and Susannah follow suit.

"Do you want our help or not?" Alice asks.

I don't move.

"We're not going outside," Susannah says. "Honest."

I push back my chair, and we make our way out of the lunchroom in a mass of black. There isn't a pair of eyes that doesn't watch us go.

Alice winds us through the halls and stops in front of a nondescript door.

"Got it," Mary says, and it swings open. *Did she pick the lock?*

Susannah looks both ways down the hall. "Go." And we do. We file into the dusty room and close the door behind us.

Alice flips on the light. It's a storage room full of file cabinets. Mary pulls out her black wool blanket and spreads it on the floor. Does she carry that thing everywhere, just waiting for something witchy to pop up?

"How do you guys know about this place?"

Alice shrugs and sits down on the blanket. We all follow.

"How'd you know how to get in?"

Mary opens her mouth. Alice puts a hand on her arm and she shuts it again.

"Why should we tell you anything if you don't want to join our circle?" Alice asks.

"Why should I join your circle if you don't want to tell me anything?"

Alice and I stare at each other.

"You've barely talked to us these past six months," Alice says with a frown.

I hesitate. Did she want me to talk to her? I didn't figure I mattered to her. "I know. I just . . . I needed a little quiet."

Everyone is silent for a beat.

I adjust my position on the blanket. "So can you guys help me make this weird stuff stop happening? Make everything go back to normal?"

"You're a descendant of Cotton Mather living in Salem who can do magic. There's nothing normal about your situation," Mary says.

"Touché," I say.

"Why do you think we always keep to ourselves?" Alice asks.

"You? To look cool," Mary says.

Alice actually smiles. "No, our cool points come from me being so personable."

Mary rolls her eyes.

Susannah's expression is calm and quiet. "When you first moved here, people told you that we cursed you, didn't they?"

I think back to the fall and all the rumors that started then. "Something like that, yeah."

"We don't even *know* how to curse people," Mary says. "And if we did know, we wouldn't."

"We're here to find out what Sam knows, not to tell her our life stories," Alice says.

"Because withholding information worked out so well last time?" I say.

"Samantha's right," Susannah says. "She might not have been talkative these past few months, but we set that precedent. Plus, she's seeing drenched dead people at our school. Do you really think we can wait?"

"Nope," says Mary.

"Fine," Alice concedes, and gestures at Susannah to continue.

Susannah looks at me. "We don't do spells just to do them.

Alice reads bones so we can try to prevent bad things from happening. And my readings of people help keep us from walking into traps."

I look at Mary, and she twists a curl around her finger. "Our families have been casting in Salem for a long time. There's way more going on here below the surface than anyone realizes. We do our part to keep things on the up-and-up."

Susannah nods. "Now, there's obviously something going on with you. Don't bother to try and argue that there isn't. From what Alice's bones say, it's most likely serious. Waiting is a mistake. We might already be late in sorting out whatever it is."

I pull at the hole in the knee of my jeans, considering her words.

Mary leans forward. "What's the problem? You don't want to do magic?"

"That's definitely part of it."

Mary smiles. "Then what did you mean when you asked us to help you stop seeing spirits?"

"I just thought . . . I don't know what I thought. I just need it to stop."

"Magic," Mary says.

Shit. "I guess so."

Mary stands up. "Good. Well, now that that's settled, let's go eat lunch. I'm starving."

Did I just get outsmarted? I stand up, too. "There's no other way?"

"No," Alice says, grabbing the door handle and peering into the hall. "All clear." She opens the door wide.

Only the hall isn't empty. The little girl in the pink dress is standing in it; she's got the same amused expression she wore in my dining room. I slam the door shut.

Alice flinches. "What the hell was that?"

Mary grabs Alice's arm. "Please tell me it isn't the drowned guy."

"No. A girl. Old-fashioned dress." My voice is hushed.

"Wait, you're seeing two ghosts?" Alice looks at Susannah.

There is a small knock on the door. I jump, but no one else reacts. I can tell by their faces that they didn't hear it.

"What can we do?" Susannah asks.

I pace in the small dusty room. "You can come over to my house tonight and help me make this stop."

I take a deep breath and open the door again. The girl leans against the opposite wall, examining the end of her braid. The Descendants follow me out.

"Go away," I say in a low whisper.

"Ada," she says, and drops her braid. "My name is Ada." She frowns at my expression. "Are you mad because I laughed about the blueberries?" She has a British accent.

"No. I just need you to leave."

Ada seems unfazed. "My brother Fredrick has a bad temper, too. His cheeks get red just like yours. Once, he slammed the bedroom door on me. But his sleeve got caught on the latch and he fell, putting a huge hole in it. Papa was furious." Ada giggles.

The Descendants fan out around me, blocking me from view of anyone who might wander into the hall and see me talking to thin air.

I lean down and make my voice stern. "Go away and don't ever come back. I don't want you here."

Her bottom lip trembles. I try not to notice it.

"I only wanted to know if you found my boot hook. Mum will be mad if I lost it. It is the only one we packed to take to America," Ada says with a wavering voice.

To America? How does she not know where she is? I

examine her old-fashioned clothes more carefully. I swallow. "How . . . are you getting to America?"

She wipes at her eyes with the backs of her hands. "The *Titanic*. Papa says it is the largest ship in the world."

My head spins. "And you're here because you're looking for your boot hook?" My voice is less confident than it was a few seconds ago, and my thoughts drift to the hooked metal rod I found in my shoulder bag yesterday. With a shaky hand, I reach into my bag and dig it out.

Ada takes it and disappears. I wish I could disappear, too.

CHAPTER SEVEN

Those Voices

I lie awake in my four-poster bed, which is carved with black-eyed Susans. My phone sits next to me, and I stare at the armoire. I haven't checked to see if Abigail's letters are in the hidden compartment. The possibility that they're there makes me feel like some part of Elijah is still around. And lying here in the dark, I can almost believe that he could blink in.

He would look serious, like he always looked. I would tell him about my dad and about my dream. He would listen and offer advice that I would refuse to take. And every once in a while I would catch him watching me when he thought I wasn't paying attention.

I twist the empty vase on my nightstand, the one he used to put a freshly cut black-eyed Susan in every day.

A text lights up my phone: 12:27 a.m.

Susannah: *Here.*

I grab my flashlight and pull open my bedroom door. My black fluffy slippers mute my footsteps in the hallway, and I'm careful to step around the creaky boards. I head down the carpeted stairs and pause. This is the first time I've ever snuck around my dad.

I tiptoe down the hall, into the kitchen, and stop. Mary, Alice, and Susannah stand on my patio, peering through the window.

"I still don't understand why we couldn't do this at my house," Alice whispers as I open the door. "My parents wouldn't even notice."

I put my finger to my lips and Alice rolls her eyes. They follow me silently to the library. I turn on the flashlight, illuminating the floor-to-ceiling dark wood bookshelves.

"Okay, I need your word you won't say anything about what I'm about to show you," I whisper.

They all nod without hesitation.

I weave around a reading table piled with books and stop at the old fireplace. I guess if there's one thing I can count on these girls for, it's secrecy. I reach into a niche in the brick, grab an iron hook, and pull. The wall paneling to the left of the fireplace pops open to reveal a door. Mary squeals quietly and clamps her hand over her mouth. Susannah smiles.

Alice runs her fingers over the paneling and pushes the door open. "Are you kidding me? You have a secret passageway?" She and the others step through it.

I follow them into the narrow brick hallway, shutting the door behind us and taking a lantern off the wall. I turn the little knob. Flame shoots up inside the old glass, and the bricks glow a warm red.

"I'll go first," I say at normal volume, and hand the flashlight to Susannah. "You want to bring up the rear?"

"Sure thing."

"The steps are steep and twisty," I say. "So no one trip or everyone will go down."

The stairs groan under our feet all the way up into my grandmother's secret study. I haven't been here since everything happened. I can almost see Elijah, with his furrowed brow, bending over a stack of old journals—his black wavy hair falling on his cheeks and a pencil lodged between his teeth while he tries to hold three books at once. It was his study, too.

"This is like something out of an old British manor," Mary says, and runs her fingers along the exposed wooden beams on the sloped walls.

"When did you find this?" Susannah studies the heavy desk piled with papers.

"Not long after I moved in, maybe a day or two. This is where my grandmother kept all those records about the Witch Trials you guys were surprised I knew about."

Alice wipes the dust off an antique candleholder that's perched on a stack of books. "This is definitely worth traveling over here in the middle of the night for."

I open the leather trunk near the wall and take out a cloth-wrapped bundle. The Descendants join me on a faded rug. I pull back the folds of white linen to reveal a well-worn leather book with silver accents.

"You've got to be shitting me. Tell me that's not a spell book." Alice is practically giddy.

I open the cover and flip through the soft handwritten pages, skimming the spell titles as I go. "It's from the late sixteen hundreds."

Alice smacks her knee. "How are you acting all casual about this? You have a secret study and a freaking spell book from the sixteen hundreds!"

Mary laughs. "Wow, Alice, who knew you had such a thing for antiques. I can get you a job in my aunt's antique store if you want. But you'll have to promise not to make out with her armoires."

Susannah and I grin.

"Laugh it up, clowns." Alice points to the spell book. "But *this* is a big deal."

Susannah pushes a piece of wavy auburn hair off of her face. "Where did you get one this old?"

"Elijah found it," I say without looking up.

"The spirit guy? Do you still talk to him?" Mary asks.

I open my mouth, but stop myself before the words *I wish I did* come out. "Okay, I think this one should do it—'Warding Off Unwelcome Spirits,'" I say, pointing to a spell and shaking away my thoughts of Elijah. "Unless you guys have something better."

I place the book in the middle of the rug so that the girls can read it. Alice practically pushes Mary out of the way to get closer.

"This spell's a great choice," Susannah says.

I scan the page. "Good. I'll get these herbs tomorrow from Mrs. Meriwether's garden and we can give it a try."

"I'm not so sure we need to wait until tomorrow," Susannah says, and looks up at me. "There's more than one way to cast spells."

"Ingredients and potions are for when you're first learning. And, well, potions are really handy to have for certain things, like picking locks," Mary says so nonchalantly that I almost think I misheard her.

What are these girls getting into in their free time? An image of Susannah scaling the side of my house six months ago comes to mind.

"With a group of four," Alice says, "also known as a *circle,* you can bypass the ingredients and go straight to the words of the spell. More efficient."

"And eventually, you can cast without either of them. But we're not there yet," Susannah says. "From the skill you showed in the woods, though, I'm not so sure about you."

I brush off her last comment. "So we can try this now?"

"Yes, but . . . ," Alice says.

"But what?"

"But I'm gonna need to come back here and read this entire book," Alice says. "And I want you to reconsider our offer to join our circle. You think I'm asking you to get involved with some mysterious riddle. But my bones never tell me anything unless it's important."

"Oh, I'm definitely going to say yes, now that I know you want to hang out with me for my spell book."

"That's what you took from that? Idiot," Alice says.

Susannah interrupts before I can respond. "We wanted you to be part of our circle before we ever knew about this book. But that doesn't change the fact that we've been searching for one of these since we were ten. The one we use is only from the late eighteen hundreds. Alice just takes it as a sign."

Mary nods.

I look at Alice, who has stubbornly set her jaw. "You can read the book and I'll consider your offer. Let's just do the spell."

Mary pulls out four black candles from her bag and places them around the book. Susannah lights the wicks and I turn off the lantern. The room looks better in candlelight, like it was always meant to be that way.

Alice offers her hands to Mary and Susannah, and we form a circle.

"Read us the words," Susannah says.

I clear my throat. "Lingering spirits old and new, walk the paths that you once drew. Avoid me now and evermore, unless our tales have tangled lore. From now on I will only find the spirits whom I need to mind."

"Again," says Alice, and I repeat the words.

By the third repetition, they say the words with me. Nothing happens.

They all look at me.

"What?" My voice is self-conscious.

"The more you focus and mean the words you're saying, the better it works," Susannah says. "You can't lead a spell if you're apprehensive."

"So stop judging magic and get over yourself," Alice says.

"I . . ." But there's no point. They're right. "Okay."

I take a deep breath and close my eyes for a second. I start the words again and they all join in. Our voices meld together like a song, ethereal and layered. "From now on I will only find the spirits whom I need to mind."

A breeze bursts through the room, but not from a door or window. It swirls around us in circles, lifting our hair as it buzzes past. The pages of the spell book turn by themselves. I squeeze Susannah's hand. Mary's already white-knuckling my other one.

The wind carries pieces of whispering voices, male and female. They murmur, like they're far away. The buzzing intensifies, and our hair swirls more violently. The voices get closer, more precise.

A journey . . . to start . . . help . . . no stopping . . . yet in my dreams I'd be nearer. Yet in my dreams I'd be nearer. They're loud now, verging on wailing. *Yet in my dreams I'd be nearer!*

Mary clamps her eyes shut. The wind is frantic, twisting in and around us, flapping our clothes. Our hands vibrate.

The candles waver, but strangely don't go out. Then all at once, the air whooshes away and there's complete stillness. Our hair settles back around our shoulders.

Mary's eyes widen. "Those voices."

I drop Mary's and Susannah's hands as though I could drop the whole experience.

For a second we all sit there watching the dust settle in the candlelight.

"Are you convinced now that something's going on?" Alice asks.

"You can't be sure what that meant. It could be total nonsense," I say, but my voice betrays me by shaking. "It might have nothing to do with your riddle."

Before I even finish my sentence, the candles go out.

"Alice!" Mary yells.

"Samantha, the lantern," Susannah says quickly.

I pat the rug around me. Something slams onto the floor with a bang. Susannah screams. I catch the edge of the lantern with my hand and turn the knob. The small room lights up.

A book lies open on the floor.

"Maybe it fell off the desk?" Mary says, gripping Alice's wrist so hard I'm sure it hurts.

I close the book, and the black-and-white photo of Archibald Gracie's *Titanic* cover looks back at me. I hold it out for the girls to see. The upper left corner is frayed. My stomach sinks all the way to my toes.

"We got that in literature class today," Alice says.

"This is definitely my copy," I say.

"Were you reading it up here?" Susannah asks.

"No."

"It was a ghost?" Mary asks with a high-pitched voice.

"This spell was supposed to keep spirits away, not attract them," I say, trying to convince them as much as myself.

Alice's brow furrows. "Didn't you read the description? It's supposed to chase away the riffraff, keep you from interacting with every dead person from here to Timbuktu. But there's no way you're gonna avoid the ones you're supposed to see. You could royally screw things up if you did that."

I put the book facedown, hiding the cover.

Susannah studies me. "You know something about this, don't you? Something you're not saying?"

Great. She's reading me again. I make eye contact with her. "I had a dream."

CHAPTER EIGHT

I Need to Talk to You

I peer out my window at the maple tree, whose red buds glow in the early-morning light. My dad woke me up an hour ago. I was crying in a full sweat, and I haven't been able to go back to sleep since.

Gracie's *Titanic* book peeks out of my schoolbag on the window seat. I can't understand how it showed up during a spell for spirits to leave me alone. Was it the spell that moved it, or was Mary right that it was a spirit? Elijah once left a book in the library for me to trip over. It couldn't be him, could it? And yet for just a split second the idea of having Elijah back is thrilling, however far-fetched it might be. My stomach does a quick somersault.

I frown. Didn't I just say I wasn't going to think about him? "I swear, Elijah, if this is you . . . if you've been around and didn't tell me, I'll be . . . I will *not* forgive you."

I turn on my side and jerk the covers up to make a point. I lose my grip on the comforter, though, and my fingers spring back, smacking me in the face. There. If that's not an accurate metaphor for my life, I don't know what is.

There's a knock on my door and I sit straight up. "Come in."

"Was told to tell you we're eating at my house," Jaxon says as he pushes my door open. "Am I interrupting something?"

I glance at my clock. There's still another ten minutes until breakfast. "Just the usual, talking to myself."

"Oh, well, in that case . . ." He sits down on my bed and kicks off his slippers. "So what's up?"

I smile. "I don't know, Jaxon. You're the one in my bedroom at six-fifty in the morning."

"I just mean . . . You were acting a little jumpy yesterday, and your dad told me you woke up all shaken again today. You haven't done that in a while."

I try to smile. *I don't want to tell him why. I want that spell we did to work and for these strange things to disappear. Return to the life I've been happy in recently.* "I know there's a normal out there, and I'll be damned if I don't find it."

He pushes his sun-kissed hair out of his eyes. It's only April, and Jaxon already looks like he stumbled off a beach. "You mean doing witch training with my mom isn't at the top of your 'normal' list?"

I laugh. "Can you even imagine?"

"Yes. Yes, I can. When I was in fifth grade, my mom decided that I needed to learn how to cook, and she invited my entire class to her bakery. Great in theory. Everyone stuffed their faces. But by the time the next week rolled around, there was a whole group of guys calling me Muffin."

"So you're saying that if I did witch training with your mom, people might start calling me Witchy-poo or something?"

"Actually, you do kinda look like a witchy-poo."

"Shut up, Muffin." I push him lightly.

He picks up one of my pillows and smacks me in the face with it.

My mouth opens. "Oh, you're so dead."

I jump on him, and he falls back into a mound of down comforter. He grabs my wrists and rolls on top of me, pinning me under his weight.

He smells like pine trees. "You're stronger than I thought. I mean, not that strong, but still."

"You mean I'm dangerous."

"I mean good thing for me you suck at fighting."

I laugh, and for a brief second my stomach flutters under his. "You just better hope I don't learn magic, or I'll give you a tail."

Jaxon grins. He adjusts his weight off me and onto his side, supporting his head with his hand. His eyes are focused, and the flutter in my stomach intensifies.

"Will you go to the dance with me?" he asks. "I have a sneaking suspicion we would make an awfully good *Titanic* couple."

Titanic. "Wait, what?"

"The Spring Fling."

Is Jaxon asking me out? Maybe he was flirting the other day. Not jokey fun flirting, but I-want-to-stick-my-tongue-in-your-mouth flirting. I reach out to touch his arm, but take my hand back. "Don't you want to go with a date or something?"

Jaxon looks out the window for a brief second, and when his eyes return to me, his smile has tension in it. "I would much rather go with you. Doesn't have to be a big deal. I just, well, I think it would be good for you to have a little fun for once. Socialize."

The flutter in my stomach turns to anxiety. *Please don't do this.* "I don't know. I just . . . I don't know."

Jaxon pulls back to get a better look at me. "You're not going with someone else, are you?"

I wish I could laugh at that. I wish that the major problem of my life right now was too many dance invites. "It's not that. I just don't think I'm gonna go at all."

"Come on, Sam. I know it's been a little weird at school these past few months. But you have to jump in at some point."

I slide away from him and sit up. "It's not just that." It's Ada and the dream, Alice's bones, and a slew of weirdness that tells me I shouldn't go anywhere near a *Titanic*-themed dance right now.

Jaxon's eyes focus on me like he's trying to sort something out. "Well, what's it about, then?"

I pull at the edge of my comforter. Maybe I should tell Jaxon what's going on. He'll hate it, but at least I won't have to hurt his feelings about the dance.

Jaxon frowns. "You're acting the same way you did right after . . . Does this have anything to do with that dude ghost that left?"

My heart immediately and annoyingly starts pounding. *Stop it, heart.* Why should I care that Jaxon brought up Elijah? I stand up and step into my black slippers. "We're gonna be late to breakfast."

Jaxon stands up, too. "I'm guessing by your reaction that's a yes."

"It's . . . I'm just not going to the dance. I don't want to go," I say with more frustration than I intended. Great. Now I've made it sound like it *is* because of Elijah. I turn away from his look. I *hate* that I'm flustered and that Jaxon can see it.

"Do you still have feelings for him?"

I walk into the hall. "I *really* don't want to talk about this." How did we even get on this topic anyway?

"That figures." No more jokes and smiles.

"What's that supposed to mean?"

"You can't even look at me when you talk about this."

I move fast down the stairs, my pulse quickening. I can't explain everything to him while I'm like this. I need to calm down, think it through. "He's gone, Jaxon. And he's not the reason I'm saying no to you. I'm just saying no. I don't have to give you a reason."

"Real nice, Sam." His frustration matches mine. "I'm the closest friend you have as long as we don't talk about anything important. But the moment I ask you a personal question, you run away."

Damn him for being right. I cross the foyer and open the side door. "Jaxon . . ." Alice stands on the other side with her hand raised to knock. "Alice?"

"I need to talk to you," Alice says, and steps in.

Jaxon looks from her to me.

"Seriously, Sam. Alone," Alice says.

"Right, you'll talk to *her*," Jaxon says under his breath. He walks out the door, and it slams shut behind him.

How did that fight even happen?

"Looks like your morning is going as well as mine is," Alice says.

"You have no idea," I say.

She walks straight for the living room and I follow. We sit down on one of the white fluffy couches, and she drops her bookbag on the coffee table, which is actually an old trunk.

"I found this on my nightstand this morning." She pulls an antique key from her pocket and holds it out to me.

I examine the metal tag. Engraved on one side is 1ST CL ST RM D33. Some of the detail is rubbed smooth. "What the . . . ?"

"It was just there staring at me when I woke up," Alice says, looking at the key like it has some nerve.

"Could it have come from someone in your house?"

Alice shakes her head.

"Are you saying you think someone snuck in and left it in your room?"

"It wasn't there when I went to sleep. And no one got into my room overnight without me noticing. I'm a light sleeper. As in a piece of dust lands on my cheek and I bolt upright."

"So you're saying . . ." A chill runs down my back.

"I don't see another explanation." She twists a black onyx ring on her finger. "It had to be a ghost."

I look at the key. "Spirit," I correct her.

"Okay, well, I want you to teach me how to see them."

"What? No way. I just asked you to do a spell to help me *not* see them anymore."

"You can't just stop seeing spirits, Sam. That isn't a door you can shut. And if one was looming over me in my sleep, which is very possibly what happened last night, I wouldn't even know it. *You* can see spirits. Maybe you're not interested in taking it as an opportunity. But I'll be damned if I'm not going to try. Yes, I want you to join our circle, and yes, you would make us stronger. But whether you do or you don't, you have to stop being such a baby and realize what a gift you have."

I set my jaw. "I get that you're freaked out. I am, too. But do *not* guilt-trip me after everything that happened."

"By 'everything that happened,' I assume you mean your stepmother trying to kill us."

I stare at her hard. "Don't do this, Alice."

"I'm gonna do this. We've been keeping your secret about her. You deserve that for what you did for us. It goes without saying. But we don't deserve you shutting us out. You're act-ing like you're the only one this happened to."

I hand the key back to her and stand up. "I *really* don't want to have this conversation." Which is now the second time I've said this since I woke up.

She grabs my wrist. "Look at Lizzie. She couldn't deal with what happened, and she shipped herself off to some boarding school. Hiding yourself away in a made-up normal world you think you want is just the same. You can't make what Vivian did go away no matter how much you avoid us or how much you avoid magic. And yeah, there's a price you pay for having power and keeping secrets. So stop being self-ish! You can't do this alone, and neither can we."

I pull her hand off my wrist and walk away from her. Screw school. If Murphy's Law is running the show today, I'm going back to bed.

CHAPTER NINE

Just a Bad Night of Sleep

I examine the glossy black-and-white-checkered floor below my feet. The fancy French-themed café is filled with white wicker furniture and women wearing delicate lace gloves. Green vines wind their way up white-latticed walls. A quartet plays classical music over the din of luncheon conversation, and the many windows stream light and fresh salty air.

Salty air. I tense. Outside the windows, the sunlight glistens off the water. What is this? Another dream? This doesn't feel like the last one. My thoughts are clearer.

I want out. I wind through the tables of finely dressed families toward a door leading to the deck. As I pass two men at a table, I accidentally brush against one's shoulder. I stop. He has a white beard and is wearing a bow tie.

"Sorry," I say, but he doesn't respond.

"I hear President Taft invited you himself, Mr. Stead," the other man says, and stirs sugar into his tea.

"Right you are," Mr. Stead says.

I walk right up to the table. "I said I was sorry." But they don't so much as glance in my direction.

I wave my hands between their faces. No reaction.

"Heeelllooo!" I don't even get to be part of my own dream?

I smack the table between their plates, but oddly, it doesn't make a noise. I try to lift a plate, but it's as though it was cemented to the table. That's it. I'm going to get their attention if it's the last thing I do.

My gaze falls on a small silver sugar spoon. I grab it with both hands and pull. Nothing. I concentrate harder, and picture lifting it with my mind. It sways slightly. "Gotcha!" I tighten my grip and focus more energy at it. It lifts six inches into the air.

The men stop talking at once.

"Ya see me now, don't you?" I ask, rather satisfied with myself, even though I know they're looking at the spoon and not me.

They push their seats away from the table. Mr. Stead's chair collides with my side. I try to step away, but I lose my balance. And as I fall toward the checkered floor, I take the spoon with me.

"Hey!" My eyes fly open. "Watch what you're . . ." I'm in my bedroom. There's no one to yell at.

"What the hell?" In my right hand is a small silver spoon. Whatever residual sleepiness I had immediately disappears.

This isn't supposed to happen. No one takes things from their dreams. There's nothing to take—dreams aren't real. I close my eyes for three seconds and open them again. The spoon is still there.

I jump out of bed. *I need to tell the girls; I need to . . .* My argument with Jaxon this morning and my fight with Alice come rushing back to me. And even if I wanted to talk to them, they're both at school.

I shove the spoon into my nightstand drawer and pace in my room. I need air.

I throw on some clothes and walk into the hall.

"Dad!" I yell.

"You okay?" he calls up.

"Yeah," I yell back, making my way down the stairs. "Just going for a walk."

He enters the foyer at the same time I do. "Want some lunch before you go? Or a snack? Banana?"

I pull my hair into a messy ball on top of my head and put my jacket on. "Nah. I'm not hungry. I think I spent too much time napping. I'm starting to feel antsy."

"You have a minute? I want to show you something."

I hesitate, looking at the door. "Yeah. Of course."

I follow him into the hall, and he opens the door to his old-fashioned office, complete with a sepia-toned globe and tall bookshelves.

"Did you know this study was my dad's once? For most of my childhood, it was off-limits. Of course, that didn't stop me and Mae from snooping through his drawers when we saw the opportunity." He winks at me and walks behind his enormous desk.

"Were you and Grandpa close?" I know even less about him than about my grandmother. He died when my dad was in college, and Dad almost never talked about him when I was growing up. Come to think of it, he's been doing a lot of reminiscing recently. As long as he doesn't want to reminisce about Vivian, I'm fine with it.

"He didn't talk to me much." He laughs. "I used to take it personally and try to goad him into conversation. But he said what he thought and that was that. Even when he got mad at me." He points to the plush armchair on the other side of the desk. "Whenever I did something wrong, he'd have me sit there and retell what I did, using only the facts. No feelings, no reasons. Then he'd ask me what kind of punishment I thought I should have."

"That sounds like a sweet deal."

"Not even close. He would look at me with those we-both-know-what's-right eyes until I named something way too severe. Mae used to laugh until she cried when I told her how those conversations went. And I know you think she's nothing but sweet, but don't let her fool you. She's an expert troublemaker." He pulls out a drawer of the desk and hands me a photo. "*That* is proof."

In the picture my dad looks about nine years old. He's tied to the tree in the backyard and covered head to toe in mud. And there's a girl around his age standing a few feet away, holding a mud ball.

I start laughing. "Way to go, Mrs. Meriwether."

He pauses. "So about staying home today—"

"I'm fine," I say too quickly. "Just a bad night of sleep. I figured I'd be passing out in class. Not a big deal."

"You'd tell me if it was a big deal?"

"Yeah." I put the photo on his desk and pull my sleeves down farther than they're supposed to go. "I think I'm gonna take that walk now."

His eyebrows knit together.

I stand up and force a smile. "Dad, stop worrying. I'm fine."

He doesn't look entirely convinced. "When you get back, I'll cook us up some of those pumpkin raviolis in sage butter you love and garlic bread. I have a couple of stories about Mae that will make you fall right out of your chair."

I laugh. "Extra garlic?"

"Is there any other way?"

"I'm so in for that." I blow him a kiss and head out of his office and out of the house.

I exhale loudly into the crisp spring air as I zip my jacket closed and turn down my street toward town. Maybe I'm being stupid. Maybe Dad wouldn't freak out the way I think he would if I told him I was seeing spirits. No, he definitely would. What am I even thinking right now?

Tree roots fight to break through the old brick of the sidewalk and small purple flowers are just beginning to appear in gardens. I once told Elijah that purple flowers were my favorite because they were unapologetically bold. And all he said was "Like your language." I smile at the memory.

The shops are busy, even at this time of day. People are starting to get that spring itch where they just want to be outside, even though it hasn't truly warmed up yet. I can tell by the double takes from some of the pedestrians that they know who I am.

"Girl," a voice says, and I turn to my left.

An older woman with salt-and-pepper hair down to her waist has her door cracked open. Her face is mostly shadowed, and she's wearing a drapey black dress. She stares at me pointedly and waves me to come in.

There's nothing indicating what kind of store it is. The windows are blacked out. There isn't even a sign, just old brick and a worn black door.

"Um, I'm good, thanks," I say, and stick my hands in my pockets.

"You're not good or well," she says. "Come inside."

People pass me on the street and shoot sideways glances at us.

"Thanks, but I . . . I don't have any cash."

Her face wrinkles into a frown. "You think I want your money?"

"I just meant . . ."

A couple of pedestrians have stopped to watch us. The

weird part is, they look more shocked to see her than me. She opens the door wider and retreats into the dark room. *Screw it.* I slip inside, and the door clicks shut behind me.

"Hello?" I turn from side to side. "It's pitch-black. I can't see a thing."

"Come in, come in," she says with a muffled voice.

"I am in."

No response. *You've got to be kidding me.* I put my hands out in front of me and take careful steps in the direction her voice came from. My hands hit a wall, and I follow it down a dark twisty hallway. The farther I get from the door, the more uneasy I get.

"I'm going to leave," I say, not entirely confident that I could find my way out of this maze. What did I just get myself into?

"Brave but impatient," she says just as I collide with a curtain.

I'm not sure I like being analyzed out loud. I push the curtain aside and step into a perfectly circular room lit by candles in chest-high, wrought-iron candelabras. The walls are covered with black velvet curtains, and the floors are a mishmash of colorful rugs and pillows. There's a faint smell of lemon and ginger.

She sits in the center of the room on a pillow next to a low round table. *Did I make a mistake?*

"So what's all this about?" I say.

"You."

I shift my weight from one foot to the other, ready to bolt if need be. "Me?"

"This is exactly my point. You're not paying attention. Do you think I invited you off the street randomly?"

"No, probably not, but—"

"Obviously not. Now stop hovering and sit, because I'm only going to say this once."

"Say what?" I eye her multicolored pillows.

"You started something with that spell of yours. Now sit down!"

And I do. "The spell we did last night? How do you even know about that?"

"Don't bother asking me that question. I *know*. I've been around a lot longer than you have, and that's that. Now, what I was saying was that you and your friends started something last night, and you all must finish it."

I scratch my forehead. "We weren't starting anything. I was trying to *stop* seeing spirits."

"Well, that's ridiculous. There is nothing that will stop you from seeing spirits. You either see them or you don't."

Who is she? Alice's older twin? "Yeah, I'm getting that."

She inspects me. "You think you have it hard, do you? Feel sorry for yourself? You have a *gift*. Knock it off."

I meet her eyes, my temper sparking. "I definitely didn't come in here for this."

"You disagree?" she scoffs. "You have a natural ability with magic *and* you see spirits. You're young, rich, white, and healthy, for crying out loud. You are *privileged*. You have every opportunity to do spells because you live in Salem in a time when no one will jail you. That's just the short list. Now use your brain for a moment and think about how much more difficult it could be. If you were half as smart or right as you think you are, you wouldn't be arguing with me, you'd be *listening*."

I stare at her, my jaw clenched, but I don't say a word. She's right.

She rests her arms on the table, and her silver bracelets

-59-

clink against the wood. She shakes a finger at me. "This is why I don't help people anymore. You know what Sartre said? He said, 'Hell is other people.' And I quite agree."

I half laugh. "You have a funny way of trying to help people."

She lifts an eyebrow. "I'm trying to warn you. You and your friends are about as subtle as drunk monkeys. And you'll pay for it. So will lots of others, if I'm reading things correctly."

My pulse quickens. Maybe she's not just a cranky weirdo. "What do you mean? Is someone in danger? Are *we* in danger?" All the sarcasm has left my voice.

She grabs my hands. Her expression is dead serious. "Stop being so blind. You need to think past yourself, past your friends and your problems."

I try to pull my hands back, but she has a firm hold. "What did we do with the spell last night? What do you think we started?"

She leans even closer to me. "You know that better than I do."

I swallow. "Does this have something to do with the key Alice found or the dreams I've been having?"

She releases my hands, and I pull them back quickly. "I've said too much already. And I promised myself I wouldn't get involved."

Now I lean toward her. "You haven't said anything specific."

She sighs. "I don't know the specifics and I don't want to. All I know is that the course you're all on right now will bring death. There—I've told you, which means I can thoroughly wash my hands of this whole mess." She stands up. "It's time for you to go."

"Wait a second, you can't just say we're headed toward

death and then not explain it." I stand up, too. "Who do you think is going to die?"

She frowns. "It wasn't clear."

"Me?"

She hesitates. "Possibly."

"My friends? My family?"

"I said it wasn't clear."

I follow her to a different black curtain from the one I came through. "Yeah, but you also said 'possibly' when I asked about myself. Do you know something you're not saying?"

"No. Now stop badgering me with questions I don't have the answers to." She pulls the curtain aside and grabs a door handle. "And you're welcome for the warning."

Her straight thick hair slides over her shoulder. It smells like lavender. The door clicks open and bright light streams in. I squint against it.

"Hang on, I don't even know your name," I say, but she pushes me onto the sidewalk. The door closes behind me. I jiggle the knob, but it's locked.

CHAPTER TEN

It Wasn't Like the Other Dream

I kick at the loose pieces of asphalt near Mary's black Jeep in the school parking lot and check my cell phone. The last bell rang more than fifteen minutes ago.

"Sam?" someone says, and I tense. I look up from the ground to find Dillon, Niki, and Blair. But no Jaxon.

"I thought you were out today. I didn't see you in history," Dillon says.

I scan the parking lot, looking for the Descendants. "I was."

Niki examines her nails and acts like I don't exist.

"Man, I wish my parents would let me stay home," Dillon says. "I have to do full-on theatrics and throw myself on the floor when I'm sick. And most of the time they still say no."

"Same," Blair says. "And with all this dance planning and organizing, Niki and I barely have a minute to breathe. After it's all over, I'll probably collapse."

"Exactly. So don't come near us if you're contagious,"

Niki says with more force than she needs to, and rubs her glossy lips together.

"I'm not sick," I say.

"In that case, you wanna join us? We're gonna grab a bite with Jaxon at his mom's bakery," Dillon says.

Niki gives him the death stare.

They're going to Sugar Spells? I'm liking Dillon dating Blair even less now. I point to Mary's Jeep. "Thanks, but I'm meeting Alice, Mary, and Susannah."

"Ohmigod, don't tell me you stayed home because you had to confront a ghost or something," Blair says, like I'm a fascinating headline. "I can't even imagine."

Before I can respond, Matt rounds the corner of the big SUV parked next to Mary's Jeep and bumps into Niki's bookbag. He doesn't apologize.

"Ugh! Watch where you're going. This bag's suede," Niki says with a good dose of drama.

"Wait, 'old on," Matt says, and stops walking. "It's made outta *suede*?"

And here we go.

Matt smiles. "You want to tell us 'ow much it costs, too, Niki? I'm sure we'd all be impressed."

I think I like this guy.

"If you're jealous that I'm going to hang out with Jaxon, just say it," Niki says, looking quite pleased with herself.

Was that for my benefit or his?

"Jealous of Jaxon?" Matt looks at me pointedly and back at Niki. He laughs. "Nope."

Niki turns red as Matt walks away. "You're such an ass, Matt," she calls after him.

"And 'ere I thought you had dibs on that," Matt says without turning around.

An embarrassed Niki glares at me, and I realize I'm smiling. "You think he's funny?"

How did this get turned on me? "Whoa—"

"I know I do," Alice says behind me. "Now move it before Mary undoes your nose job."

Mary winks at Niki as she comes to my side. Niki's hand shoots to her face protectively and her lips tighten.

Blair pulls Niki away from us. "Let's go." Blair looks at me. They saunter off with their matching white jeans and knee-high boots.

Dillon rubs his neck, looking guilty. "Sorry, Sam. Really."

"It's fine," I say, and he walks away.

"They've been acting entitled like that since they could talk," Mary says.

"We haven't gotten along with them since third grade," Susannah says with a grin. "Not since Alice tarred Niki's playhouse with a bucket and a broom."

Alice looks at me. "We're neighbors. She thought it was funny to dangle my kitten in front of her dog."

I open my mouth. "Completely deserved."

"Agreed," Alice says, and pauses. "So . . . let me guess, you're here to tell me I'm right and you need us?"

I hold my hands up in concession. *One order of humble pie.* "I do need you. Do you guys know anything about an older woman in town who wears lots of silver jewelry and has blacked-out windows in her shop?"

Mary's mouth opens. "Shut up, you saw Redd?"

"She's a local legend," Susannah says.

Alice unlocks the Jeep and gestures at the doors. "Get in. I have no intention of having private conversations in the midst of these morons."

Susannah and I slide in the back, and Mary takes the passenger seat.

It takes Alice all of two seconds to screech out of the parking space. Startled students jump out of the way.

I grab the car door. "So what do you guys know about her? Why are her windows blacked out?"

Susannah straightens her black skirt. "That building used to be Redd's store. She sold herbal creams and tonics—they were the absolute best. Half the town went to her instead of the doctor. But she got fed up one day and basically said the town didn't deserve her help anymore. At least, that's what my mom says."

"Now," Mary says, turning around from the front seat, "no one knows what she does in there. A couple of shop owners complained about it last year, and the fire marshal went in to check it out. But the marshal reported it was just empty rooms."

Alice swerves onto her street. "Redd's a Descendant."

If I didn't have my seat belt on, I'd probably soar right out the window. "Redd . . . as in the accused witch Wilmot Redd? Why wouldn't she tell me her name, then?"

Alice slams on her brakes by the curb in front of her house and we fly forward. "We all have our secrets."

"Tell us everything," Mary says.

I open my door, grateful to be out of the Jeep. "It was all pretty mysterious. She plucked me off the street and told me we started something last night with that spell and—"

Alice shushes us as we approach her massive white colonial house with pillars. Her front door opens before she lays a hand on it. A tall man in a suit and white gloves stands on the other side. He's not the butler I remember from Alice's party last semester. How many people does her family employ?

We step into the entrance hall, and our shoes echo off the shiny stone floors.

"Alice darling," a woman's voice says from a hallway to the left. She's dressed in a flowing floral dress, and her blond hair is pinned into a twist.

"Mom," Alice says.

"We're having the Coreys over for dinner tonight. Wear something appropriate." She pauses. "Unless you're not coming, which is fine."

Whoa on so many levels, where people call other people "darling."

"I'm not coming," Alice says flatly. No wonder Alice doesn't sugarcoat.

Alice's mom continues down the hall, and Alice marches straight through a formal sitting room decorated with Victorian furniture. She opens a door at the back of the room and we file through.

Mary hits a light switch controlling two Tiffany floor lamps. The room is upholstered with black fabric from floor to ceiling. Heavy black curtains snuff out any light from the windows, and it smells faintly of the herbs the girls burn in their spells. There's a black area rug, a desk, and a cozy black couch with a matching love seat and armchair.

I sit.

Susannah plops down next to me. "Did you soundproof this room?"

"Yup," Alice says. "My parents don't care. And there are always people in and out of this place. No one can stand to work for my mother for more than a month. I don't want every new person in my private business."

"Redd's room was lined with black fabric, too. You guys are the same brand of suspicious."

Alice rolls her eyes at me. "There are all kinds of spy spells, genius, and this helps block them."

"You really think people want to know what we're talking

about?" My question doesn't hold the oomph I want it to. Salem's nosy, and everyone pays particular attention to the Descendants.

Mary sprawls out on a love seat with her arm behind her head. "Someone in town started tracking Alice last year. He tried to poison her because we caught on to the scam tour he was running."

Of course the people I make friends with would be almost as prone to dangerous situations as I am. And who poisons anyone in the twenty-first century? No wonder the Borgias was a dance theme favorite.

Susannah kicks off her shoes and pulls her legs up under her long black skirt. "So what did Redd tell you?"

I lean back into the pillows. "She said that we started something with that spell and now we need to finish it."

"Started something how? Did you mention the key I found in my bedroom?" Alice asks with an uneasy edge to her voice.

"She wouldn't give me any details. She said we would know better than she would."

"Great. Typical cryptic Descendant," Mary says.

"She also said that the course we're on would bring death. Possibly mine. She wouldn't say. And then she shoved me out the door. It sounded like she felt guilty not warning us, but also that she wanted nothing to do with the whole thing."

"Death," Susannah breathes, and looks at Alice. "My mom always said Redd was the honest type. She never told you something worked if it didn't. I think we have to assume she means what she says."

"Which also makes me think that when Alice's bones said darkness would be over us and our rest would be a stone, it was most likely ominous," Mary says.

"Don't you know all of the Descendants?" I ask.

Alice scratches her shoulder. "We don't follow around every Descendant in town and put them on a naughty-or-nice list. We're definitely not all the same. And again, we're secretive."

"What she means," Susannah says, "is that some Descendants form groups, like us. Some go solo, like Redd. Some have no interest in magic. And others become amazingly good. Take our parents, for instance. They never cared about it. The three of us and Lizzie learned spells from our grandmothers. They were friends, just like we are. And it's not only witches. There are lots of warlocks in Salem as well."

"So you think Redd was telling the truth?" I ask.

Susannah nods. "From what I know about her."

"At the very least, if Redd bothered to talk to you, then she thinks whatever we just got ourselves involved in is a big deal." Alice bites her nail. "When she said we would know better than she would, what were you talking about *exactly*?"

"The spell we did last night. She compared our subtlety to drunk monkeys."

Susannah leans forward. "But how could a spell to keep spirits away have started something?"

"That's what I wanted to know," I say. "And I've been playing it over and over in my head. The spell said that spirits should ignore us unless we have 'tangled lore,' and the last line was 'From now on I will only find the spirits whom I need to mind.'"

"You think we found a spirit we need to mind?" Mary says with no enthusiasm.

"Possibly," I say. "What if we not only pushed spirits away, but *drew* some to us? There was that book that appeared right after the spell finished, and Alice thinks a spirit left her that key."

"Hmmm." Alice leans back in her armchair.

"Also, I brought a spoon back from my dream this morning."

Mary pops up. *"What?"*

"You wait until now to tell us this?" Alice says.

I push my hair behind my ear and rest my elbows on my knees. "I fell asleep and dreamt I was on the *Titanic* again, only it wasn't like the other dream. It didn't have that dream-like shifting quality to it. Everything seemed clear. But the weird thing was that no one could see me. I was an observer. I got pissed and tried to move things on one of the fancy lunch tables. I grabbed a spoon. When I woke up, it was still in my hand."

Alice and Susannah share a look. "That's not a dream," Susannah says. "I don't know what that was. But it definitely wasn't a dream."

"But I was sleeping."

Mary's eyes widen. "Wait, are we now saying that not all dreams are dreams? That's so not gonna work for me."

Alice taps her fingers on the armchair. "We only did that spell last night. Yet I woke up to a key with some strange letters on it, and Sam had a nondream where she took a spoon. Redd says the course we're on will bring death, and so far this all makes not one ounce of sense."

For a second we're quiet.

"Should we do another spell?" I ask. "Is there one that might give us more information?"

"No. Not yet," Alice says. "The last one we did backfired. We need to go over what's happened so far. Figure out how everything connects." She pauses. "And look who's suggesting magic all of a sudden."

I shrug. Alice knows she's won.

Susannah smiles. "So you're joining our circle?"

They turn and look at me.

"Yeah, I guess I am." And without meaning to, I find myself smiling, too. "Also, I need you to see a painting in my house."

CHAPTER ELEVEN

———

I Might Lose You

My dad leads the girls down the sconce-lit hallway toward the . . . ballroom? I can't believe I'm calling it that now—or more accurately, that I even have a room like that in my house. As I pass the painting that I'm convinced has changed, I scowl at it.

Susannah glances back at me, and I pull my eyes away from the woman's face. "This place is huge."

"Perfect for a party. We *love* planning parties," Mary says.

"Some of us more than others," Alice says.

Mary ignores her and pats her stomach. "I just wish I wasn't so full. I think I ate a loaf of garlic bread by myself. And those chocolate-dipped cannoli . . . wow."

"You were eating like you've been starved half your life," Alice says, even though she did the exact same thing. "And I know your mother keeps your refrigerator full."

"Correction: she keeps it stocked with organic vegetables and granola parfaits, and *no* cannoli."

"You're welcome here anytime. We have enough sweets to feed the whole town," my dad says as we enter the ballroom. It's obvious he's thrilled they showed up to eat a meal with us and even more thrilled they asked for a tour of the house.

Mary smiles.

"I'd be careful with that offer, Mr. M," Alice says. "Mary may look small, but she's got the metabolism and food capacity of a Tasmanian devil."

The girls stop as if on cue and take in the room.

"This is like a time capsule from the eighteen hundreds," Susannah says. "It's gorgeous."

"Well, feel free to have a party in here anytime you like," my dad says.

Mary walks to the middle of the room and turns around twice. Her eyes widen. "What if we all meet here before the Spring Fling? It's ideal for pictures."

My dad lights up. "I think that's a great idea."

"I wasn't going—" I start to say.

But Mary cuts me off with a squeal. "Is there a way to play music in here?"

My dad grins. "Sure thing. There's an old record player over there, and we could easily bring in a stereo with some speakers."

I cringe, remembering my fight with Jaxon. On impulse I pull out my phone and check my texts, but there are none. I usually hear from him ten times a day. I type a text and press send: *Can we talk?*

Mary walks up to the old gramophone. She lifts the lid and places the needle on a record. Scratchy classical music fills the room, and Mary bounces on the balls of her feet. Something about the music feels oddly familiar, and not good familiar. She picks up the needle and the room goes quiet.

The doorbell chimes. *Jaxon?*

"I'll get it," I say. Would he really come over that fast?

I speed-walk down the hall to the foyer and peer through the brass peephole. No one's there. I open the door and squint into the darkness. A long glossy white box with a black bow sits on our steps with a card tucked into the ribbon.

I step outside and look around. "Hello?" But there's no answer, and no delivery truck leaving from the curb.

I pull the box inside and open the card. It's written in beautiful cursive, not as loopy as Elijah's calligraphy, but close. It reads:

> *To my dear niece,*
> *I do hope you will join us for dinner soon.*
> *With love,*
> *Aunty Myra H.H.*

Niece? Myra H.H.? "Daaad?"

My dad comes down the hall so quickly I feel bad for having yelled his name. The girls are right behind him.

"Sam?" he says, and looks down at the pretty box. He's on edge about every little thing. It's almost like he's waiting for something bad to happen the same way I am.

I hand him the card.

His brow furrows. "Huh. Well, that's odd, considering your mother and I were only children. And I don't know anyone named Myra. I suppose 'aunt' could be loosely referring to someone from my mother's extended family? I just didn't think we had any Haxtun relatives left."

"Haxtun?"

"Your grandmother's maiden name was Haxtun. That

could be what one of the *H*'s stands for. No other *H* names in the family that I can recall. Maybe this is one of her second cousins I don't know about?" He looks at me. "Come to think of it, that painting we talked about in the hallway—she might have been a Haxtun. Was this all that was in the envelope?"

"Yeah. No address or phone number of any kind."

Alice steps past Mary to get a closer look at the card.

"Go on. Open it, Sam. I can't take all the suspense," Mary says.

I untie the elaborate bow and slide the white lid off the box at arm's length, not entirely convinced something won't jump out at me. Inside, there is rose tissue paper and an emerald-green silk dress with short white lace sleeves. *My dream! That green dress on the deck!*

I rub my thumb against my palm and avoid looking at my dad.

Susannah lifts it up, and the skirt falls all the way to the floor. The fabric hangs in complicated folds, and the lace looks fragile.

"Why would someone send me a fancy dress?"

"This isn't just a dress," Mary says. "It's an Edwardian *evening gown*."

Alice's eyebrows go up. "Like *Titanic* Edwardian?"

Mary nods, and we all stare at the gown.

"Isn't that the theme of your school dance?" my dad asks.

"Yeah, maybe our Haxtun relative sent this for the dance?"

"I don't know the Haxtuns. It does seem odd for one of them to send you a dress out of the blue like this, though." My dad laughs. "And we were just talking about you girls meeting here for pictures."

I swallow. Does he have any idea how weird this is? Or does he just think it's a strange coincidence?

"My mom's sisters do this constantly," Alice says quickly,

and I'm extremely grateful to her for normalizing it. "I think I had seven different dress options for my tenth birthday."

"If this Myra knows about your school dance, she must live nearby. Want me to ask Mae about her?" my dad asks.

I shake my head. "Don't worry. I'll ask her. That way I can send a thank-you card or something."

"Whoever saw someone look so gloomy after getting a beautiful dress." He smiles at me. "You used to love them when you were little."

My shoulders relax. "They're uncomfortable and I always trip," I say. I couldn't be more thrilled he thinks I'm upset only because it's a dress.

"Here." He hands me back the card. "I'll check outside for a delivery slip."

Or maybe I'm wrong. Maybe he does think it's weirder than he's letting on. My dad opens the door, steps outside, and closes it behind him.

The girls move in so close, all of our shoulders touch.

"I *saw* this dress in my dream. The very first dream I had. It was on the deck of the ship," I say fast and nervously.

Alice rubs her forehead. "And we were talking about the dance when it showed up. Another item appearing out of nowhere. And I don't believe in coincidences. I think Redd was right that we started something. Don't mess with this dress until we decide what to do with it." Even in a whisper she sounds bossy.

"We need to track down this Myra H.H.," Susannah says. "I'm gonna ask my mom. Mary, you do the same."

"I'll look in my grandmother's study. Maybe she has some sort of record of our extended relatives. And not to change the topic, but as far as meeting here before the dance goes . . . Do you really think we should be going anywhere near something *Titanic*-themed?"

"We can't be sure the dance is even connected. But if it is, there's no question that we have to go. We need all the information we can get." Alice gives me a warning look. "And I'm serious about not touching that dress, Sam."

If Alice is right that the dance is inevitable, I need to talk to Jaxon. Everything's changed since this morning. The door opens, and we all jump a foot apart.

"No delivery slip," my dad says.

"Yeah, I'll give you a call later with the homework assignment," I say to Susannah.

Mary picks up her bag, which was resting near the mail table.

"You girls get home safe," my dad says. "And come over soon so we can plan what to do for those pictures."

"Sure thing, Mr. M," Mary says.

The door shuts behind them, and it's just me, my dad, and the awful dress.

My dad wraps his arm around my shoulder. "That was fun."

I look up at his chin, which has a little bit of stubble on it. "You're just basking in the fact that you're hosting the predance get-together, *Mr. M*."

"That was all your friend Mary's idea. I'm only the hired help around here."

"Uh-huh."

He smiles. "It was nice having them over, though, wasn't it? You've finally met a group of people who avoid brightly colored clothing the way you do. I better not take you girls anywhere at night. I might lose you." He winks at me.

CHAPTER TWELVE

———————

My Brain Is in a Thick Fog

I blow on a hot cup of strawberry-mint tea and stare at the dress box on my window seat. My phone buzzes on my nightstand.

Jaxon: *Talk tomorrow. Going to bed.*

Okay, he's officially mad at me. He waited four whole hours to tell me that? And I get it; I'd be frustrated with me, too. I don't even know how that conversation spiraled out of control this morning or how we wound up talking about Elijah.

I exhale audibly. "Why are you so hard to forget? I didn't even like you at first, and here I am getting into arguments about whether or not I still have feelings for you? Total bull. And here I also am talking to myself for no good reason. You suck."

I put my phone down, and my eyes move back to the box. I'm just gonna put my jams on and not think about any of this until tomorrow.

I walk to my armoire, grab the latch, and pause. I look back at the box. We opened it before and nothing witchy happened. We took the dress out and everything. I let go of the armoire door. It can't be that dangerous to touch it if Susannah already did, right?

I take off the box lid and grab the emerald-green silk dress. The box falls by my feet as I spread out the delicate fabric on my bed. A piece of white lace peeks out from the rose tissue paper on the floor. I push it aside, and there are lacy shorts, a bra, a slip, and a skirt. Who sends someone historical underwear?

I run my fingers over the silk and down the seams. I'm not usually a dress fan, but even I have to admit this one is beautiful. Would it really be so bad to try it on?

I slip off my jeans and sweater and step into the dainty shorts. I slide each layer on as though I know instinctively how they fit together. Weird. Last time I tried on a dress in a store, I got my shoulders caught and had to yell for help from the changing room.

Once the delicate layers are on, I pick up the dress, pull it over my head, and—

My vision blurs, and for a split second I panic. But the panic leaves just as quickly as it came. And with one blink, the world comes back into focus, a more vibrant world than I remember.

I'm standing in front of a long oval mirror in my many undergarments. A girl just a couple of years older than me is tightening the laces on my corset. She wears a dark gray wool dress, and her curly brown hair is tucked into a white cap.

Am I supposed to know who she is? I must; she's dressing

me. How could I not know someone who's dressing me? My worry returns, but is quashed before it can take hold. I touch my stomach as the girl gives the corset laces a strong pull.

"How am I going to eat in this thing?" Am I going to eat?

The girl winks at me. "Small bites, miss," she says with an accent. British? No, Irish, I think. She pulls an emerald-green dress off a pink satin hanger and holds it above my head for me to slip my arms into. "This must be the prettiest dress on the whole ship."

My brain is in a thick fog, and my mouth is answering when it shouldn't. "Do I seem like myself to you?"

The long skirt glides to the floor, and she works on fastening the small buttons in the back. "Just like yerself. Only maybe a wee more elegant in this." She examines me in the mirror and runs her hands along my sides to smooth the fabric.

Her voice is reassuring, and I smile at her. "I'd be more elegant if I didn't trip in dresses."

She laughs. "Nonsense. Ya've made a singularly good impression here. There are a number o' ladies talkin' about yer fashion. And one young man in particular seems quite smitten. Come, sit down. I'll fix yer hair."

The girl has freckles that form a speckled cloud under her eyes and across her nose. For the life of me, I can't remember her name. That's awful that I can't remember her name when she seems to know me so well. My nervousness comes back for a third time, only it's so weak that I brush it off entirely.

The girl leads me to the vanity, and I sit down in the chair, careful not to catch my dress on anything.

I watch in the mirror as she twists and pulls my hair into elaborate patterns. "Where did you learn to do hair like that?"

"Me mum taught me. I was never quite awake in the mornin' before school, and by the time I was dressed and ready, I'd missed me breakfast. She used ta say, 'Mollie, do yer hair quick and yer eatin' slow.' " She smiles to herself, and I smile with her.

Mollie, her name is Mollie. She grabs a hairpin from the vanity and pushes it into my hair.

"Sooo, who is it?" I ask.

"Me mum, miss?"

I laugh. "No. Who's the guy who's smitten?" What in the hell kind of a word is "smitten"?

Mollie's freckled cheeks lift in a smile, and she leans close to my ear. "Mr. Alexander Jessup Jr. I heard from one of the waiters that he could barely hold a conversation over lunch with his pa for seein' ya. He nearly toppled his chair once, tryin' ta get a better look atcha. But ya didn't hear it from me. Yer uncle would box me ears if he knew I was gossipin'."

"I won't say a word." I run my fingers along the brown bristles of the hairbrush in front of me. "I don't remember meeting an Alexander. Will you point him out to me?"

There's a noise in the adjoining room.

Mollie stands straight up like someone pinched her in the butt. "I would be happy ta walk ya to the dinin' room, miss," she says at normal volume, and winks at me in the mirror.

My messy hair has been transformed into an elaborate updo with more pins than I can count. Mollie lifts a gold lace ribbon with tiny pearls on it and weaves it into my hairstyle like a headband.

I turn around once in front of the long mirror to make sure everything's in order. This corset might be the end of me.

A bugle belts a tune.

"Time fer dinner, then." Mollie holds out a long white coat and I slip my arms into it.

We leave my bedroom, with its canopied bed, and make our way into the burgundy-colored sitting room, which has plush armchairs and a fireplace. Mollie holds the door for me. The moment I step into the hallway, I realize I'm unsure which way to go. It looks familiar and foreign at the same time. Maybe I ate something I shouldn't have and it's making me sick?

"Left, miss," she says, and I listen. "Through this archway on yer right."

I smile at her. I'm glad she's here. I would feel strange wandering around with all these fancy people, asking for directions. We walk through a long room with couches and a sprawling grand staircase shaped like a lady's fan.

Mollie opens a door that leads into an extravagant dining room. The tiles on the floor look exactly like Persian carpet, white columns come down from the ornate white ceiling, and women wear jewelry fit for museums.

I grab Mollie's hand. There must be more than two hundred elegantly dressed people in here, many of whom turn to inspect me as we pass.

"On yer left," Mollie whispers, "three tables ahead of us. Alexander Jessup Jr."

I count up three tables and make brief eye contact with a handsome guy around my age with brown hair and blue eyes. He smiles at me, and my heart leapfrogs.

"Yer uncle Harry is watching, miss," Mollie whispers, and leads me to a table on my right.

I immediately shift my gaze to a distinguished middle-aged gentleman, who rises from his seat. "You look beautiful this evening, niece. That dress suits you perfectly."

"Thank you, Uncle Harry." His name sticks in my mouth like I've never said it before. I hope he doesn't notice. Maybe the motion of the boat is affecting me? Actually, I'm sure that's it. I'm not used to sea travel. I exhale, relieved to have located the probable cause of my strange feelings.

Mollie takes my white coat and gives it to a waiter. Behind my uncle is a youngish-looking man with handsome brown skin and strikingly attractive features.

My uncle follows my line of sight and turns to the man. "That will be all, Hammad."

"Yes, sir." Hammad bows and makes eye contact with me before he walks away. He's got an accent that I can't quite place.

My uncle brings his napkin to his lap.

A waiter appears to my right. "May I serve you wine, miss?"

I almost say no, that I'm not old enough. But I look at my uncle, and he doesn't seem to object. "Yes, thank you."

The waiter fills my glass without spilling a drop on the crisp white tablecloth.

"Since it is only the two of us for dinner tonight, I thought we might invite the Jessups to sit with us. Yea or nay?" His amused grin lets me know Alexander's feelings are not a secret. But if he's inviting him to our table, then he must approve, right?

I nod into my wineglass, and my uncle waves them over.

A man around my uncle's age, tall and lean with a hard face, approaches with Alexander behind him.

"May I present Mr. Alexander Jessup and his son, Alexander Jessup Jr." My uncle gestures toward me. "My niece, Samantha Mather. Her aunt and I have just taken her on a tour of Europe and Asia."

Europe and Asia? But as they both bow to me, my question fades from my thoughts.

Mr. Jessup claps my uncle on the back and takes the seat

next to him. "What a treat that we can join you both tonight, Mr. Harper."

Alexander sits next to me.

The older men start talking immediately, and I read my menu, which has "RMS TITANIC" stenciled at the top. I frown at it. I have a nagging sense I can't remember something. Something I don't like.

"Did you enjoy your tour, Miss Mather?" Alexander asks.

I look up from my menu to find dark blue eyes focused intently on me. For a second I forget he's asked me a question.

"Call me Samantha."

He smiles, and it's hard not to smile back at him. His brown hair is combed perfectly, and his suit is obviously expensive. "And you must call me Alexander."

"I will. I don't like formality. Do you?"

He laughs. "Do not say that too loudly in here or a couple of old women might faint."

I smile now, too. "They might not be the only ones. If I breathe too hard in this corset, I might pass out. Good thing these chairs have arms."

"If they did not, I would catch you."

Mollie was right. He's definitely flirting with me. I clear my throat. "Where do you live?"

"New York City. Not far from the Harpers. I met you a couple of years back at one of their Christmas parties. Do you remember?"

Christmas party? I don't remember. But New York City is right. "I'm sorry. I don't. But then, I'm usually quiet at parties." I pick up my crystal wineglass.

A waiter places a plate of grilled asparagus with lemon and olive oil in front of me.

"Did your uncle tell you the story of how we bought our way onto this liner at the last moment?"

I'm grateful for a subject that isn't about me. "He didn't. You tell me. Does it have some good scandal in it?"

He laughs. "Why, yes, I believe it does."

My body vibrates slightly. Nausea? I put my glass down on the table.

Alexander frowns. "Samantha?"

I push my chair back, and all the men look at me. My body vibrates more violently. "I'm sorry. I need to be excused."

I walk away as fast as my dress will permit. My arm jerks in front of me. The corset limits my air supply and the room spins. I push through the door and—

Someone leans over me, gently shaking my shoulder. I blink. His dark wavy hair casts shadows on his cheeks in the dim light. His lips part slightly and he exhales, the tension in his eyebrows lessening. He's beautiful.

I sit straight up in my bed. *How could he . . . I don't understand.* I rub my eyes just to make sure what I'm seeing is real.

"Elijah?" I say, my tone unsure. Could I be dreaming?

"Samantha," he says with his old-world accent, and pauses. "Why would you put that dress on when you do not even know who sent it?" His look is accusatory.

Well, that clears that up. It's Elijah, all right. But how? I examine my legs. I'm no longer wearing green silk, only my antique frilly undergarments. The corset is off, too. I can't quite make sense of it all; my brain still feels foggy. "Did you *undress* me?"

"I could not wake you while the dress was on." He stands. "How could you not think it might have a spell on it? Of all the—"

"Wait, hold on a minute." I stand up, too. My familiar room suddenly looks surreal with Elijah in it.

"How could you be so reckless?" Elijah continues in a disapproving tone.

I brush off his question, my own thoughts so tangled that I can only address one confusing situation at a time. "You're *here*? How can you be here?"

Elijah opens his mouth, but before he can say a word, I'm talking again.

"Have you been around this whole time?" My tone has turned from surprise to indignation.

"No."

"Part of the time?"

"Yes."

"And you didn't tell me?" My volume is steadily rising.

He stares at me with his proud expression.

My cheeks are hot and my breath is fast. Six months he's gone without a word, and then he just appears out of thin air like . . . "The book." I point at my backpack. "The *Titanic* one that appeared in the study. Was that you?"

He doesn't respond, but by the look in his eyes, I know it was.

"Did you see the package arrive, too?" I say, daring him to say he did.

His silence holds.

"You've been watching me." I take a step toward him. "And you said *nothing*." I swipe at him. "How could you?"

He dodges my right hand, but I come at him with my left. Then my right again. I get a few good hits to his chest before he catches my wrists. We're inches apart.

"I hate you," I say.

But then I'm kissing him.

He pulls me into his body so hard and so fast that it almost knocks the wind out of me. I wrap my arms around his neck and tangle my hands in his hair. His tongue touches mine, and his fingers dig into my back until—

Knock, knock, knock. "Sam? Is everything okay?" my dad asks through the door.

Elijah disappears, and I'm left grabbing the air where he just was.

CHAPTER THIRTEEN

Cycling Through Thoughts of Elijah

I run down the hallway to my homeroom, dodging people as I go. Three hours of sleep, no breakfast, and a brain that keeps cycling through thoughts of Elijah and that terrifying dress. If someone took a match to my nervous energy, I'd launch to the moon.

I yank Mrs. Hoxley's door open and head directly for the Descendants, sliding into the seat next to Susannah.

"Big problem," I say with zero attempt at sugarcoating. They all turn toward me. "I put that dress on."

Alice clicks her tongue off the roof of her mouth. "You did *what?*"

"I put that dress on and—"

"Wow. We can't leave you alone for two seconds," Alice says.

Blair walks past me, and I scrunch my nose at her vanilla perfume.

Mary dismisses Alice's comment with a wave of her hand

and leans toward me, her curls in Alice's face. Alice frowns. Susannah and I lean in closer, too.

I lower my voice to a whisper. "As I was putting the dress on, my room dropped away. I swear it was like I was on the *Titanic*."

"Like in your dream?" Susannah asks.

"Different. More real. I was in a bedroom with a maid dressing me. Everything was disorienting. I kept feeling like I was supposed to be there and not supposed to be there at the same time."

"So you could touch things this time?" Alice whispers.

I nod. "I drank and ate and talked to people. I was getting dressed up for dinner with my uncle. . . ." Those words feel comfortable, but they shouldn't. I don't have any uncles. "And everyone there knew me. Like I had a whole different life. Even some of the things I said were old-fashioned. I felt, I don't know . . . happy? But wrong happy, like the calm before the storm. And I can't shake the feeling that it has something to do with Redd's death warning. All morning I've had this feeling in the pit in my stomach."

Mary is practically falling out of her chair, she's listening so hard.

Alice narrows her eyes. "Back up. What do you mean, your *uncle*?"

"His name was Harry Harper. . . . I'm telling you, it's like I had a separate life there. I could feel my brain trying to remember who I was, especially in the beginning. But the longer I stayed, the more that dropped away. I had family; people knew me. I sat down to have—"

Susannah sits bolt upright. She puts her hand on my arm. "Stop."

We all look at her. Usually Alice is the one telling me to stop talking.

Alice scans the room, which is quickly filling with students. Mary looks out the windows.

Susannah squeezes my arm. "Something's off. Let's talk about this later."

Susannah's face looks focused and serious, like someone is giving her important information from the next room and she has to strain to hear it. Alice and Mary might be used to her reading people, but I've never been around when she's had a "feeling," or whatever it is. It's unsettling.

The bell rings.

Mrs. Hoxley claps her hands together to quiet us. "It's not Friday; it's Thursday. Look alive, people. Blair has an announcement to make about the Spring Fling."

Didn't we cover this on Monday?

Blair makes her way to the front of the room with an uninterested-looking Matt. His hands are full of small white slips of paper. Blair flashes the class a toothy smile and grabs the top one from the stack. She hands it to the first guy in the row nearest the door. "These are raffle tickets. Everyone should write their name on one. And at the dance, three names will be chosen for prizes."

Blair hands four raffle tickets to me. I take one and pass three of them back.

"Third prize is a homework pass," Blair continues. "Second prize is a dinner for two, and *first* prize . . ."

An approving murmur ripples through the room, and everyone hangs on her words.

"First prize is a *sur*-prise."

I can't deny that I would love to get my hands on that homework pass.

I examine the raffle ticket. There's a drawing of a ship, with "RMS TITANIC" printed above it. The drawing looks familiar, like I may have seen it somewhere before. Maybe something from my homework? I write my name on the blank line labeled PASSENGER.

The guy behind me leans forward and hands me the signed raffle tickets from our row.

To my left, Susannah drops her pen. It rolls to the floor and she grabs her desk. Her head droops and she squeezes her eyes shut.

"Susannah?" Alice and I both say at the same time.

"Is something the matter, Ms. Martin?" Mrs. Hoxley asks.

"Water," Susannah squeaks. She looks like she's beyond nauseated.

Alice stands up. "I'll take her to the bathroom."

"I'll help her," I say.

"I think you'd better," Mrs. Hoxley says, and all eyes in the room are glued on us.

Alice and I hoist Susannah out of her seat.

Blair wears a smug smile, and Alice glares at her. We push through the door, leaving the whispering students in our wake.

"What the hell is going on?" Alice asks.

"Everything looks like it's swaying—the people, the desks, the walls," Susannah says as we guide her to the bathroom.

"You look like you're going to throw up," Alice says.

"Worse. The floor was rippling under my feet like it was made of water."

"Is it still happening?" I ask.

Susannah touches her forehead with her fingertips. "The farther away we get from that class, the walls become more solid and the floor sloshes less."

Alice pushes the bathroom door open. Susannah heads for the sink, turns on the cold water, and splashes it on her face.

I check the stalls to make sure we're alone.

Susannah pats a paper towel over her face. "It was a spell.

At least, I think it was. It started the second I touched the raffle ticket. And I could practically smell the ocean. Almost like seasickness."

Alice cracks her knuckles. "But how could it have been the ticket? We all got them and no one else almost puked, so it makes it less likely or more difficult. Blair would have had to set you up to get a specific one. She's not a Descendant, and she doesn't know jack about magic. And Matt isn't even from Salem."

"I know," Susannah says. "But the feeling went away as soon as I left the ticket behind."

"Just like the dress," I say. "I mean, it can't be a coincidence that two times in the past twenty-four hours we've come into contact with objects that have spells in them."

The bell rings.

"No, it's not," Alice says. "And *if* someone is doing magic that way, that person could be clever enough to deliver the objects through other people. It's not easy, but it's also not impossible."

The bathroom door opens and Mary walks through, holding our bags. "Please tell me that wasn't a spell." She looks at Susannah and then at Alice for confirmation. "Damn. But it's gone, right?"

I take my bag. "Gone. But I think we should avoid anything *Titanic*-related for the rest of the day to be safe."

"Agreed," Alice says.

Susannah frowns. "A weak spell is almost worse than a strong one. It's like someone's just toying with us. . . . And casting it in public like that? The person either doesn't think they'll get caught *or* doesn't care. Like the way serial killers send letters to the police."

The warning bell rings. Mary opens the door.

We say our goodbyes, and I speed-walk to Wardwell's

history class. The bell rings just as I enter. I freeze. Jaxon's laughing with Niki, who is sitting on his desk.

"Seats, everyone," Mr. Wardwell says.

Niki slides from her perch, grinning at me. What is it with these girls recently? She flicks her ponytail over her shoulder and touches Jaxon's arm. I plop down in my chair.

Wardwell grabs a stack of thick paper packets. He drops a few of them on each of the front-row desks; they make a weighty clunk as they land. "These packets are divided by categories. You'll be expected to learn or, better yet, memorize them." *Clunk.* "Because . . . next Friday we're having a *Titanic* trivia contest. And the winning team will be excused from the test with an automatic A."

There's a murmur of excitement from the students. Raffles and trivia contests. I've got to hand it to this school; it has have the carrot method down.

"Let's get you used to the *Jeopardy!* categories by starting with some of the passengers we learned about this week. I want a name, what you know about the person, and if they survived."

A few hands shoot up around the room. Wardwell points to Dillon, who is once again in his lacrosse jacket. I don't think I've ever seen him without it.

"Joseph Laroche," Dillon says. "He grew up in Haiti and was working as an engineer in France. He's thought to be the only black dude on the entire ship. His wife and two daughters were on board with him. They got into a lifeboat, but he didn't. He went down with the waves."

"Correct." Wardwell nods and points to a girl in the first row.

"Margaret Brown. She was the only first-class passenger who came from nothing. She and her husband got rich in the mining industry. She was a feminist and suffragette and known for her philanthropy. She helped load passengers into lifeboats, and even rowed in her own boat. She survived."

"Great, perfect," Mr. Wardwell says, and points to Niki.

"Henry Harper," Niki says.

I jerk my head up. *Harper. Uncle Harry. Harry could definitely be a nickname for Henry.*

"He was one of the owners of the Harper and Brothers publishing house and one of the few men who survived with his entire family. I think because they were in one of the first boats and everything hadn't gone crazy yet? Anyway, Henry, his wife, and even his Egyptian valet survived."

All the blood drains from my face. Seeing Elijah threw me for such a loop last night that I didn't consider that the man who called himself my uncle on the *Titanic* could have been my actual ancestor. I raise my hand.

"Exactly right," Mr. Wardwell says. "Samantha?"

"What was his wife's name? Henry Harper's, I mean." My tone is urgent, and a few people turn to look at me.

Mr. Wardwell tilts his head. "Huh, good question." He picks up a packet off his desk and flips through the pages. He runs his finger down one of them. "Henry Sleeper Harper and Myra Haxtun Harper."

The room spins. *Myra H.H.* Either dead people are sending me packages now, or someone knows my family history better than I do.

"Samantha?" Mr. Wardwell says with slight annoyance, and I look up at him. "A name?"

I zero in on Niki. "Why did you pick Henry Harper, Niki?"

She turns around in her chair. "Huh?"

Jaxon stares at me.

"Why did you pick him? Did you have a reason?"

Niki looks at me like I might have lost my mind. She opens her mouth, but Mr. Wardwell interrupts her.

"Samantha, I'll ask that you stay on topic and not disrupt the class." His eyebrows are up, and he looks like he means business. "A name."

I shift my eyes to him. I have the subtlety of a foghorn. "A name?"

"Of a passenger."

"Uh." My mind races. I do know some, but for the life of me I can't think of anything right now except Myra and Henry. And I would bet anything that the painting in the hallway is of her. "Um."

Mr. Wardwell frowns. "Samantha, whichever team you're on isn't going to want a weak link. You'll be first up tomorrow. You'd better study tonight."

CHAPTER FOURTEEN

I Didn't Run Away

The last bell rings, and everyone pushes their way out the classroom door. The dance committee has set up a table and is selling anchor and ship-wheel bracelets. The sign reads: HELP US MAKE THE SPRING FLING UNSINKABLE! GET BOTH BRACELETS AND GIVE ONE TO YOUR DATE! The table is swarmed. Excited conversations about costumes and arguments about who gets to be which passenger fill the hallway. It's strange to me that with more than two thousand people on that ship, everyone wants to be the same ten famous ones. Privileged in life and privileged in death, I guess.

I turn the corner toward my locker. Jaxon's leaning against it. My stomach twists up into one of those complicated nautical knots that are impossible to undo.

"Hey," I say, and stop short in front of him.

He looks as uncomfortable as I do. "Ride home?"

I twist the dial on my lock. "Yeah, maybe we—"

"Yo, Jax!" Dillon yells from down the hall. "You coming with me and Blair to Niki's later?"

Niki and Blair are seriously threatening my last inch of calm.

"Depends," Jaxon says.

"Yeah, depends on whether you grow a set." Dillon grabs his pants for emphasis.

Jaxon laughs. "Dude. Really?"

Dillon's hair is messy, and his backpack is slung over one shoulder. He stops next to Jaxon and grins at me. "Man. Sorry, Sam. I didn't see you there behind Jax's fat shoulder."

I close my locker. Dillon's a total goofball, but I've always liked that about him. What you see is what you get.

I smile. "Don't apologize to me. Jaxon's the delicate one here."

Dillon laughs and punches Jaxon in the arm. "I see why you spend so much time with her."

Jaxon gives him a warning look. "Seriously, dude. I'm gonna have to insist that you shut up."

Mischief tugs at the corners of Dillon's mouth. "Nah, it's cool. Respect. I'm *definitely* not gonna say anything about—"

Jaxon takes a swipe at Dillon, but Dillon jumps out of the way and raises his hands in surrender.

"Okay, man," Dillon says through a laugh. "I get it. Just be at Niki's tonight." Dillon walks into the crowd pushing toward the door.

Jaxon rubs the back of his neck with his hand. "Sorry 'bout that. He thinks he's funny."

I half laugh as we walk toward the side door. "He is funny."

But Jaxon doesn't laugh in return like he normally would. We exit into the parking lot and head for Jaxon's truck. An awkward silence replaces our usual banter.

"So you're going to Niki's tonight?" I ask.

"Does it matter?"

I look at him. "What do you mean?"

"Do you not want me to go to Niki's for some reason?"

Besides the fact that she doesn't like me and would probably make me disappear if she could? "How do you want me to answer that?"

"Words would be best. I'm shit at charades."

I stop next to Jaxon's truck. "How are you this mad at me?"

Jaxon shrugs.

"Words would be best. I'm shit at shrugs," I say.

"I tried words."

"You're frustrated because I won't go to the dance with you? You don't even *know* why I said I wouldn't go." And this is definitely not the moment to tell him that I will go with him. It's going to look like it's for all the wrong reasons.

"How could I? You don't talk to me, Sam."

"Are you kidding? We talk every day. I talk to you more than I talk to anyone besides my dad."

"Small talk. Every time I try to talk to you about something personal, you change the subject. Especially if I bring up Vivian running out on you guys, or what happened in the woods."

"So our friendship doesn't count because I won't talk to you about terrible things I'd rather forget?"

Jaxon shakes his head. "You can twist my words all you want. I'm just saying that right now we have a pretty low standard for friendship. And yesterday morning was a perfect example. You literally ran away from me."

He gets in his truck, and I'm left standing there with my mouth open.

I get in the passenger side. "First of all, I didn't run away; you wouldn't let it go. Second of all, just because I don't want to go to the dance doesn't mean it's about you or our friend-ship."

Jaxon starts his engine. "Not what I'm talking about. If you're honest, you know I have a point."

It takes me several tries to slam my seat belt into its buckle. "Did it ever occur to you that I'm not super open with you about certain things because you're so judgmental? And when something comes out that you don't like, you get all moody. Like this." I gesture at him.

He drives through the parking lot. "Right. I'm the prob-lem. Glad we sorted that."

"I'm not saying I'm not the problem. I'm just saying you are, too. You *hate* magic and anything supernatural."

"That has nothing to do with it."

"That has everything to do with it. You have no idea what you're asking me to tell you, and you're acting like I'm ri-diculous."

"No, I *don't know* what I'm asking you to tell me, because you don't communicate."

"You want me to communicate? How's this for commu-nicating? My *stepmother* was the crow woman!" My hand flies to my mouth.

Oh no. What did I just do?

Jaxon screeches to a stop behind a parked car. *"What?"*

"Forget it." *Damn my temper! I'm such an idiot.*

"I'm definitely not going to forget it." He stares at me, and I stare at the dashboard.

"You're serious, aren't you?"

"Don't you dare tell my dad."

"Hold on. Your *dad* doesn't know?"

I shake my head. "He knows that she was the woman in the woods, but *not* that she was the crow woman. That's the name he associates with my grandmother's death, and I just couldn't lay that on him after everything else that happened. And I swear, if you tell him, I'll . . ."

Jaxon rubs the back of his neck. "I won't tell him. But what about the police?"

"No."

"And she's . . . gone now?"

"Dead. She's dead now."

"Holy shit, Sam. I never imagined . . . You told me she was after your dad's money. It just seemed to fit her personality."

Jaxon pulls away from the curb and turns left onto Blackbird Lane. "I wanna hear this."

I twist my hair up into a messy ball, for no other reason than to occupy my hands. "You want to hear about my stepmother?" *Please don't let me regret this.* "You're not gonna like some of it."

Jaxon pulls into his brick driveway, which is just as uneven as mine is, and turns his engine off. "Let's grab dinner tonight. Out. We definitely can't talk about all this stuff in your house, and I'm pretty sure my mom has superhuman hearing."

I nod without looking at him. "Pizza or something?" I get out of the truck.

Jaxon closes his door and leans against it. "I'm always up for pizza. I'll pick you up at eight?"

"Works for me," I say, awkwardly waving goodbye to him and walking across his driveway to mine.

My dad's car is gone. I pull out my cell phone. Sure enough, I have a text from him saying he went to grab groceries with Mrs. Meriwether.

I also have texts from the girls.

Alice: *Come to Mary's for dinner?*

Mary: *We're getting takeout.*

Damn. I can't cancel on Jaxon. Not after that conversation we just had. I lock the front door behind me.

Me: *Can't come for dinner, but can meet after.*

Susannah: *We'll come to you. Maybe help you go through family records? See if we can find anything on Myra and Henry?*

Me: *It's a plan.*

Alice: *But do NOT touch that dress again, genius.*

I slip my phone into my hoodie pocket and drop my bag by the door. I open my mouth to yell for my dad and remember he's gone. I'm alone. I crack my knuckles. *Should I?*

My stomach does a quick flip. "Elijah?" I say, my voice unsure as I walk through the foyer and down the hallway. I step into the ballroom.

"Elijah?" I say more clearly.

No response.

"I know you hear me." Still no response. I walk past the piano and the beautifully laid-out crystal, used for old-timey cocktail parties—the kind where everyone smokes with those long cigarette holders.

"Elijah, come on." Nothing.

I rub my hands over my face and exhale. "You can't just show up last night after being MIA for six months and then not respond to me."

Silence.

"So you're scared to talk to me?" I say.

"I hear you," he says in his old-world accent.

I whip around. He's in front of the fireplace in a white button-down shirt, a black vest, and black dress pants. His dark hair falls in waves around his face, framing his gray eyes.

We're both quiet for a long couple of seconds.

"Sit." He gestures toward the couch behind me and walks to an armchair on my right. He waits for me to situate myself on the couch before sitting himself. Our knees face each other. I don't know what to do with my hands. I'm still having trouble believing he's actually here, that my brain isn't playing a trick on me.

"That dress," he says. "Tell me all that you know about it." His voice is slightly strained, like he's fighting the urge to leave.

I blink at him. "Wait. Slow down. That's not why I . . . You want to talk about the *dress*?"

He looks uncomfortable. "If it had a spell on it, as I suspect it may have, then yes, I certainly do want to talk about the dress."

I laugh a short laugh. "The dress?" He comes back with no explanation? No greeting, nothing? "Maybe you want to talk about the card, too?"

"I do."

"Or football?"

He raises an eyebrow at me.

"Well, the message on the card is all I know." My tone is clipped.

He sighs like he's trying very hard to not react. "Then you do not know who Myra H.H. is?"

"My great-great-something-aunt who survived the *Titanic*," I say, and wave my hand in the air with frustration. "And speaking of the *Titanic*, why did you throw that book into the secret study?"

"I had begun to suspect that the *Titanic* was an important factor."

He's been watching this unfold and hasn't said a word to me. My chest tightens. "And you said nothing?"

"I did not intend to interfere with your life again," he says, like he finds this whole conversation painful.

My mouth opens. "Too late."

He hesitates. "Samantha, I am sorry that I kissed you last night. I should never have done it."

Wait, what? I stand up, pushing my hair back from my face. "Don't apologize. I haven't been sitting around pining for you, whatever you might think."

"I did not think you were," he says. "Now, if you will just tell me what information you have thus far, I—"

"I don't need your help." I glare at him and his perfect posture. If he won't talk to me about why he left, then I won't talk to him.

His calm wavers. "You do not know what is happening any better than I do."

"I'll figure it out with the girls!"

He stands, looking more agitated than I've ever seen him. "I will leave you, then."

I don't say anything. I don't want him to go, but there isn't a chance I'm going to admit that after he offered no explanation and a kiss apology.

Elijah blinks out.

———

CHAPTER FIFTEEN

Don't Get Me Wrong

I lie in my bed staring blankly at my homework and refusing to look at the bedroom furniture Elijah designed for his sister. Our conversation from earlier plays on a loop in my head. Where has he been all this time? Why didn't he say something if he was here?

I smack my hand down on my bed. *No. I'm not doing this. He's here. I don't care. That's it.*

A hand touches my arm. I look up quickly.

Ada. "Go away," I say.

"Mum always told me that if you come across someone sad and you do not try to make them smile, then you have disgraced your own humanity," Ada says in her British accent. "'Everyone deserves happiness,' she says."

"I'm not sad. But I'm also not in a smiling mood," I say.

"We shall see."

My bed moves as Ada steps over me and plops down. The ruffles on her dress billow before settling in layers around her legs. Ada puts her head on my other pillow, her hand tucked under her cheek, so that we're looking at one another.

"Is it a boy?" Her expression is serious, and her little eyebrows are furrowed. She's so genuine about it that I almost do smile.

"What makes you think it's a boy?"

"My sister did just what you are doing after she found out we were moving to America. She said that she had no friends in Florida and never would." Ada nods her head against her hand. "But it turned out she was just upset to leave a boy. Well, that is what her diary said, anyway."

I lift an eyebrow. "You read her diary?"

Ada's eyes widen, like it's me who said the shocking thing. "She was crying. No one was doing anything to help her, so it only seemed right that I take matters into my own hands. In life-and-death situations, it is acceptable to read other people's diaries."

"When you put it like that, it makes perfect sense."

"Exactly." Ada giggles, mischievous satisfaction dancing in her eyes. "I saw it, you know."

"Saw what?"

"Your smile."

"Did not."

"Did so. It was small, but it was there."

Now I do smile, but Ada disappears.

There are footsteps in the hallway moving closer to my room.

"Sam?" my dad says just outside my door. "Jaxon's here."

Jaxon? I look at my phone: 8:01 p.m. Crapola.

My dad knocks. "Sam?"

"Tell him I'll be right there."

I open my armoire. *Stupid Elijah.* I trade my hoodie for a black slouchy sweater and grab my knee-length black coat.

Vivian bought it for me and was always trying to get me to wear it instead of my vegan leather jacket. *Stupid Vivian.*

I open my door. The sconces give the hallway a soft yellow glow. Paintings of long-dead relatives loom over me as I walk. I grab the banister and take the steps quickly. Jaxon waits at the bottom with my dad.

"Ready," I say as my black boots thud dully from the Oriental rug onto the wood floor.

"There she is," my dad says, and takes a good look at me. I can feel him trying to assess my mood.

I force a smile. "Rough homework night. I lost track of the time."

My dad kisses me on the forehead. "Have fun. Call me if you need anything."

I follow Jaxon out my door and into the fleeting light. The air smells of new grass, and the chill wakes me up.

Jaxon opens the door for me and I climb in his truck.

The more I breathe in the fresh air, the more I think getting out of my house is the best thing I've done in hours. And coming clean with Jaxon about Vivian is a relief. I'm so sick of secrets. "I'm glad we're doing this."

Jaxon gets in and starts the engine. "Yeah, me too. It's nice to see you go out for once. You should come out this weekend, too. I mean, I get why you've been at home with your dad. But Salem in the spring is pretty fun. All the crazies come out of hibernation. The ghost tours start back up, and the street fairs. There is even wand-making."

I smile. "How did you grow up in this town and turn out even remotely normal?"

"Sheer willpower."

"Did you ever make a wand?"

"Totally. It's the highlight of every year."

I laugh. "I call bullshit."

He pretends to look shocked. "That's it. I'm showing you my wand collection when we get back, and you're gonna feel *pretty* ridiculous."

As we near the edge of town, we turn down Derby Street toward the harbor. The tall masts of the *Friendship* stand out like black webs against the soft glow of lights from boats in the distance. The houses in this section of town are old and beautiful. And the narrow streets have a personality, like you can feel the centuries of families and international traders who lived and died here.

"Wait, there's a pizza place down this way?"

Jaxon rolls to a stop at the curb. "Right here."

I get out of the truck and look at the hand-carved wooden sign of an upscale Italian restaurant. Small tea lights frame the windows. "Um, do you mean this fancy place I'm not dressed properly for?"

"Trust me, when you taste their pizza, you'll be thanking me."

He opens the door, and a woman with long hair and weathered skin smiles at us.

Everything is dark wood and candlelight. The walls are a faded brown with burgundy grapevines painted on them. Shelves are made from old shipping crates, and they hold small glass bottles and antique postcards. *When I have a house, I would love it to look like this.*

The woman leads us to a table and gives us our menus.

Our table has a wine bottle on it with a portrait of an Italian villa painted on the glass. A candle sticks out of the top, and wax drips down the sides.

I scan the room. "Okay. I'll hand it to you. This place is beautiful."

Jaxon grins.

"*Ciao, bella. Ciao, signore,*" says our waiter, a cheery man with an apron. "What can I bring you young people on this wonderful evening?"

Jaxon gestures to me.

I look over the drink menu. "Can I have your hot chocolate with a scoop of peppermint gelato?"

The waiter kisses the tips of his fingers and lifts them in the air. "Gelato before dinner—a woman after my own heart." He looks at Jaxon.

"I'll have the house-made root beer. And actually, you can bring your arugula-and-parmesan salad, fettuccine ai funghi, and your burrata-and-basil pizza with pink sauce."

The waiter nods approvingly and takes our menus. "Very well, signore."

"Did you just order for me?" I ask as our waiter walks away.

"Yup," he says.

I stare at him, trying to decide if I should object. But since I like all those foods, I'm not sure that arguing is to my benefit. "Okay, what gives? I mean, I'm impressed. Don't get me wrong. But this is way more than casual pizza so we can chat about . . . everything."

Jaxon smiles. "Take it as an apology. I definitely could have been nicer earlier. I got my back up. Also," he laughs, "I'd like to note that any other girl would be oohing and aahing over me right now for planning all this. And here you are searching for ulterior motives."

"Vivian taught me to be suspicious of nice people," I say before I catch myself. It just popped out.

Jaxon's smile fades. "You cool?"

"Uh, yeah. I just didn't mean to say that. I forget sometimes."

The waiter returns with my hot chocolate. The peppermint gelato floating in it is a thing of beauty. "After your father died and your mother was having all that trouble, how long did it take before you felt normal again?"

Jaxon's blue eyes soften. "Man, I think it took me about a year before I felt like myself again. I was depressed for a while."

I sip my drink. "Some days sail by and I think I've never been happier. Then all of a sudden I'll remember everything that happened and I feel, I don't know, like I'm kidding myself."

The waiter returns with our arugula salad, which has the tangy scent of lemon vinaigrette and is teeming with shaved Parmesan.

Jaxon spears some salad with his fork. "You know how I told you that after my dad died, my mom was convinced that he was still around?"

I chew the spicy leaves. "Yeah."

"Well, I was, too."

I pause, my fork halfway to my mouth. "Was he?" Is Jaxon saying he used to believe in spirits?

He shrugs. "I don't know. But the town never liked that my mom dabbled in herbs and potions, and they especially didn't like that she was so close to your grandmother. The way she used to talk to my father like he was still there pushed them over the edge. And I got caught in the crossfire."

"But I thought people in Salem live for that stuff. You said it yourself . . . wand making is a *thing* here. How could they come down on your mom and you for that?"

"Yeah, but Salem's selective. Also, my mom's not a Descendant. Lizzie's family was one of the ones that didn't like her. So as I'm sure you can imagine, I became a target in school. Public humiliation was an everyday thing for a while, and as you know, when it's about people you really care about, you can't brush it off. It hurt every time someone brought it up. Dillon was actually my only friend through the whole thing."

I never considered that Descendant politics would affect people like Jaxon, and definitely not in this way. "That's horrible."

Jaxon studies my face. "That's why I have no patience for all this supernatural stuff."

The waiter returns, placing the fettuccine on the table and the pizza on a stand. The smell of cream and mushrooms and fresh dough swirls around me like a hug.

I grab a slice of pizza. "I get that. My introduction to Salem magic wasn't exactly gentle. And my dad would flip if he knew how intense things got."

"So you don't talk to him about it?"

I look at my food, not completely comfortable with the truth. "No. I basically act like it didn't happen. We don't talk about Vivian."

"I get it," he says, and I look back up at him. "Protecting your parent through selective information, I mean. I used to do the same thing." Jaxon takes a sip of root beer. He sets his glass down and taps his fingers against it like he's trying to decide something. "Also . . . what about the noise at breakfast the other morning? Was denying it about protecting him, too?"

I take a deep breath. "Yes."

Just then an awful briny smell fills my nose and I drop my fork. The drowned man appears next to our table, dripping salt water all over the floor. He has stubble on his cheeks, and his hat shadows his eyes.

My heart beats a muffled thrum in my ears.

"Sam?" Jaxon says, but I'm not looking at him.

The drowned man extends his arm toward me, holding an old-fashioned dog collar in his open palm.

I stand, shoving my chair away from the table.

"Sam, what's going on?" Jaxon asks, standing now, too.

The drowned man steps forward, pushing the dog collar at me. "Don't be daft. Take it," he says in an accent that sounds Irish.

I step backward, colliding with the chair. I reach for the table to steady myself but secure only the tablecloth and manage to pull it and all the food down with me as I fall.

I hit the floor so hard it knocks the wind out of me. The drowned man tosses the dog collar under the table and blinks out. Jaxon is at my side in a flash, and the whole restaurant is staring. I pluck a napkin off the floor and wrap up the collar before Jaxon can see it.

"Sam? What happened?" Jaxon helps me to my feet. "You're bleeding."

There's a patch torn out of my sweater, exposing a cut. "I have to go."

CHAPTER SIXTEEN

I Just Need a Minute to Think

I race down the sidewalk toward the harbor. The cold air seeps through my clothes.

"Sam!" Jaxon yells, running after me. He grabs my arm, pulling me to a stop. "What the hell just happened in there?"

I look back at the restaurant, disoriented. "I don't know. I don't know."

Jaxon takes note of my jittery hands. He unzips his coat and puts it around my shoulders. "Let me get my truck. I'll bring it to you."

"Yes. No. I can't go home yet. I don't want my dad to see me like this. I just need a minute to think."

Jaxon looks over his shoulder. "How about we go to my studio?"

I nod.

I follow Jaxon down the brick sidewalk through the moonlit streets and work on slowing my heart rate. He stops near a streetlamp, pulls out a key, and unlocks an old door.

The house is two stories tall with charcoal-gray trim around the windows. The arched roof has dark shingles, reminiscent of a cottage, that are spotted with greenish, mossy patches, I guess from being so close to the water.

He pushes the door open.

The house has a stronger version of Jaxon's pine scent. He flicks on a light switch and closes the door behind us.

The room has high ceilings with exposed beams, hardwood floors, and walls whose chipping paint reveals other colors behind the cream top coat. It's filled with workbenches and beautifully carved furniture.

I run my hand along a rustic wooden table with a complicated grain.

"That's one of my new favorites," he says, and comes to stand next to me. "See how there are no seams? It's one piece of wood. It took me a long time to find it. It's the type of thing my dad used to make for my mom. I'm a . . . I'm giving it to her for her birthday."

I look up at Jaxon. He rarely talks about his dad. "It's perfect. She'll love it."

He beams at the compliment. "Come, sit down."

I make my way to a navy-blue couch in front of a fireplace, and I sink into the soft cushions. He flips a switch and flames shoot up in the hearth.

I type into a group text I have with the Descendants.

Me: *I just saw the drowned man again. Can we meet up sooner?*

Jaxon grabs a first-aid box off the mantel and sits down next to me. "Let's take a look at that arm."

I slip his coat off. "Sorry I ruined our dinner."

"Actually, you didn't ruin it at all. I got a few good bites in before you took down our table." Jaxon adjusts my sweater, trying to get at the cut. "Can you take this off? I mean, do you have a T-shirt or something underneath?"

"No, but . . ." I pull my arm out of the sleeve and readjust the fabric around my side so that my bra isn't showing.

The cut isn't deep, but it's a good three inches long. What did I land on? A knife? A piece of glass? Jaxon dabs the cut with an alcohol wipe and I wince.

His sandy hair falls in his eyes. "You saw another ghost, didn't you?"

"He was dripping salt water."

Jaxon tenses. "Hold on, what?"

"Honestly, I don't know. He smelled like he'd walked straight out of the ocean. I saw him once before at school, and he scared the crap out of me then, too."

"So you've been seeing ghosts a lot, then?"

I pause. "Define 'a lot.'"

"I'm pretty sure that answers my question. Besides looking creepy as hell, though, is there anything they can do? I mean, can they blow out all the lights or—"

"Actually . . . I'm not sure. What I do know, though, is that spirits feel exactly like living people to me. Solid."

"So this guy could've hurt you?"

I nod. "Probably. Hence the backpedaling and destroying the restaurant."

"So any dead lunatic could wander in and potentially do something to you? Do you even know what this guy wanted or who he was?" Jaxon squeezes antibiotic cream onto my arm and covers it with a piece of gauze.

I help him hold it in place while he tapes it up. "It's complicated."

Jaxon lets go of my arm, and I slip it back into my sweater. "Okay, start from the beginning. We both know I'm not great with all the magic stuff, but I'm gonna do my best."

I consider his offer. "You know what, it might be nice if you knew."

"Let's make a deal," he says. "We'll be honest with each other, even if it's weird and uncomfortable."

"Deal." I smile. "Oh, and about our conversation yesterday morning, I changed my mind. I am going to go to the dance."

Jaxon reaches out and pulls me into a hug. His warm hands grip my back. He doesn't come off as the guarded type, but in some ways he is. He laughs and jokes with everyone, but there is a lot more to Jaxon than his humor.

Jaxon pulls back and looks at me. He doesn't take his arms from around my sides. *Oh no.* His look is focused. *He's not going to . . . I . . . Shit.* He leans forward, his breath hot on my lips.

I put my hand on his chest just before his lips touch mine. "Wait."

Jaxon lets go of me and rubs his neck. "Sorry, I definitely didn't plan to do that. I don't know what . . . Sorry." He laughs, but his expression shows his disappointment.

My cheeks are blazing. "No, it's fine." I shift uncomfortably. "It's not you. I'm just . . . I don't know. We're friends. I like our relationship the way it is." *Why did he have to do this now, when we're finally talking?* "Today has just been intense. And last night. There was this thing with this dress, and Elijah showed up." The moment the words leave my mouth, I realize my mistake.

His embarrassment disappears. *"Elijah's back?"*

Great, now he's going to assume I just dropped that information to explain not kissing him. Smooth.

Jaxon's frustration is obvious. He scans the room. "Is he here now?"

"No." I pull at my sweater sleeves.

Jaxon focuses on me again. "And ghosts can touch you."

I meet his eyes. "What?"

"Nothing." Jaxon stands up so quickly that I wince.

"Hold on. Are you mad right now?"

"No."

"You're pacing."

Jaxon picks up my coat. "How 'bout we call it a night."

My mouth opens. "What happened to wanting to help me figure things out? Was that all about kissing me?"

"Don't be stupid. I just need . . . Let's just go."

"You want me to tell you things, be honest with you. Just not the things you don't want to hear?"

He exhales and hands me my coat.

I yank it from his hands.

CHAPTER SEVENTEEN

Could This Be Real?

I sit on my bed frowning at the dog collar and chewing on my thumbnail. What does this thing mean? Why would the drowned man give it to me? It seriously makes no sense. I can't help but think about Redd saying "possibly" when I asked her if I was going to be the one to die.

My cell phone buzzes on my nightstand and I jolt.

Alice: *Takeout was a disaster. Food poisoning happened. Are you okay?*

Mary: *You're welcome to come over. But fair warning that we're paying homage to the toilet bowl.*

I check the time: 10:27 p.m. *Damn, I was really hoping seeing them would calm my nerves.*

Me: *Don't worry. The drowned man story can wait. Just get some rest and feel better.*

Susannah: *Text us if you change your mind. Sleep is unlikely.*

I drop my phone in my blankets. Crap. That means I'm

gonna have to look for those family records alone. Or I could ask Elijah? *No. Definitely no.*

I slide off my bed and grab the flashlight out of my night-stand drawer. I make my way quietly into the hall, listening for my dad. There are no lights on besides the small sconces. He's probably still downstairs in his office. And if he's down-stairs, then sneaking into the study isn't the best idea. I guess I could start in the attic?

I tiptoe down the hallway where my dad's room is and press the flashlight on. Mostly, the rooms at the back of the house are unused or have become a place to store extra furni-ture. But behind one of these doors is a staircase. I discovered it when I first moved in and made the rounds.

I stop at a door with a wrought-iron latch instead of a knob and unhook it. "Bingo."

The signature musty smell that inhabits attics wafts out. I grab the wooden railing and latch the door behind me.

The room is bigger than the secret study and much less re-fined. There are boxes stacked in piles and loose floorboards. Nails stick out of the slanted walls at all angles like a torture device from the Dark Ages. *Please, please don't let me trip.* The thing that's noticeably absent, though, besides good light, is spiderwebs. Shouldn't they be all over this room? I swear, if Elijah was cleaning the attic instead of spending time with me, he'll have officially achieved a new low.

I shine the flashlight at the stacks of cardboard boxes. Most of them have labels like MATHER CHINA and CANDLEHOLDERS. Nothing so far that looks like it might contain old family documents. Against the far wall is an open wooden crate with about ten cloth-wrapped squares in it. *Paintings? Hmmm.* Waving the flashlight around me to be sure I wasn't wrong about those spiders, I walk to the crate and peer inside. Yup, definitely paintings. All neatly packaged and tied up . . . except the one on the end.

I pull at the cloth, and it comes off in my hand. I almost drop the flashlight. It's *the* painting. The one from the hall with the woman that changed.

A chill runs down my spine. Did my dad move this up here? Maybe I didn't hide how creeped out I was about it? But still, wouldn't he have said something? I look quickly over my shoulder at the musty room. Nothing's there but shadows.

"So was I right? Are you Myra?" I ask the painting as I examine it.

I tip the frame forward and shine my light at the brown paper backing, looking for one of those note cards my grandmother sometimes used to catalog things. But I find a small plain envelope instead, taped to the bottom corner, and poke it tentatively with one finger. Nothing happens. I put my hand on it and leave it there for a second.

Seems safe. I carefully dislodge it, brace my flashlight under my arm, and open it, only to discover an older envelope inside. It's written in my grandmother's cursive and reads:

Letter to Grandmother Haxtun
(Maria DeLong Haxtun)
from her cousin Helen Hopson.
Account of the Titanic disaster.

My heart beats faster. Aren't letters like these supposed to be in museums? Could this be real? I carefully pull out the folded paper.

TWO HUNDRED TEN RIVERSIDE DRIVE
NEW YORK, N.Y.

Dear Cousin Maria,

Aunty Myra and Uncle Harry are both home safe and fairly sound considering all they have been through, which means that they are nervously tired out, though otherwise well.

When their ship struck the iceberg Aunty Myra saw the great wall of ice scraping along past her porthole for the lights were turned on still, and she knew just what had happened, so she got Uncle Harry + valet up to dress him. He had been so ill with grippe he had to be helped up and almost carried onto the deck. They made their way to an upper deck where were very few people, and were the last to leave that deck. Both were warmly dressed so did not suffer from exposure but the boat was so crowded all the men could not sit down, and in that state they waited and watched for the first steamer. It was so clear that all through the night they could see stars so near the horizon they thought must be ships' lights. When daylight broke they seemed to be completely hemmed in by a field of ice and yet that other little steamer made straight for them. The people on it did their utmost to make things comfortable for them, gave up their beds, took off their clothes for them almost and saw that every thing possible was done to relieve their suffering. But I do feel that we have a true miracle come our way this time in having our own people so wonderfully saved.

Mother knows everything now, and has stood it very well, but the rest of us are pretty well worn out. You see we didn't get any real news from them until Thursday evening just before they got home and what a relief it was!

I'm sorry this is so short + sketchy. Perhaps I'll have time to write more fully later, and hope it hasn't been so long either as to make your poor bruised head feel any worse.

Mother says to tell you that she means someday to send you a picture of my father *and will try to find one of herself to send too.*

This letter is a disgraceful one to send to anyone who writes such lovely ones as you do, but I didn't want to wait any longer to send you even a scribble if it was a good news one.

Lovingly Helen T. H.

A board creaks behind me, and I whip around to find a black cat staring at me. It's pear-shaped and squints at my bright flashlight. Is this a joke? I head for the stairs, full speed, letter in hand.

I take the steep wooden steps so quickly my heel misses one, and I slide down three of them on my butt. I land unceremoniously with a clunk in the hallway, holding the letter away from my body so I don't crease it. The pain sharpens everything into focus.

I latch the door behind me and instantly feel guilty for leaving the cat.

"Sam?" my dad calls from what sounds like the bottom of the main staircase. "What was that noise?"

"Nothing. I just tripped! Don't worry!" I yell back, staring at the attic door.

Of all the ridiculous . . . I'll just run up, scoop up the cat, and come right back down. I grab the latch, and something moves by my feet. The cat walks right through the door and into the hallway, its fat belly swinging between its legs.

"Oh, you've got to be kidding me."

CHAPTER EIGHTEEN

The Question Disappears

I stand by the railing, watching the porthole lights reflect off the dark water. A salty breeze blows a couple of wisps of my hair free from their pins, and they tickle my cheek.

"I thought you might need this," says a familiar voice, and I turn around.

Alexander holds my long white coat. I'm surprised to see him after I embarrassed myself in the dining room. But I'm happy he came looking for me.

"Thank you. I'm sorry I ran out on you during dinner like that." Why did I run out on dinner? I open my mouth to ask him what he remembers, but the question disappears from my thoughts.

I slip my arms into the sleeves as he holds my coat up for me.

"It is of no concern. Lots of passengers are unused to the motion of the ship. I will admit that even I ran from the dining room on the first day."

He watches me intently. I focus on fastening the small silk buttons on the bodice of my coat, but my lace gloves make it nearly impossible to hold on to the slippery things.

"I'm pretty sure the world would be a lot easier if I didn't have to wear these confounded gloves." I shake my hands in the air. Since when do I use words like "confounded"? I frown. Why don't I sound like myself?

He laughs, breaking my train of thought, and my worry disperses like smoke.

"That is precisely why I make it a point never to wear lace gloves when I have buttons to do," he says.

I laugh, too, and breathe in the ocean air. What was I just thinking about? It must not have been that important. "You were going to tell me a story before I ran away earlier, I believe."

"Ah, yes. The story of how I wound up here with you instead of stuck in France with my insufferable aunt for another week. Shall we walk?"

He offers me his arm and I accept it. My dress limits my movements, and we walk at a slow pace.

"As you know, many transatlantic ships were canceled because of the coal strike, and everyone was rescheduled to board the *Titanic*."

I nod. That does sound like something I know.

"Well, my father and I had gone to Paris for business and somehow got coerced into staying for my aunt's birthday. We tried every excuse we could think of, but she would not hear of our leaving." He looks at me as we walk. "Samantha, her children screamed all day and all night, her friends were world-class snobs who talked about nothing but diamonds and hat feathers, and she kept finding ways to bring over young women she thought would be good marriage material for me."

"That does sound bad. Especially the marriage part." I examine his face. "How old are you, anyway?"

"Seventeen. I'll be eighteen in January."

"Um, yeah. You're much too young."

He smiles. "Is that so?"

"Not even a question."

"I wish you would tell that to my aunt." A few men in top hats pass us, arguing over which of them is the best card-player. "Because there I was in Paris, one of the greatest cities in the world, having a perfectly miserable time. And it was no better for my father. My aunt was trying to arrange introductions for him, too."

"Are your parents divorced?"

Alexander looks shocked. Did I say something wrong?

Alexander smiles, and again my question drifts from my thoughts. "My mother passed when I was small."

I look down. "I'm sorry. I had no idea. I really need to learn to think before I speak."

"I actually quite enjoy your frankness. It is rare that you meet someone who says what they think without trying to manage your impression of them."

His words feel almost familiar, like I've heard them from someone before. "So how did you ever escape your aunt?" I ask.

"With trickery and plotting," he says, and raises his eyebrows dramatically. "I paid the butler to deliver a note to my father at dinner, pleading for his immediate return to New York to handle urgent business matters. Of course, he recognized my handwriting, and he scolded me for it later, but he took advantage of the opportunity without pause."

"But how did you get on this liner? I heard it was completely booked up."

"Aha, well, that is a whole other drama." He gestures toward large windows that look into a gorgeous room with intricately carved walls and velvet armchairs. "Shall we sit for a while in the lounge?"

"Certainly. But then I must retire to my room." Is it wrong for me to be spending so much time with him? Will my uncle disapprove? Why am I even worrying about this?

For a moment disappointment flashes on Alexander's face. "Well then, I must dedicate myself to making my conversation so interesting that you want to stay a bit longer."

A butler opens the door for us and we enter the lounge. Inside, there's a buzz of conversation. We navigate through tables of people playing cards, drinking after-dinner tea, and telling jokes. Near a wide bookcase, an older gentleman with a white beard and a bow tie sits by himself, reading.

"Good evening, Mr. Stead," I say as we pass. How do I know his name? Wait, I met him in the café, right?

The man looks up from his book and smiles. "Good evening. Never a more beautiful night, if you ask me."

"I could not agree more," says Alexander.

Mr. Stead's smile widens, and he returns to his book. Alexander leads me to a velvet couch that's isolated from the loud socializing groups. He helps me take off my coat and drapes it over a nearby armchair. We sit.

For a second he watches me without speaking.

"What?"

He doesn't break his gaze. "I was just thinking how if I had not finagled my way out of my aunt's house and bartered my way on board, I never would have spent this evening with you."

Before I can respond, Alexander's father approaches us.

"Well, good evening, Miss Mather," he says, and bows. "I hope my son isn't boring you with too many stories."

"Not at all," I say. "Only exciting ones."

"Yes, well," he says, and frowns at me. "Alex, do come find me when you are done. I imagine you will be retiring to your room soon, Miss Mather." His intonation implies it's a statement and not a question.

Is he suggesting that I leave? "Of course," I say.

He bows again and walks away.

"I don't think your father likes me," I say to Alexander in a hushed voice.

He laughs. "Sometimes I wonder if he likes me. Now, what were we saying?"

"I believe you were going to tell me how you bartered your way on board?"

"Ah, yes. My father paid an Italian immigrant and his brother an unreasonable sum to give us their steerage tickets. The White Star Line told us the first-class cabins were full. But of course, once we arrived on board, we were able to talk to Bruce Ismay and arrange other accommodations. J. P. Morgan and Alfred Vanderbilt canceled their trips at the very last moment, and their suites were available."

"Bruce Ismay?"

"One of the *Titanic*'s owners."

"Oh, right. Well, weren't you fortunate."

He smiles. "I do feel very lucky right now."

His happiness is so infectious that I feel lightened by it myself. "And what will you do with all your newfound luck?" I ask.

"Use it to make a bet."

I raise an eyebrow. "What kind of a bet?"

"A bet that before we reach New York, you will dance with me."

I laugh. "You know there's no dance floor on this ship."
For a brief moment my confidence falters. How do I know
that? Maybe Mollie told me?

"I do," he says, and my lightness returns.

"I'll take that bet. But I—"

CHAPTER NINETEEN

What a Mess

". . . hope you are prepared to lose."

There's a loud beeping noise, and I stab at my phone with my pointer finger until it goes away. There's also a text.

Alice: *Got no sleep. Not coming to school. Meet us in Ropes Mansion Garden when you get out.*

I squint at the dim light shining through the white lace of my bedroom curtains. *White lace, white gloves . . .* I sit straight up in my bed and a pit forms in my stomach. The box with the green dress is on the floor next to my trunk, where I put it two days ago. What's the deal? That wasn't a dream like the other dreams about the *Titanic*. That was exactly like what happened when I put on the dress. I didn't know myself there; I couldn't remember who I was. And that guy, I was flirting with him. What the hell?

The blankets move at the end of my bed. I launch out of my covers and onto the floor so fast that I barely get my legs under me. A black paw emerges from a mound of down comforter, followed by a furry head. The pear-shaped cat stretches and then dedicates itself to licking its wobbly belly.

"So you're sleeping in my bed now? Why not on my head? Might as well just sleep there. I have zero privacy anyway."

The cat doesn't bother looking up.

I open my vanity drawer and take out the *Titanic* letter and the dog collar. I tuck the letter into my Gracie book for safekeeping and knot the napkin around the collar so I don't accidentally touch it.

I grab the black sweatshirt draped on my chair and carefully pull it over my bandaged arm as I head into the hall toward the stairs. I try to shake off the icky feeling I have about my nondream. It's not like anything bad happened per se, but my gut tells me that place is dangerous. I can feel it in my bones, something terrible looming there right outside of my view.

I shudder and grab the banister. Also, what a mess last night with Jaxon. Six months with no flirting or anything, then the moment my life goes haywire, he does, too. I just hope that attempted kiss doesn't screw everything up.

"Hey," my dad says from the foyer as I reach the bottom of the stairs. "I was just coming to wake you up."

I couldn't be happier to see my dad. I walk straight up to him and hug him. "I love you."

He smiles and wraps his arm around my shoulders as we walk down the hallway. "There is no one I love more on this earth than you."

I nod my head into his side. "We eating here?"

"We're eating alone this morning. Mae had to go to the bakery to handle some business, and Jaxon had to leave early to pick someone up."

Pick someone up? I don't buy it; he's avoiding me.

My dad releases me in order to push open the kitchen door. The smell of bell peppers and onions greets me.

"And since we're all alone, I figured we could have good old fried-egg sandwiches."

"Yes and yes," I say, sitting down at the small breakfast table we almost never use, now that we do so many meals with the Meriwethers. I've always liked it, though, because it's in front of an arched window that looks out over the backyard.

I pour myself a mug of coffee and stir in half-and-half and a scoop of cocoa. Eggs sizzle in the frying pan.

Egg sandwiches were always our guilty-pleasure breakfast. Vivian hated them. I think it was because Dad once told her they were my mother's favorite food. "Did Mom like living in Salem?" I ask, and sip my coffee. Nothing better than the first sip.

My dad flips the eggs. "Your mom *loved* Salem. Her family owned a bookstore here for generations. And your mother made it her personal mission to read all the books in it. Getting her out of that store for a date always made me feel like I'd achieved something." He smiles at the memory and wipes his hands on the dish towel draped over his shoulder. "Although, she was never gentle about letting me know when hanging out with me was *less* interesting than her current book." He laughs.

"And the bookstore got sold after her parents died, right? Did it stay a bookstore?"

He carries over two plates and places one in front of me. He made the pepper-and-onion hash browns in the shape of pancakes and put them on hard rolls with fried eggs and cheese.

"Yum," I say.

He pours himself some steaming coffee in his #1 DAD mug

and sits down. "I don't think so; I'm pretty sure it became a beauty shop or something. Honestly, I didn't investigate it. At the time it held too many memories."

I nod with a mouth full of egg sandwich.

My dad sips his coffee. "Oh, you know what? Another package arrived this morning from the mysterious Myra H. H."

I choke on my food. "What?"

"Only, I assume it was for me this time. I thought the Mathers were eccentric, but the Haxtuns are clearly giving them a run for their money."

My pulse quickens. "Can I see it?"

"It's in my office." He pauses. "What's the thing? You look worried."

I force my shoulders down. "Nope. Just curious. Did you get a dress, too?"

He laughs. "Almost. I got a bowler hat. I've never worn a bowler hat in my life. I'm starting to wonder if this Myra, whoever she is, is cleaning out her closets and sending antique clothes to her distant relatives. Wouldn't surprise me."

My stomach knots up. "Yeah, I bet you're right. I hope she sends jewelry next or a cool pocket watch."

My dad nods. "There was no return label on my package, either. I asked Mae if she knew of any Haxtuns in Salem. But no luck there. I did find contact information for a cousin Mom had listed in her address book, though. I've never met her, but I'm going to give her a call later today."

My mind spins. I one hundred percent can't have him researching Myra and figuring out that we're getting packages from a dead person—or someone pretending to be a dead person. He'll flip. "Dad, you really don't have to do that. I'm sure if she wanted us to respond, she would have listed a return address."

"I'm curious, though. Aren't you?" His eyes search mine.

"Yeah. For sure," I say. But I can't have my dad poking around in these presents or they'll lead him to ask questions about the *Titanic*. And I don't want him even thinking about that, not with Redd's ominous warning—and her unclear answer—about who was at risk of dying. The girls and I are just going to have to move faster. Spells, whatever it takes.

CHAPTER TWENTY

What's Going on Here?

I walk down the hall toward history class and pull out my phone. There's a reply from Alice in response to my rant over the bowler hat.

Alice: *Either both packages were actually sent by a generous dead relative, or someone wants you to think that. I almost hope it's the first, because the second means there is some hidden agenda. Not good.*

Me: *I know. Agreed. We need to make a plan today.*

Alice: *As opposed to not making one? Brilliant thinking.*

My shoulder collides with someone and I drop my phone. It slides a few inches and stops near a pair of guy's shoes. Matt stares at me with an amused look and bends down to retrieve it.

"Sorry," I say.

He hands me back my phone. "Truthfully, I wasn't watchin' where I was goin', either. It wasn't all you."

I check my phone for damage.

"You're Sam, right?" he says.

"You know I am," I say flatly. This line is usually followed by a question about the woods or me seeing spirits.

He laughs. "Amazin'. You care almost as little as I do."

There is a beat of silence. "So you're the exchange student staying with Blair," I say, not sure how to respond. "How are you liking Salem?"

"Who do you think this school gossips about more: you fa bein' able to see ghosts and do magic, which I can only assume is complete rubbish? Or me, for 'avin 'ad multiple kamikaze-style endin's to my relationship wif Niki?"

I laugh. No one ever calls out the rumors like that, at least not to me. "I'm leaning toward you, considering those hall-way screaming matches you guys have had recently."

"Hmmm. Well, there's always time fa you to catch up. Just turn a teacher into a frog or somefin'. Be'er yet, turn Niki into one."

"So you say now. But come next week, I bet you two will be all over each other again."

Matt smirks. "Do I detect a li'l jealousy?"

"What? No," I say quickly.

His smirk widens. "Relax. I'm kiddin'." He pauses. "Do you mind if I ask you somefin'?"

"You don't seem like the asking type."

"Good point. So then, why did you run away from me and Niki the other day when we were outside? You looked seriously bothered by somefin'."

"Oh, um, yeah. It was a bad day."

"Also, you were talkin' to an empty bench."

I laugh awkwardly. "It's like you said, I don't exactly have a reputation for being normal in this school."

Matt smiles. "You say that like it's a bad thing." The

bravado has left his voice. "Believe me, as someone who didn't grow up 'ere, I don't think you should want to fit in. You're way be'er as you are."

I look at him, shocked by how genuinely nice that was.

"Anyway, the bell's about to ring. See you around," he says, and continues down the hallway before I can reply.

I open the door to AP History. Niki's sitting on Jaxon's desk.

"You guys should come over again tonight. Kick off the weekend," Niki says.

Wait, he went to her house last night after we fought? I sink into my hard seat.

The bell rings.

Niki jumps down from Jaxon's desk, leans over, and whispers something in his ear before walking off. I look at Jaxon, but he's busy pulling out his homework.

"Settle down, everyone," Wardwell says. "Sam, you're up first for trivia. Give me a name of a famous passenger, a brief description, and whether or not they survived."

I clear my throat. "Hammad Hassab. He lived in Cairo, and he was twenty-seven years old. Henry Harper hired him as an interpreter while he was traveling there and then offered to pay his fare to come to America as his valet. He survived." I looked him up after I saw him that night at dinner. "He was the only full-blooded Egyptian on board *and* he was the only non-Lebanese Arab passenger to survive."

Wardwell nods. "Correct. Also, speaking of Hammad and the Harpers, who you were asking about yesterday . . . Did you know that they were one of the only families that survived without casualties? And even more remarkable, their dog survived with them."

I drop my pen and glance toward my bag, which holds the dog collar. Could Wardwell's comment be a coincidence? Unlikely.

"Well, I thought it was interesting, anyway," Wardwell continues when I don't answer. "Anyone else?"

Niki raises her hand and Wardwell points to her.

"William Stead. He was a newspaper editor for years in England and built a reputation because of his political writing. His articles were responsible for expanding the navy's funding and exposing child prostitution and raising the age of consent to sixteen. But later in life he started a paper called *War Against War* and became committed to peace through arbitration. He was on the *Titanic* because President Taft had invited him to be a part of a peace congress at Carnegie Hall. He died on the ship."

Okay, what's going on here? First the dog collar, and now this. The morning after I meet Henry Harper, Niki names him in class. Now Wardwell mentions the dog, and I just saw William Stead in my nondream last night. I look from the back of Niki's blow-dried head to Wardwell. All of a sudden, I don't trust either of them.

CHAPTER TWENTY-ONE

I'm Standing Still and Staring

I close my locker. No sign of Jaxon and no text. He wouldn't have left without saying anything, would he? To be fair, I don't need a ride right now. But still. I'll just swing past his parking spot on my way out.

I pull out my phone and text Alice.

Me: *Headed over now.*

As I move through the hall, I slip my arms into my jacket and sling my bag over my shoulder. I go out the door that leads to the student parking lot and stop short. Jaxon is talking to Niki next to his truck, and she's holding on to his shirt. In the rare instances that Jaxon is mad at me, he still offers me a ride; we just drive home listening to music instead of talking. I really don't want to watch this. But I am watching it, and I'm standing still and staring.

Oh no. He saw me. He's looking directly at me . . . and waving? Am I supposed to wave back? *I will not wave at you like everything is normal!* He looks at me for a second longer and goes back to his conversation with Niki.

I lift my chin and walk as fast as I can in the direction of Essex Street.

I arrive at the Ropes Mansion Garden in record time. As I pass under the vine-covered trellis, I spot the Descendants. Alice, Mary, and Susannah stand around the sundial in the center of the circular garden, just like the first day I had a real conversation with them. Back when I still believed that there was a logical order to the world and that magic was something you found in bedtime stories.

They turn and watch me approach. Three gothic-chic stunners in a sea of spring green.

I drop my bag on the ground and join their circle. "Are you guys feeling better?"

Susannah tucks a stray piece of auburn hair into her bun. "Much better."

"Speak for yourself," Alice says. "While you were being cared for by your mom and your girlfriend, Mary and I had to fend for ourselves."

"My parents were visiting my aunt," Mary explains. "They didn't get home until late."

I look at Susannah. "Hang on, you have a girlfriend? How did I not know this?"

"Because you've barely talked to us in six months. What were you expecting, a memo of updates?" Alice's matter-of-fact harshness hits me like a slap.

"I . . ." I have no idea what to say. She's right. It didn't occur to me, when she said it last time, how distant I've been. Actually, that's why Jaxon was frustrated with me, too. Maybe I really have been closed off.

Susannah dismisses Alice's comment with a small wave of her hand. "I'll introduce you to her."

"Now, moving on . . . ," Alice says.

Wouldn't it be amazing if we *did* spend our time talking about the awkward things we said on dates, rather than the weirdo packages delivered by dead people who may or may not want to harm us?

Susannah pulls her already slim-fitting black coat tighter around her body. "Even though we were sick, we did find out something about that key Alice got."

"Oh?" I ask.

"The engraving IST CL ST RM D33 is old shorthand for 'first-class stateroom D33,'" Alice says. "It was Mary who figured it out. Before we ate that death food, she went to her aunt's antique shop and asked some questions."

I almost don't want to ask. "And room D33? Was that a room on the *Titanic*?"

"You bet," Mary says.

I press my lips together. "Was it the Harpers'?"

"It certainly was," Susannah says. "At the very least, there's a connection between some of these strange occurrences."

"Actually, there's another connection to the Harpers. . . . So I told you I saw the drowned man last night. I was in a restaurant with Jaxon, and he blinked in right next to my table."

Mary's eyes widen. "Oh, you've got to be kidding me. That's so creepy."

"Beyond. He shoved a dog collar at me. And I think he had an Irish accent?" I pull the cloth restaurant napkin out of my pocket and unknot it. "I didn't touch it just in case."

Susannah examines the old leather collar with dulled metal accents. "It looks like an antique."

I nod. "And take a wild guess whose dog survived the *Titanic*?"

Mary frowns. "The Harpers'?"

"They had a Pekingese. And guess how I found out?

Wardwell told me—not the class, *me*—right in the middle of his lesson. Only to be followed up by Niki talking about William Stead, who I saw in my *Titanic* dream last night."

Alice's eyes widen. "That's it. I don't care what you all thought you were doing this weekend, 'cause you're not doing it anymore. Someone or something is trying to communicate with us, and we need to figure out what it means before Redd's warning becomes a reality."

CHAPTER TWENTY-TWO

I'm All In

Susannah leans against the soft cushions on Alice's black couch. "How physically close to us is this person that they can do things like put a spell on a raffle ticket or tamper with the paintings in your house? And why haven't I been able to sense who they are?"

"You don't always sense people," Mary says. "And right now our entire school is exploding with *Titanic* mania. If someone is casting spells related to the *Titanic,* it'd be pretty easy to cover up or blend in."

"I mean, it's kinda genius to saturate our school with the *Titanic* right as these weird things are happening," Alice says. "That can't have been accidental."

"Is there anyone at our school who could do this kind of magic?" I ask.

Susannah sighs. "Honestly, no one we know of. The packages, the paintings, your nondreams, the key, the seasickness spell that someone put on me. Whoever is orchestrating this is *excellent* at magic. That's not someone we would have missed."

"So then what if it's not one person? What if it's a group and some of them happen to be at our school?" I ask.

"Interesting." Alice sits in her black armchair with her feet on the coffee table. "Now, *that* is a possibility. Although as far as we know, no one else at Salem High does magic besides us. But that doesn't mean we couldn't have overlooked some low-level caster."

"Maybe Wardwell?" I say.

Mary shakes her head. "There *was* an accused witch with the last name Wardwell. But this Wardwell isn't related. It's just a name coincidence. And we've never sensed anything magical from him."

"Well, what about Niki and Blair?" I ask.

Alice grunts. "Niki's closest connection to any magical family line is that we go to the same dentist." Alice looks at me. "So basically, nada magic over there. And Blair wouldn't know a spell book if I hit her in the face with one." Alice grins. "Although maybe we should test that theory?"

"If I can do a spell, anyone can do a spell," I say.

"Ehhht." Alice makes a buzzing noise like I got the wrong answer on a game show. "Not even close. You're a Descendant, and I saw you in the woods doing complex spells when you didn't even know how. You could probably fart wrong and a spell would come out."

Mary giggles. She's burritoed in a blanket on the love seat, and her curls bounce as she laughs.

"Well, I would never have suspected my stepmother," I say. "And it wasn't just me. Susannah talked to Vivian and didn't suspect her. And, Alice, you thought it was me for the longest time, which it clearly wasn't," I say. "Blair gave

Susannah that raffle ticket. Niki mentioned both Henry Harper and William Stead the day after I saw them in my nondreams. How do you explain Niki saying those things in class? You said yourself that you haven't really known her since third grade. Can you be sure what you know and don't know?"

"I'm with Sam," Mary says. "I think we should take any shred of evidence we can get. I think this has already escalated to a guilty-until-proven-innocent-level situation."

"Same," Susannah says. "I could have absolutely been sensing Blair yesterday morning in homeroom and just not been able to pinpoint it."

Alice sighs. "Okay, okay. Let's look into them. But let's talk more about these nondreams. There's got to be clues there we're not seeing."

"I've told you basically all of it." I run the events of the nondream back through my thoughts.

"Does it feel like you're going back in time?" Mary asks. "I mean, I know you're not, but you said you feel like some old-fashioned version of yourself."

"It feels real while I'm there, but the moment I wake up, I can see how not real it is. But it doesn't feel like a dream, either. I'm not sure how to explain it. It's like an idealized version of the *Titanic,* too bright and happy to be factual. The telltale sign that something's off about it is that I have obviously never been on that ship and yet the people there act like I have."

"Hmmm." Susannah presses her lips together. "I'm not positive, but it could be a spell. Magic has a way of being almost right, but not quite."

I shudder. "*If* it's possible that it's a spell, what does it mean that my mind wasn't as conflicted this time? After the dress, it was like the two halves of my brain were fighting, one accepting being on the *Titanic* and the other sensing something was wrong. But this last time, I was more . . . comfortable, like I was acclimating."

"Maybe that the spell's working?" Susannah says. "That your resistance to it is wearing down?"

"That is just downright creepy," Mary says.

We're all quiet for a second, and Susannah and Alice share a look. I can't help but think about my conversation with Redd.

"What I want to know is how you got there?" Alice says. "You said you weren't wearing the dress this time."

I shake my head. "I did touch the painting and the letter, but I wasn't instantly transported there like with the dress. Unless the dress has lingering effects? Also, I was dreaming about the *Titanic* before the package with the dress in it showed up, just not the same way. That first dream was more like the ones I used to have about Cotton, like a premonition. I saw the painting and the dress and a little silver book. Two of those three things have already shown up."

"Maybe that first dream was a warning?" Mary says.

I look at Gracie's book sticking out of my bookbag. "Possible. Also, the dress, the painting, the dog collar, the key, *and* the letter all point to Henry and Myra. There's no ignoring those connections."

"I totally agree," Alice says.

"We should go through my spell book. Maybe there's a spell in there that could help us," I say.

Mary grins. "You're all about spells these days."

"I draw the line when dead people send packages to my dad. I'm all in."

Alice raises an eyebrow at me.

"So here's the thing about that spell book," I continue. "When everything weird was happening last fall, Mrs. Meriwether and I used it to make a potion to reveal the identity of the person who was casting against me. I'm pretty sure she still has the leftover potion. But I can't just ask her for it without my dad finding out. All the same, we might want to have it for worst-case scenario."

"You know a potion that will tell us who cast a spell against us?" Susannah asks. "I've never heard of anything like that. It must be a really old spell."

"Yeah, and you're just telling us this now?" Alice looks dumbfounded. "Even though you knew *yesterday* that there was probably a spell on that dress?"

"It's not that simple," I say. "It didn't give me the first and last name of the person who made the spell. It showed me a feather, a symbol that I didn't even fully understand at the time and definitely didn't associate with my stepmother. And right after I used the potion, she rushed home and tried to get me to go somewhere with her. When I wouldn't, she took you guys. I'm fully convinced she knew I was trying to figure out her identity. So I think we can pretty much assume the moment we use that potion, we'll send the person doing these things into action. I don't know what the consequences of that would be, but I'm pretty sure I don't want to find out."

"Huh," Alice says. "*That* I get. But you're right. We should have it on hand just in case."

"I know." *And how am I going to get it without my dad finding out?* I hesitate. "Have you guys noticed anything else weird about me? Anything at all? I mean, if I'm not resisting the *Titanic* in my dreams, I just want to make sure there's nothing in my waking life that's off."

"We would have told you," Alice says.

Mary looks at me sympathetically. "I'm thinking a sleepover at Sam's. Since that's where most of the action is"—she smiles—"and, well, the food."

I smile, too. I haven't had friends sleep over since I was tiny. "I think that's a great idea."

CHAPTER TWENTY-THREE

I've Trapped Myself

Alice screeches to a stop in front of my house. "Figure we'll be back here in an hour or so, once these two get their stuff together. Mary is the slowest packer of all time."

Mary rolls her eyes.

"Are you sure you don't want to come with us?" Susannah asks.

"Yeah, I wanna talk to Mrs. Meriwether before dinner," I say.

"Just . . . don't do anything magical without us," Mary says.

I get out of the Jeep. "Don't worry. I'm not going *near* anything *Titanic*-related until you get back."

Alice lifts her eyebrow. "You say that, and then you try on a dress and touch a painting, a letter, and who the hell knows what else."

"Be careful, Alice, or your face will get stuck in that scowl," Mary says.

"Are you really saying that right now? What are you, five?" Alice says.

"Scared you, didn't I? You're relaxing your mouth." Mary points at Alice's lips. "Right . . . there."

Alice bats Mary's finger away. "You seriously need to work on your personality. It's embarrassing," Alice says, but her eyes smile.

Alice pulls away from the curb. One look at Mrs. Meriwether's empty driveway and I turn on my heels and head toward town.

Potted plants are just starting to appear on porches, and there is a new energy to the air. The streets are buzzing with people.

At the rate I'm walking, I reach Sugar Spells Bakery before I've sorted out my strategy. Mrs. Meriwether is in the window, crafting an elaborate forest of flowering trees and wood spirits out of sweets. I pull the door open and bells chime. The scents of melted chocolate and warm pastry dough waft toward me.

"Samantha!" Mrs. Meriwether says. "What a lovely surprise." She steps away from the window and rubs her hands on a floral tea towel.

"Do you have a minute to chat?"

"Always." She uses sign language to talk to Georgia, the tall middle-aged woman behind the counter, and leads me to the only empty table.

Her café looks exactly like the inside of a thatched fairytale cottage in the woods inhabited by a happy witch who can't stop baking. Old glass lanterns and bundles of dried flowers hang from the ceiling. The walls are covered with arched shelves filled with worn books and twine-wrapped bottles of spices. And there's an occasional crooked broom hiding behind a trunk or a birdcage filled with candles. Tourists practically faint from joy when they find this place.

I take my seat at the rustic wooden table. I wonder if Jaxon made the furniture in here?

"What a treat to see you," Mrs. Meriwether says.

I stare at her. And for the life of me, I can't think of a single sentence to lead into this conversation that isn't totally awkward. "Um . . . so . . . I wanted to ask you . . ." *Can I have that potion we made? Not because I'm doing magic . . . obviously. What would make you ever think that . . . because I asked for a potion? Sheesh. Judgy. I don't see the connection at all. Also, if you could never tell my dad this, that would be great.* "Um."

Mrs. Meriwether smiles. "You act like you're going to propose."

"Well, I actually . . ." I'm officially an idiot for not planning this out better. "The other day at breakfast you said I should have training. Did you ever have training?"

Mrs. Meriwether laughs. "Oh gosh, no. I really don't do magic. I make some mean spell-inspired desserts and healing poultices, and I used to help your grandmother with her protection spells. But that's all. I wish, though. I always wanted to learn magic as a little girl. I was just never good at it in a traditional sense." She studies me for a second. "Are you thinking about what I said? About practicing and learning?"

Georgia walks up with two steaming coconut-rose milks. Mrs. Meriwether signs thank-you to her. I copy the motion.

"I don't think my dad would like it if I learned magic, to be honest. And by 'not like,' I mean hate."

Mrs. Meriwether blows on her drink. "You know, after your mom passed away, your dad didn't want anything to do with Salem. I think he blamed this place for her death. And, well, he blamed magic, too."

I sip my rose milk. "That's kinda what I always figured. I just . . . I was thinking about that 'Origin of a Spell' potion we made last fall. Do you still have that, by the way?"

Mrs. Meriwether puts down her drink and focuses on me. "I do."

"I was curious about it, how I even made it work. Do you think I could take a look at it?"

She pauses. "This wouldn't have anything to do with those mysterious packages I've been hearing about, would it?"

I swallow a hot gulp of my drink and cough. "The ones from our eccentric relative? No. I'm just thinking about what you said about the training, and I thought I might check out the spell."

Her look is questioning. "So you *were* thinking about the training, then?"

Crap. I've trapped myself. "Yeah."

"Should we talk to your dad about it? I'd be happy to be there with you if you want."

Double crap. "Maybe not yet?"

"No problem. Whenever you're ready. You just give it a good think, and then we'll tell your father and I'll give you the potion."

It's times like these that I wonder if Mrs. Meriwether has some secret supermom handbook. She totally backed me into a corner. My choices are now what? Either tell her there's a problem I need the potion for, or tell my dad I want witch training? "Great."

CHAPTER TWENTY-FOUR

A World of Things Could Go Wrong

Susannah helps me put an extra comforter on one of the four-poster beds while Alice works on the other one. My dad comes into the spare bedroom carrying a pitcher of water and four glasses on a silver tray. He sets it down on a round table between two armchairs.

"Silver tray, huh? I can see why Mom called you 'Charles the fancy.'"

He suppresses a grin. "Hmmm. Maybe you're right. And *maaaybe* I should just take this box of homemade Meriwether éclairs down with me when I go. They might be too fancy."

"What?" I stop tucking in the comforter and look at him.

Mary comes into the room, freshly changed into maroon plaid pajamas.

My dad pulls out a pink pastry box tied with string from behind the pitcher. "It's a real shame I'm going to have to eat these fancy éclairs by myself. We'll just tell Mary that you didn't want them."

"Um, no. Sam, whatever you did, I need you to fix it stat," Mary says with such a serious face that even Alice smiles.

I put both hands up in the air and do my best surrendering voice. "Okay, okay. I concede. You're not fancy. Not even a little. Éclairs are an everyman's food."

He chuckles and puts the box back down on the table. "You girls sure you'll have enough space in here? We have more bedrooms if you want them."

"Two queen-sized beds are more than enough. And besides, we work better as a unit," Alice says, and I warm. I'm part of a unit.

"Fair enough," my dad says. "I'm headed to bed now, but just let Sam know if you need anything."

"Night, Dad. Love you."

He closes the door behind him, and it takes Mary all of two seconds to grab the éclair box.

She pulls the string and opens the lid. "Wow. Just, wow. They're decorated with rosebuds. They look like little works of art." Mary tilts the box so we can see. In her plaid pajamas, with her dark curls piled on top of her head, she looks just like a little kid.

Alice raises an eyebrow. "If you even think about eating mine, I will push you out of bed while you're sleeping."

Mary curls up in an armchair with a mouth full of éclair. "What? I can't hear you; I'm busy."

Alice takes the other armchair, and Susannah and I sit on the bed near them. Mary hands us the pastry box. There is a meow behind me.

"Really?" I turn around, and sure enough, the black cat is sitting on the bed, staring at me from under its Neanderthal brow.

"What?" Mary asks.

"That cat I told you about. For unknown reasons, this

black behemoth slept in my bed last night. And by the way it's all spread out now, I think it might be here to stay with us tonight."

Susannah turns around and scans the bed. "Where?"

Alice leans forward in her black silk pajamas to get a better look. "Just to be clear, you're saying there's a black ghost cat on that bed with you?"

"Yeah, right here." I put my hand out behind me, and it rubs its head against my fingers.

Alice smirks. "Leave it to you to become a witch cliché in less than a week."

Mary claps her hands together and lets out a little squeal. "I love this. Spirit cats I can totally deal with, spirit humans . . . not so much."

"Actually, speaking of spirits, I have a suggestion," Alice says.

"Oh no." Mary frowns. "Don't ruin my happy moment."

Alice looks at Mary. "You haven't even heard it yet."

"I don't have to. If you were sure about it, you would just tell us we're doing it. If you're suggesting it, that means it's either super uncomfortable or risky."

"Hear, hear," Susannah says.

"Everyone just untwist your panties for a second," says Alice. "Nothing we're doing right now isn't risky. If we wanted to be safe, we would've locked ourselves up in my protected room all weekend. We're at Sam's house, which is clearly a hot spot for weird shit. And we need information."

Alice swallows her last bite and wipes her hands on a napkin before continuing. "Tomorrow we'll research Myra and the weird objects that have been showing up to see if we can connect the dots. But what if we go a step further than research and try to talk to her in person? Maybe she can tell us what the deal is with the hat and why all these objects are appearing."

"Like try to summon her spirit?" Mary pulls her knees a little closer to her body.

"Yeah. With Sam's abilities, it makes a lot of sense," Alice says.

Susannah's eyebrows push together. "We have no idea what side of this Myra's on. Yes, we need information. But we could be walking straight into a huge problem. And Samantha can see spirits, but they can also hurt her. We're specifically putting her at risk. Or maybe setting ourselves up for a trap."

"It's less risky than using that potion on the dress," I say. "And Myra is the common denominator in most of these clues. Believe me, the last thing I want to do is see more spirits, but I'm fully with Alice on this one."

Mary frowns. "But that spell's in the gray area."

"Gray area?" *Do I want to know?*

"It's not good or bad magic, but somewhere in between," Susannah says. "Gray spells leave lots of room for error. You can't exactly control them, and you don't know what you're gonna get. Not everyone can do gray spells. Alice is banking on your natural ability, I think. And since you're *untrained,* a world of things could go wrong."

"You are certainly *not* doing that spell. Is this the type of nonsense you have been discussing all day in that room where I cannot watch you?" Elijah stands by the door, his jaw set.

I jump. "You do *not* just get to pop in here and criticize like that. If you wanted to be included, you should never have let me believe you left!" Even as the words leave my mouth, I'm surprised by how raw they sound.

For a split second Elijah seems unsure. "Samantha, this is not the time for that discussion."

I slide off the bed. "Because you chose to blink in while my friends were here? Not my fault."

"Um, what's going on?" Mary's eyes are wide, and her voice is high-pitched.

Elijah looks flustered. "This is not any more comfortable for me than it is for you."

"Samantha?" Susannah says, and looks back and forth between me and the door I appear to be yelling at.

I lift my chin. "We're doing the spell. And I don't need your input."

Alice's mouth opens. "So, not the drowned man, then."

Elijah's stubborn expression intensifies. "You are not doing that spell and that is the end of it."

"Oh yeah?"

"Indeed." Elijah blinks out.

I'm left standing there with my hands clenched and my chest rising and falling emphatically. The girls stare at me.

"That"—I wave angrily at the door—"was Elijah. Alice, set up the spell," I say with force.

Alice heads for her overnight bag and digs around in it for a moment. She pulls out a black cloth pouch. "Sam, I really think—" The cloth pouch disappears from her hand. Alice's eyes widen. "What the hell?"

I shake my hands in the air. "Give that back!"

Nothing.

"Alice, is there another way to do the spell without whatever was in that bag?"

The lights go out. Mary screams.

"Damn it, Elijah!" I march over to the light switch and flick it up and down. Nothing. I open the door. The dim light from the hallway floods in. I peer inside my floor lamp. He didn't just turn the light off. He took the bulb.

"Sam?" My dad comes to the door, concern written all over him. "What happened? I heard someone scream."

I steady my voice. "Lightbulb blew."

He examines the lamp. "You mean gone?" He sounds unsure.

"We took it out."

"Oh. Well, let me get you another one. You girls get in bed."

"Okay, thanks, Dad."

Mary doesn't hesitate. She looks all kinds of relieved we're not doing that spell and jumps under one of the comforters.

My dad leaves the door open and makes his way down the hall.

I pull the covers up over my shoulders.

"So Elijah's back?" Susannah asks.

"Apparently," I say.

"Wasn't he a pretty important part of figuring out what was going on with your stepmother?" Susannah asks.

Damn it. "Yes."

"Screw Susannah's gentle approach. I don't know what happened between you two, but are you really that stubborn?" Alice asks. "You know we're already in the danger zone with this. Weren't you the one just saying you're all in?"

"Point taken," I say begrudgingly. The black cat curls up against my side and blinks at me. "Move over, cat."

"Maybe you should call the cat Spirit," Mary suggests.

"Or bed hog," I say, rubbing its head between the ears.

"His name is Broome," Elijah says.

I scowl into the blackness.

CHAPTER TWENTY-FIVE

That's Why You Love Me

I stand in front of the mirror in my cabin. Mollie repositions the lavender sash on my white afternoon dress. I look like a giant doily.

"Now yer hat, miss." Mollie holds up a wide-brimmed white hat trimmed with purple flowers.

"Are you sure I need it?" I ask, eyeing the hat like it's a foreign object.

Mollie smiles, and the freckles on her cheeks rise. "Unless ya want ta get sunburned while yer walkin' round the promenade deck?"

"I can handle a little sunburn."

"And get me in trouble? Not likely." She places the hat on my head without hesitation and pins it in place. A sheer veil drops over my eyes.

"Done?"

"Just yer parasol and ya can be on yer way." She holds out a frilly umbrella.

"I'm sorry, Mollie, but I have to draw the line somewhere. There are only so many accessories a person can wear, and that thing pushes me over the edge."

Mollie puts her hand on her hip. "Never in me life have I come across a lady that dislikes getting dressed as much as you do."

"That's why you love me." I smile at her and head for the door. "You coming?"

She sighs and puts down the parasol.

We walk side by side through the hallway and out onto the deck. The sun is shining, there's a cool salty breeze, and everything sparkles—the water, the people, the mood.

"Enjoying the afternoon, niece?" Uncle Harry asks, and I turn. His black hat shields his eyes from the bright sun. Hammad is with him, walking by his side.

"Very much so."

"Good. Good. I am off to join Mr. Stead for lunch. I would invite you, but as I understand it, you have quite the social engagement." He smiles at me in such a kind way that I actually feel warmer.

This ship really is lovely, especially today. "Yes, of course. Please send Mr. Stead my regards."

My uncle bows. "Right-o. See you this evening."

I scan the deck, which is filled with finely dressed men and women. There is an empty bench a ways down with a good view of the water.

I turn to Mollie. "So what's this social engagement he was talking about?"

"Yer uncle arranged fer ya ta have lunch with Madeleine Astor at Café Parisien. She's only a couple a years older than ya. Lucile Carter, Gladys Cherry . . . oh, and the Countess of Rothes. There are a few others as well. I'm sure ya will enjoy yerself. They are absolutely the who's who of the ship."

I laugh and do my best English accent. "Lots of tea sipping and 'Oh, isn't that dress *darling*. And this hat, I just couldn't live without it. It simply matches everything.'"

Mollie almost laughs, but catches herself. "Yer just terrible."

We arrive at the bench at the same time as a middle-aged man with a black mustache.

"Pardon me, miss," he says in a thick Spanish accent, and bows.

"Samantha Mather," I say.

"Manuel Uruchurtu," he says.

"Are you taking a trip to New York?" I ask.

He shakes his head. "Mexico City. I am quite looking forward to seeing my beautiful wife and our seven children. I've been gone for nearly two months."

"You were visiting Europe, then?"

"Visiting old friends in France. I was actually scheduled to take another ship altogether, but a friend of mine persuaded me to trade tickets with him. Please take the bench, Miss Mather," Manuel says, looking from Mollie to me. "I will find another one."

"No, no, you take it. I have a lunch soon anyway. You can enjoy the view for both of us. I insist," I reply.

We share a smile, and Mollie and I continue across the deck.

"How much time do we have, Mollie? Before the lunch, I mean."

"A little under an hour, I would guess," she says.

We stop at a chain marking the end of the first-class promenade area.

I run my fingers over the metal links. "An hour? Hmmm." I smile mischievously at Mollie. "Have you been to any of the other decks besides the first-class ones?"

"Aye."

"How about we go exploring?"

Mollie watches me. "I don't like the look in yer eyes, not one bit."

"Steerage is in the front and the back of the ship, right?" By Mollie's expression I know I'm right.

I bend down and duck under the chain, careful not to catch my hat on it.

"Miss!" I stop at the concerned sound of Mollie's voice. "Ya know that part of the ship is sectioned off."

"If it wasn't, it wouldn't be any fun," I say.

She looks over her shoulder.

"Don't worry, you don't have to come with me. I'll tell my aunt and uncle that it was my idea and you had nothing to do with it." I turn around and walk as fast as my dress will allow me toward the front of the ship.

Before I get ten steps away, Mollie is at my side.

"Oh, really?" I say, smiling at her.

"Better ta be actin' foolish with ya than ta be lonesome." She smiles, too. "Besides, ya wouldn't last ten minutes without me. We need ta get off this main deck before we draw attention."

She winds me through back hallways and empty passages. And when one of the ship's crew members comes along, we jump out of sight.

Mollie stops in the center of a quiet hall and lowers her voice. Not that there is much chance anyone would hear us over the roar of the engines in this part of the ship. "We have two options. Around this corner is a locked gate leadin' ta third class. The guard is young and would probably be easy ta convince, but ye'll have ta be real firm. Or, we can take the longer way around, which includes some passages only used by crew. However, if we get caught, it'll absolutely look like we're doin' somethin' we shouldn't."

"Hmmm. Okay. Let's go with the first option."

We round the corner and walk toward a ceiling-high gate with an eighteen-year-old guard in front of it.

He stands up a little straighter when he sees us. "Is everything okay, miss? Are you lost?"

"Everything's just fine. If you would unlock the gate, please, we'll be on our way."

His eyes widen. "The gate, miss? I cannot do that."

"Of course you can," I say with a smile.

He starts fidgeting. "It is against immigration regulations."

"It would be against regulations if ya let steerage passengers out, not if ya let us in," Mollie says.

He seems unsure.

"If you don't let us move through quickly, I'll be late to my lunch with the Countess of Rothes. You wouldn't want that, would you?"

"No, miss." He fumbles for his key and slips it in the lock. "Just be quick."

The moment the gate shuts behind us, Mollie and I grin at each other. She grabs my arm and leads me away from the boy before he can change his mind. As we turn the corner, the hallway bursts with life. People speak Italian and something I'm pretty sure is Swedish. The clothes and complexions vary greatly.

Mollie knocks on one of the cabin doors.

A woman in her early twenties wearing a white blouse and a floor-length black skirt opens the door. She squeals and grabs Mollie in a hug. "Mollie! What'er ya doin' here in the middle a the day? Ya haven't been made redundant, have ya?" Her Irish accent is strong, stronger than Mollie's, and I love it.

"No, Nora," she says, looking a little embarrassed. "Miss Samantha wanted to see steerage."

Nora turns to me and smiles. "A course ya did. There're three types a people in this world: those that create division, those that enforce it, and those that tell the first two ta kiss their bloomin' arse." She winks at me.

I laugh. It's hard not to like her.

"Nora!" Mollie attempts shock.

"Smile." Nora puts her arm around Mollie's shoulder and whistles. "A little language never hurt ya." Her grin is mischievous. "And as me pa always said . . . why worry over small problems when the worst is yet ta come."

"Mollie!" says a young woman coming out of a nearby room and walking arm in arm with a young man. Mollie hugs her.

"Kate and John Bourke. Newlyweds, they are," Nora says to me.

I nod. I can tell just by the way they look at each other. "Are you traveling with them?"

"Them and twelve more. Fifteen lads and colleens all from County Mayo. The noise they make when they get ta singin' after dinner is a thing a beauty." Nora grins at me.

Three kids come running down the hall, weaving in and out of the adult passengers. A girl about ten years old stops abruptly in front of me. Her mouth hangs open.

"How can you be real?" the girl asks. Her hair is braided and she's wearing a pink dress. There is something so familiar about her.

"I know you, don't I? We met in a . . . Where did we meet?" The sparkling happiness that filled the air a moment ago wavers.

The girl continues to look at me with wide eyes. "In my dreams, you . . . you . . ." And then she faints.

Nora rushes to her and lifts her head off the ground. "Ada?"

Ada. "Is she okay?" I ask, leaning over Ada, too. There is something about not being able to place her that makes me anxious.

Nora pats Ada's cheek, and a voice yells my name from down the hall.

I turn around to find Alexander rushing toward me.

"What are you possibly thinking coming down to steerage?" His eyes are accusatory. "You do not belong here."

"I . . . well . . ."

He shifts his focus to Mollie. "Was this your doing?"

She looks terrified. "I'm terribly sorry, sir."

I step between them. "No, it wasn't her doing. It was mine." I put my chin in the air. "If you must know, I tore my favorite lace dress. And as you probably *don't* know, lace is incredibly hard to repair and very few people can do it well. I wanted to wear it to dinner tonight, and Mollie said she knew a woman down here who might be able to fix it. I insisted on coming down myself, even though Mollie begged me not to." I give him a hard stare, daring him to challenge me and my desperate need for the right wardrobe.

His face softens. "Oh, well, I suppose . . . But you really should never have come down here by yourself."

"Miss, I can mend it fer ya if ya leave it with the gate boy. I just need ta get this lass to 'er mum first," Nora says from the floor, where she's crouched down.

I release my breath. "Thanks. I'll have someone bring it down. Tell Ada I hope she feels better." I focus on Ada. *Who are you to me?*

"Shall I escort you back above deck, Samantha?" Alexander asks.

I nod and take his offered arm.

"You are just lucky I was the one who found you and not your uncle."

Merde. My uncle. I hope he doesn't tell him.

CHAPTER TWENTY-SIX

Maybe This Is a Good Thing

There is a loud knock. "Girls? Breakfast's ready." My dad opens the door and pushes it a few inches. "Sleep much longer and the sun's going to set."

I sit up and rub my eyes. "What time is it?"

"Eleven."

"It smells delicious, Mr. M," Alice says with a scratchy morning voice, propping herself up on one elbow.

"Come on down when you're ready."

I slide out of bed, pulling my leg from under Broome, and put my feet in my slippers. My nondream comes rushing back to me, and I almost stumble. "You guys? I . . ."

Susannah slides out of bed in her green floor-length nightgown. Her wavy auburn hair is messy around her face instead of in its usual neat bun. "You went back?"

"Yeah."

"That's the third night in a row," Susannah says.

"I know," I say with anxiety in my voice. "I don't understand how . . . but I saw Ada—you know, that little spirit girl? She recognized me and was so shocked I was there that she fainted. But before she did, she said something about me being in *her* dreams. . . ."

Alice holds up her hand. "Back up. You're saying the spirit girl was there last night and she somehow thinks when she visits you here in Salem that you're in *her* dreams?"

"That's exactly what I'm saying. She was a passenger on the ship, people knew her and were talking to her. How is that possible?"

Mary's face pales. "Okay, that's too weird."

Susannah's features scrunch together. "And what's stranger is that in Salem no one can see her except you, but on the *Titanic,* everyone can see her."

Alice leans against the bed. "Yeah, but she's dead. That's why we can't see her here."

"That's exactly why I think it's so weird that people there can," Susannah says.

We all look at Susannah.

"What are you thinking?" I ask. "That everyone in her world is dead and that's why they can see her?"

"Unless anyone can think of a better explanation?" Susannah says.

We're all silent for a second.

"Can someone please say Sam's not going to the bottom of the ocean with a bunch of dead people? I'm really not good with that," Mary says.

"It's not the sunken *Titanic,*" I say. "It's actually super bright and sparkly." I frown. "I really don't know why I just had a knee-jerk reaction to tell you how nice it is. Why would I do that? I don't like anything about being on that ship."

Alice eyes me. "I don't know, but tell us if it happens again. We can't let your confusion about that ship spill into your waking life."

I shudder. "Agreed."

"So if it's not the wreckage you're visiting, then maybe Susannah was right. Maybe you're going to some kind of replica?" Mary says.

"A spell ship?" Susannah says.

I push my hair back from my forehead. "Remember what I told you guys yesterday about the two conflicting sides of my brain? Well, the accepting side definitely won this time. Until I saw Ada, I'd almost entirely stopped being suspicious. It's like each time I go, I become more and more comfortable in that reality."

Susannah watches me. "Maybe the spell from the dress never actually broke? Maybe you're still under it? That could even be why you felt the need to tell us how beautiful the place is."

"I wanna say no way, and that I would know, but I'm not sure what to trust right now."

"Was there anything else, anything odd or any suspicious people?" Alice asks.

"No one strange but Ada." I glance toward the door, which my dad left cracked open. "Let's go eat before he comes back up here again," I say, and they follow me toward the stairs.

We head to the dining room, which looks like it's straight out of *Pride and Prejudice*. The walls are paneled in dark wood, the table is long enough to comfortably seat ten, and there is a brass chandelier with lights that resemble old candles. Jaxon is already at the table. I stare at him a second longer than I should. We don't usually eat with the Meriwethers on the weekends. And even with Mrs. Meriwether here, I figured there was no way Jaxon would show up. My hands start to sweat. Maybe this is a good thing. Maybe he's here because he wants to smooth everything out.

Mary walks into the room behind me, gets a look at the table teeming with delicious food, and stops short.

Alice walks into her. "Dude. You gotta warn people if you're gonna stop like that." She steps around Mary and pulls out a chair. "Actually, I take that objection back. This is completely impressive. Do you eat like this every day?"

"Most, yeah," Jaxon says.

I slide into the seat next to Susannah.

Mrs. Meriwether and my dad come through the swinging door between the dining room and the kitchen carrying a pot of coffee, a jug of hot chocolate with marshmallows melting on top, and freshly squeezed orange juice.

"Oh, good! You girls are perfectly in time. The strawberry-rhubarb cobbler just came out of the oven," Mrs. Meriwether says as she offers everyone drinks.

"This is *incredible*," Susannah says, pulling a waffle onto her plate.

Mrs. Meriwether pours me some coffee. "When I heard you girls were staying the night, I told Charlie that there was simply no way we weren't eating together."

"True story," my dad says, smiling at Mrs. Meriwether. "She wouldn't leave me alone about it."

I steal a glance at Jaxon. He's piling eggs, cobbler, and some of my dad's hash browns onto his plate and looks completely relaxed.

Alice sips her hot chocolate. "Damn." She examines her drink in awe.

Mrs. Meriwether beams. Very few people love anything more than Mrs. Meriwether loves feeding people. "I don't know if Sam told you, but I've got an enormous garden. Lots of ingredients for, oh, any sort of thing." She winks at us.

Oh no, what is she saying right now? I thought she was gonna let me broach this topic myself.

"Mom," Jaxon scolds.

"Well, I'm just saying that you're welcome anytime at all," Mrs. Meriwether says.

Concern creeps into the corners of my dad's eyes. If he doesn't like her good-natured mild comment, how will he ever accept the things I need to tell him?

"I'm coming over for sure," Mary says with a mouth full of cobbler. "I'm in total awe of you."

"Mom, I'm gonna head out after this. I'm meeting Niki down by the harbor," Jaxon says, and takes a big sip of orange juice.

The girls look at me and I look at Jaxon. How much time are those two spending together?

"No problem. Just be home by dinner."

Alice narrows her eyes at him. "You're hanging out with Niki?"

Jaxon grins like a puppy. "Yeah, we've been hanging out a lot lately."

My dad looks at us all like he's trying to work out a cross-word puzzle.

"Why?" Alice asks, and I try to kick her under the table.

"Ow," Mary says.

Crap. "Sorry."

"I like her," Jaxon says, like this is a normal conversation to be having at the breakfast table with our parents.

"But I thought you liked Sam," Alice continues without pause. There's an edge of defensiveness in her voice.

"Alice!" I choke on my coffee. "We're just friends."

Jaxon looks directly at me. "Sam likes some dead dude," he says casually. "And Niki's just a good fit for me."

I stand up so fast that my chair scrapes against the floor

as it slides backward. "What the hell are you saying?" How could he say that in front of my dad after we had that conversation about protecting our parents?

Susannah and Mary look at me sympathetically. Alice seems pissed.

I don't even know why I'm standing.

Jaxon shrugs. "Nothing. Just answering Alice's question. It's not my fault you don't like what I have to say."

"That's it!" My face turns bright red. "I will murder you with this fork."

"Children," Mrs. Meriwether says. "Now, that's fine cutlery, and I'll have trouble thinking of it the same way if it's used to murder my only child."

"Let's all just settle down for a second." My dad uses his calming voice, the one he defaults to when my temper flares.

Mrs. Meriwether motions for me to sit. "I don't know what's going on, and I don't want to. But I won't have you two being unkind to each other. If you insist on continuing, I'll put you both to work for the rest of the day." She looks at each of us to make sure we understand she's serious.

I sink into my seat. Jaxon totally crossed the line. How could he ask me to trust him and then betray me like this? And what's worse is that he's showing no signs of wanting to smooth things out. I'm starting to think our relationship may be broken for good.

"Since when is telling the truth unkind?" Jaxon asks.

"Since the invention of bad haircuts. Don't push your luck, Jax," Mrs. Meriwether says. "You're getting awfully close to having to tell Niki you're not coming."

"I'll just excuse myself now, then," Jaxon says. He picks up his plate and heads for the door.

"Jaxon Meriwether!" Mrs. Meriwether says, but he doesn't turn around.

CHAPTER TWENTY-SEVEN

We Stand in Silence

I yank on my black boots and stand up from my window seat. I'm still reeling from that crazy breakfast. I head for the spare bedroom, twisting my wet hair over my shoulder.

Just as I reach the door, Susannah opens it. "We should go. Jaxon's truck just left, and we don't know how long he's going to be with Niki."

"I don't understand."

"We'll explain in the car," Mary says.

Alice tosses me a black jacket, and I follow them down the stairs.

I knock on my dad's office door and crack it open. "I'm going out with the girls. Be back in a little bit."

"Keep your phone on and be home for dinner," my dad says.

"Will do."

I follow the girls out the front door and get in Mary's Jeep.

Alice pulls away from my house and glances at me in the rearview mirror. "So what happened with you and Jaxon?"

"Alice, you can't just go straight at a subject like that," Susannah says.

Alice shrugs. "I just say what I think. But it's not like I was trying to cause a blowup at breakfast. You know that, right, Sam? I was trying to figure out . . . I just need you to tell me what happened."

"I will," I say. "But can someone fill me in on what sent us running out of my house just now?"

Susannah turns toward me. "We're going to Niki's."

Did I hear her correctly? "When she's not home?"

"Faster and more effective," Mary says.

"Are you saying we're breaking in? Why?" My voice betrays my disbelief.

"Don't sound all shocked," Alice says. "We're not looting the place. It's just that if the *Titanic* you're going to is a spell, then we have a more serious problem than we originally thought. And with Redd's warning, I don't know. I still think it's unlikely Niki and Blair are involved, but let's just say that I'm no longer opposed to double-checking. And besides, I know where the spare key is."

Does that mean they think Redd's warning might have been directed at me, too? "What about her parents?" I ask.

"Most likely at the yacht club," Alice says. "I've lived next to them my whole life, and they're almost never home on the weekends." We pull to a stop, and she gestures toward an enormous redbrick house with black shutters. "See, empty driveway."

Mary turns around from the passenger seat and looks at me. "When we get out of the car, make sure you act like everything's normal. Don't speed-walk or look around suspiciously, and no one will question what we're doing."

The girls and I jump out of the Jeep, my heart beating so loudly I'm sure the neighbors can hear it.

Susannah nods in the direction of the brick house and I follow. Every piece of gravel under my boots is amplified.

Alice sticks her fingers through a thin opening in a tall white wooden fence and jiggles a metal latch. The gate swings open into the backyard. Rows of white flowers and bushes, all trimmed and uniform, line the house and fence.

Alice grabs a fake frog and flips it over, revealing a hiding place for a key. "They never change it." She slips the key into the back door, and just like that we're in Niki's house.

For a few awful seconds we stand in silence. I hold my breath.

Alice taps on the door from the inside. "Anyone home?" she yells.

I cringe and so does Mary. Silence.

Alice nods. "Told you they weren't here."

Mary scowls. "Jeez, you could give us a little warning before you start yelling."

"Doesn't mean they won't come home," Susannah says, and all at once we're moving full speed through the hallways and up the stairs.

Niki's bedroom door is open, and the inside matches the rest of the house, pastel blues and white.

"Whatever you touch, keep track of where it was. Judging by the neatness, she would notice immediately," Susannah says.

Alice and I head for her desk, Mary to her closet, and Susannah to her bookshelf. I leaf through a pile of books and papers, but everything mentioning the *Titanic* is just Wardwell's homework assignments. We're all super quiet and focused.

The first desk drawer is filled with pictures of Niki and Blair and a few other girls over the summer. Below the pictures are birthday cards, notes scribbled in big loopy cursive, and a wooden box. I lift the box lid. Inside is an envelope with Niki's name on it. *Wait, I recognize that handwriting.*

I set down the stack of cards and pictures and pick up the envelope. *I'll just put it back in the box and forget I ever saw it.*

Nope. I open the back flap and pull a card out.

Niki,
    Hoping you'll accept this bracelet as my invitation to the Spring Fling next week.
                                    Jaxon

P.S. I'll pick you up at 7:30 tonight.

I rub my thumb over the part of the card where the bracelet left an indent. What, it took him a whole twenty-four hours after our fight to do this? I get why he didn't tell me, but I'm also getting nervous that I'm losing my best friend to Niki, of all people.

"Sam," Alice says, looking down at the card.

I forcefully shove it back into the envelope. "It's nothing."

"Then why are you abusing that envelope?" Alice takes it out of my hands and puts it back in the box. "Dude, trust me on this one—if he likes Niki, then he's definitely not the person you thought he was."

Mary watches us. "What happened?"

"Nothing." I shake my head. "Jaxon gave Niki one of those *Titanic* dance bracelets." Everyone's quiet, as if they're waiting for me to go on, so I do. "It's not that I want to date Jaxon. It's that I feel like he just dropped me, like suddenly I don't matter to him anymore."

Mary frowns.

"I found something, too," Susannah says, and I couldn't be

more grateful for the topic change. "Niki's log of the Spring Fling committee."

We all lean over the small notebook Susannah holds. She runs her finger down the pages. "Supposedly, they finalized the dance theme options in November, and there was no *Titanic* theme. But at the beginning of the semester, Blair and Niki got Wardwell and the history department on board, and the committee made an exception to add it."

Alice grunts, like she's deep in thought.

"So the *Titanic* was more than just the theme they supported. They're the ones who actually brought it to the committee and fought for it to be admitted?" I say.

"Looks that way," Mary says.

There is the faint sound of tires on gravel.

Mary runs to the window. "Jaxon's truck. I thought he said they'd be at the harbor!"

My heart jumps into my throat. Susannah slams the notebook shut and slides it onto the shelf. We scramble to put everything back in place. And we run. Out of the room, down the stairs, and into the hallway.

The front door clicks open. Jaxon's and Niki's voices spill into the house. There are still two hallways left before the door.

"We'll never make it," Susannah whispers.

The white walls feel claustrophobic.

Alice pulls us to a stop. "Hello! Hello?" she yells.

Jaxon and Niki go quiet. Has Alice lost her mind?

"Hello?" Niki responds hesitantly, entering the hallway we're standing in. "Alice?"

I'm sweating.

"Your back door was wide open, banging against your house in the wind," Alice says. "But I guess since you're home, then you knew that."

"No," Niki says, like she has a bad taste in her mouth. "I didn't. And *all four* of you came to check on my back door for me?"

Jaxon's and Niki's hands are interlocked. He's wearing a blue cord with a silver anchor wrapped around his wrist, and she's wearing a brown cord with a ship's wheel—the dance bracelets.

Susannah tucks a loose strand of hair behind her ear. "We weren't going to let Alice check on a probably empty and possibly burgled house by herself."

Niki raises an eyebrow.

"But I thought you guys were just at Sam's," Jaxon says. He makes no effort to let go of Niki's hand.

"And I thought that when we talked about how we both protect our parents, you wouldn't bring up spirits in front of my dad and worry him," I say.

Jaxon shrugs. *Maybe he's trying to punish me for not dating him. Or worse, maybe our friendship really doesn't mean to him what it means to me.*

Niki's mouth twitches toward a smile, and she leans into his arm.

"You're welcome," Alice says. She looks at their clasped hands. "And those bracelets your dance committee's selling are ugly as shit, by the way."

Mary nods.

Niki narrows her eyes. "You know where the door is." She pulls Jaxon toward the stairs. "Let's go up to my room."

Susannah gently touches my arm. "I'm sorry," she says just loud enough for me to hear.

CHAPTER TWENTY-EIGHT

Death Is Not Always Simple

Mary turns to Alice in the front seat of the Jeep. "So you agree that Niki and Blair are involved now, right? That your friends were unmistakably right, and that you, no matter how much it pains you, were wrong."

Alice rolls her eyes and drives away from the curb. "They're involved in some way. I'll give you that. Doesn't prove they're masterminding anything."

Susannah touches her bottom lip. "They could be working with someone."

"Also, I know you guys said that he's not a Descendant, but don't you find it weird that Wardwell was involved in pushing a dance theme?" I ask. "Not only did he support it, he convinced the history department to teach it. Seems extreme."

Alice pulls up to the curb in front of my house.

"I was just thinking about that," Susannah says. "Especially after how you said he told you about the dog collar."

I open the Jeep door and get out. My dad's car isn't in the driveway. "If Niki and Blair are connected, doesn't it make sense that he could be, too?"

Alice walks next to me up my brick driveway. "At this point, I don't know what I know."

Mary's face scrunches up. "Weeell, he does have a weird story."

"Also true," Susannah says.

I open my door for the girls and lock it behind us.

Mary stops in the foyer and looks at me. "This is what happened. Wardwell was some hotshot museum director and moved to Salem ten years ago or so. He immediately started dating his now ex-wife, and they got married super fast. She thought he was a Descendant because of his last name, but two years later it came out that he actually had no relation to the Trials. It was this big scandal, and it destroyed their relationship. They divorced, and that's when he became a teacher at our school."

"You're saying he pretended to be a Descendant? And that his wife actually cared that he wasn't?"

Mary nods. "It was all really dramatic."

"Could he have a grudge against Descendants because of it?" I ask.

"I've never noticed that from him," Susannah says. "But that doesn't mean he doesn't. He *is* a history teacher who used to be a museum director. Plus, his love for the *Titanic* is obvious."

"And he's in our school; he has access to all the people we have access to," I say.

"My instinct is still to say no, but I just said that about Niki. And as Mary so wonderfully pointed out, I was wrong," Alice says.

I pause. "Oh, shit. You know what? He came to my house

once. A long time ago. Vivian said he was repairing my window. . . . He could've seen Myra and Henry's painting then and known who they were."

"Then we definitely need to look into him," Susannah says.

"It's way more risky than sifting through Niki's room," Mary says.

"Not necessarily," I say, even though I hate that I'm suggesting this. "I could ask Elijah."

They all look at me.

Susannah turns for the stairs. "Okay, then. We're gonna head upstairs and start researching Myra and Henry." The girls follow her, with Mary stealing glances at me over her shoulder.

I rub my hands over my face. How am I going to start this conversation after I told him I didn't want his help?

I walk into the living room, mumbling to myself, and stop so fast I almost trip. Elijah's already there, standing next to the fireplace with his hands behind his back.

For a second I just stare at him. "So you were listening to our conversation?"

"There is no need to make this more difficult," he says.

"*Me* make this difficult?" I fake-laugh.

"I will do it," he says. "Investigate Wardwell."

"Fine."

He turns so that he's facing me. "We can have this conversation as an argument if you so choose, but it is not the most effective option for someone so concerned about time."

"Says the person who stole our spell ingredients last night."

His expression is calm. "If you did not charge ahead recklessly, I would not have to interfere."

I have an overwhelming desire to shake my fist at him, undeniably proving his point that I'm the difficult one.

"I have been looking for Myra," he says.

I pause. "You have?"

"But I have not found her."

"What does that mean exactly?" I ask.

"Spirits who do not pass on tend to stay near their homes. But when I looked for your relation Myra, she was not in New York City. I know she traveled when she was alive, but unfortunately I cannot seem to locate any journals or letters that tell me where she frequented. I do not have any good leads as to where she might be. And then there are the other passengers—"

"What other passengers?"

"I have been looking for *all* the *Titanic* passengers. Not just Myra."

"Oh." So he was helping, even though I told him not to?

"Oftentimes with tragedies like this, spirits feel unresolved about how things ended. Many of them stay here like I did, finding it difficult to pass on. Even the passengers who did not die in the shipwreck could potentially feel bound to the *Titanic*. Large-scale traumas sometimes affect the afterlife of the entire group. I do not know why," Elijah says.

"You're really blowing the concept that when you die, things suddenly make sense," I say.

"Yes, well. I imagine that when I do pass on, everything will become clearer." There is an emotion in his voice that I can't quite place.

"After everything that happened in the woods, you had the opportunity to pass on. Didn't you? Your sister came to get you. Am I missing something here?"

"As in life, death is not always simple or easy," he says, his eyes asking for me to understand.

There is something so sad and genuine about his voice

that I suddenly have the desire to reach out to him. I frown. What's wrong with me?

Elijah must see something in my expression, because he breaks eye contact and clears his throat. "As I was saying, I have been to the passengers' homes and their towns. But I have not found any of them."

I sigh, happy to move on to easier subjects like death warnings and unexplainable missing spirits. "Maybe some of them liked to travel the way Myra did? Maybe they're just not hanging around in obvious places. Or maybe most of them passed on."

"Unlikely," he says. "With a tragedy on the scale of the *Titanic,* I should have found at least a hundred by now. I have even asked other spirits in the passengers' hometowns. None of the passengers have been seen in months. Some of them have not been seen in decades."

"I don't understand. Where could they all have gone? And why am I seeing Ada, but you can't find any other spirits? That doesn't make sense."

Elijah's eyebrows furrow. He takes a seat in an armchair. "That is what worries me. From the way you describe her, Ada always speaks in the present, as though she does not remember that she is dead. I have seen many deluded spirits in the past three hundred years, but none believed they were still living. They knew they were dead."

"So then what's going on with Ada?" I sit down on the fluffy couch. "Could she be under a spell?"

Elijah leans forward. "I have been asking myself that very question."

"And if you can't find Myra, why shouldn't we try Alice's suggestion?"

"Forcing a spirit to appear is one of the worst things you could possibly do. The only thing we have is our freedom of choice. If the spell went wrong, you could wind up with a very angry spirit, one who would consequently tell you nothing. Spirits are not missing socks. They are people."

I stiffen. "I never thought of Myra as a missing sock, and you know that. But even *you* can't find her, and she's one of the only leads we have right now. And considering how little we understand, that's saying a lot. There must be something we could do to try to get in touch with her."

Elijah's quiet for a moment. "You could try speaking to her the way you speak to me."

"By saying her name?"

"Indeed."

He blinks out.

CHAPTER TWENTY-NINE

I'll Tell You Everything I Know

Susannah and I sit on one bed and Alice and Mary on the other. Laptops, books, and handwritten notes about the *Titanic* surround us.

"I'm not finding anything else about Myra. Are you guys?" I ask.

Mary shakes her head.

"Nope," Alice says. "Your letter tells us almost as much about her as anything else I've seen."

"It's just so weird. Even Elijah couldn't find her." I chew on the end of my pen.

Alice looks over her notes. "Let's run through these connections again. It started with the dress and a note from her."

"And in my nondreams people accept me as the Harpers' niece. I've spent time with Henry, but I've never seen Myra."

"That letter you found was about her. The key Alice got was to her stateroom. And we're assuming that the dog collar could be from Myra's Pekingese," Susannah says. "It's probably fair to assume the seasickness spell is connected as well."

Mary lies on her stomach and props her head on her hand. "Didn't that letter talk about Henry being sick with 'grippe'? I looked it up. It's an old-fashioned word for the flu. And if he had the flu on the *Titanic,* he would definitely feel seasick," Mary says nonchalantly, and we all look at her.

"Not a bad theory," Alice says. "And any which way, seasickness refers to being on a boat. So that only leaves the bowler hat."

There's a knock at the door. I cover the old spell book with a pillow.

"Come in!" I say.

My dad peeks his head in. "You girls need anything? I'm headed to bed, but if you get hungry, there's enough food in the kitchen to feed the whole town. Don't stay up too late. Make sure you get some sleep."

We nod in agreement, and he closes the door behind him. We listen as his footsteps disappear down the hallway.

"Are you going to tell him about Mrs. Meriwether and the potion?" Susannah asks.

"I just don't see how that could turn out well. You guys see my dad all friendly and happy. But I'm telling you, he does *not* react well to anything magic-related."

"Whatever you do, just don't get yourself grounded. It will seriously interfere," Mary says. "Parents worry."

"Not mine," Alice says. "I'm not even sure they know what my name is sometimes."

Mary wraps her arms around Alice. "I know I should feel bad for you, and I do. But I also selfishly love that you stay at my house all the time."

Alice leans her cheek into Mary's curly head.

"Maybe we could just remake the potion from Mrs.

Meriwether's garden and save you the conversation," Susannah says. "We have the spell book."

"She would know immediately if we went over there," I say. "Plus, it's only just getting warm out, and I'm not sure she's even growing all those things yet. I'm just gonna have to figure something out." I pick up the spell book. "But in the meantime, there's a memory spell in here that might be worth a shot. Maybe help with my nondreams?"

"Can I see it?" Susannah asks, taking the book from my lap. She skims the page. "We could definitely try this tonight after we call Myra. Although it looks like a potion might be the better way to go for potency."

I glance at the spell book. How am I going to slip all this spell casting past my dad and Mrs. Meriwether?

Alice puts down her notebook. "Speaking of which, we should get started."

Mary frowns. "I just want the record to state that I *really* don't like this."

"Since we can't easily move the Myra painting from the attic, and it's where you found the letter, I'm thinking we should just do the spell there," Alice says.

"I was actually going to say the same thing," I say.

Mary groans.

"I'll grab the candles and the intensifying oil," Susannah says.

We slide off the beds, collecting our notes.

"I'd like to point out that we still don't know what side of this Myra's on. What if she does something to Sam?" Mary says. "What could we even do about it?"

"If she wanted to hurt me, she could probably do it anyway. Calling her wouldn't change that," I say, and open the door.

"But there's—"

"Mary, I swear, if you make noise and Sam's dad catches us, I will smother you with a pillow," Alice says.

Mary makes a face at Alice, but doesn't say another word.

All four of us creep through the dark hallway, me leading the way with a flashlight and Susannah bringing up the rear with a chamberstick candle, or whatever she called it.

I unlatch the attic door, and the girls follow me up the stairs. Elijah waits for us by the crate of paintings, bowler hat in hand.

"Elijah's here," I say.

He gives me the hat, and it becomes visible in my hand. Mary nervously glances around at the rough beams and protruding nails.

Alice kneels down to arrange three black candles in a triangle and Susannah lights them. Mary and I place the dress, letter, dog collar, hat, and key on the floor next to the painting.

I put down my flashlight. "We should start by saying things we know about Myra. Trying to tune in to her life and what was important to her. The painting and these items might be enough of a draw, but they might not. The more personal we can get, the more likely she is to hear us. At least, that's how it worked when Elijah first showed up."

"Got it. You want to start us out?" Alice asks.

"Sure," I say. "Myra Haxtun Harper was born in February of 1863. She was married to Henry Sleeper Harper in 1889, and for a while they lived with her widowed father in Manhattan."

"Twelve years later they purchased a home overlooking Gramercy Park. They never had kids, and they spent their time traveling," Susannah says.

Alice nods. "Myra and Henry got on the *Titanic* after touring Europe and Asia. They brought Hammad, their interpreter from Cairo, and their Pekingese dog."

"They were all saved in Lifeboat Three, and Myra lived the rest of her life in Manhattan, until her death in 1923," Mary says.

Elijah paces with his hands behind his back and his brow furrowed.

Susannah leans over the crate with her candle and peers at the painting. "Hmmm. Maybe there's something we can tell just from looking at her."

We all stare at Myra.

"Strong eyes," Susannah says.

Alice nods. "And a subtle smile."

"She looks happy," I say.

"Like she's in love," Mary says. "Which would make sense if her husband was also in this painting."

"Let's try this," Susannah says.

She links hands with Mary and me, and we circle the candles. Alice pulls a small vial out of her black blazer pocket and drops some of whatever's in it near each of the candlewicks. As the oil heats, a strong scent fills the air.

"What is that?" I ask.

"Tea tree oil and a few herbs," Mary says. "It helps with focus and intention."

"Everyone take a deep breath and close your eyes," Susannah says, and we do. "Picture Myra as she was in this painting, a proud and private woman who traveled all over the world."

I focus.

"Keep your image strong and specific as we say her name," Susannah says. "Myra Haxtun Harper."

"Myra Haxtun Harper," we all say together. "Myra

Haxtun Harper." Our voices merge and become more force-ful. "Myra . . . Haxtun . . . Harper."

I open my eyes. We all do. Mary nervously looks over her shoulder, and I can't help but do the same.

"Anything?" Alice asks.

"No," I say. Nothing but a pacing Elijah, who is looking around the room even more suspiciously than Mary. "Let's try again, maybe say her name a few more times."

We close our eyes. "Myra Haxtun Harper. Myra Haxtun Harper." Our voices weave in and out of one another like a song as we say her name over and over.

We open our eyes.

"Not here," Elijah says, and I tell the girls.

Alice breaks our handhold. "Maybe she doesn't want to come? Or maybe she never really cared about these things? Although that seems strange since someone obviously went to a lot of trouble to get them to us."

"Maybe we could look again, try to dig up more on her past that would help us connect with her?" Mary suggests.

Elijah clasps his hands behind his back. "I have looked. And if I cannot find any documents, then they likely no longer exist."

I repeat his words.

"Okay, tell us again how you got Elijah to talk to you the first time, any details you can think of," Susannah says.

I nod. "I found an old stack of letters hidden in my armoire, which had belonged to his sister, and I sat down at my vanity to read them. Halfway through, the lights went out in my room."

"And did the letters have any information about Elijah in them, personal details?" Mary asks.

"No, actually, they didn't even mention his name," I say.

"I came because I was aware of anything related to Abigail,

those letters in particular," Elijah says. "I spent many years wondering about her after she passed on. If you had said her name, I would have heard you more easily than if you had said my own."

"True. Okay," I say, mulling over his words.

Alice leans toward me, like she can somehow hear Elijah if she just gets close enough. "Does he have an idea?"

"He said he came because he was tuned in to anything having to do with his sister. If Myra won't come when we say her name, maybe she'll come when we say someone else's?"

"Like her husband's?" Susannah asks.

"It's possible," I say. "Let's try it."

We link hands again and all take a deep breath, inhaling the tea tree oil and the musty air. "Henry Sleeper Harper. Henry Sleeper—"

"Henry?" A beautifully dressed older woman blinks in at the far end of the room. *Myra!* Even from a distance, she seems weary, like someone who hasn't slept in days. "Henry?"

I let go of Mary's and Susannah's hands. "She's here." My voice is a whisper.

Myra locks me in her gaze. "Why are you calling for my Henry? Do you know where he is? Please, tell me if you know." Her words are fast and nervous.

"You don't know where your husband is?" I ask. *How can that be?*

"No. And if you have seen him, I would most appreciate your telling me so."

A chill runs down my neck. "He's not here." I take a step forward. "I did see him, though. I, um, had dinner with him on the *Titanic*."

She frowns. "Are you trying to be funny?" Myra takes note of the candles by my feet and all the items on the floor.

She assesses each one of us, stopping on Elijah. "What am I supposed to make of all this?"

"There is no bad intent. Of that, I can assure you," Elijah says.

She looks unsure.

"I know how strange this is going to sound," I say. "But I've been having dreams about the *Titanic,* whole and floating, like it was before it sank. Only they're not quite dreams. I think the people I saw there might all be . . . spirits."

"I don't understand. You say you saw my husband in your dreams, but you think he might really be on the *Titanic?* Where?"

"I'm not exactly . . . How about this? I'll make a deal with you. I'll tell you everything I know in exchange for you telling me what you know about these items." I wave my hand at the floor.

She pinches her lips together. "That does not seem unreasonable."

I take a breath. "So it goes like this . . . My grandmother was a Haxtun, Charlotte Haxtun Mather. She would have been your great-niece. And a dress was sent to my house a few days ago, a green evening gown. The card was signed with your name. Aunty Myra H.H."

Myra listens carefully.

I point at the painting. "In this crate is a painting of you. However, I could have sworn that it used to be of you *and* your husband, only he seems to have disappeared from the canvas. I have no idea how it happened. It was hanging in the hallway downstairs. Then, about a week ago, it got moved up here."

The girls watch me without saying a word, even Alice. Maybe she has more restraint than I give her credit for.

"That's very odd," Myra says, giving me her full attention.

"When I put that dress on, the one the card said was from you, I wound up on a shiny new *Titanic;* don't ask me how. And since then, every time I go to sleep, I return to the ship. Everyone keeps referring to me as your niece, even your husband. And I had dinner with him. Hammad was there, too."

"Hammad?" Myra asks, surprised. "We haven't seen him since right after the ship went down. We heard he went back to Egypt."

"And you said that currently you cannot locate your husband?" Elijah says.

Myra shakes her head. "Henry disappeared some time ago."

"And what led up to his disappearance? Did he do anything unusual?" Elijah asks.

"Nothing out of the ordinary," Myra says. "For a brief moment I thought he passed on without me. But we spent all our years after death together. Henry would never leave me by choice. It frightened me."

"What about fellow *Titanic* passengers? Have you seen any of them?" Elijah asks.

Myra furrows her brow. "Some, yes. Others, I believe, passed on. But I haven't seen any of them recently. Why?"

Elijah shakes his head. "I have not been able to find a single one. And I have been looking extensively."

Myra frowns. "So what are you saying, then? That you think something is happening to *Titanic* passengers?"

"As far as we can tell, the ship might be a spell, an illusion of some kind," I say. "And for whatever reason . . . your husband is currently with the other passengers there."

"If my Henry somehow did go to a spell ship, why hasn't he returned? I do not understand this at all." Myra lifts her long skirt and walks toward the crate. "Now, let me see what you have here. You say this portrait was altered?" She examines it, and the corners of her eyes narrow. "But how can this be? Henry *has* vanished . . . and yet the canvas looks undisturbed? Who would do such a thing?" Her tone is demanding.

"That is precisely what we aim to find out," Elijah says in a reassuring voice.

"I remember the day we had this commissioned," Myra says, her hand clenching her skirt. "We had just bought our first home. How proud Henry was in that moment. I had no idea the painting was here."

"There was a letter taped to the back of it telling how you and Unc—" I wince at the ease with which I almost called him my uncle. "Henry survived. It was written by someone named Helen Hopson."

She nods. "My niece." She bends down near the items on the floor, and the green dress catches her eye. "I've never seen this before. But I must admit that green silk was always a favorite. I wore it as often as I could." She lifts a candle, and the girls' eyes follow the seemingly floating flame. "And what is this, a dog collar? It is similar to ones I owned, but it does not belong to me."

"What about the hat? Could it have belonged to your husband?" I ask.

"It is very hard to tell with men's hats. They all look the same," she says with no humor. This must be taking a toll on her. "But do you know what this makes me think of? That fellow who filmed the *Titanic* wreckage. He found my husband's bowler hat still sitting on top of the remains of his wardrobe."

Elijah and I look at each other.

Myra places the candle on the floor next to her. The tension leaves her face. "I have not seen one of Helen's letters in many—" Myra's fingers touch the envelope, and she jumps backward, examining her hand like she just got a bad shock.

"Mrs. Harper?" Elijah says, moving toward her. I step forward, too.

Myra looks shaken. "What on earth?" She stumbles and loses her balance. Elijah steadies her.

"Are you okay?" I ask. The girls stiffen at hearing the anxiety in my voice.

"Sam?" Alice says.

Myra begins to flicker, the same way Elijah flickered when Vivian summoned him from Mrs. Meriwether's kitchen.

"What's happening to her?" I ask.

Elijah holds Myra's arm. "There must have been a spell on the letter."

Myra tries to grab on to my hand, but her fingers go right through mine. Her eyes widen in fear. She speaks, but I can't hear her. She reaches for me desperately with both arms like someone is dragging her backward against her will, and then she flickers out completely.

Elijah and I are silent, staring at the spot where Myra disappeared.

"Sam, I need you to tell us what happened," Alice says with force, jolting me out of my shock.

"Myra vanished. Not because she wanted to. A spell," I say. "It happened right after she touched the letter."

Susannah stares at the letter. "Another spell in an object."

"But I touched that letter multiple times, and nothing happened to me," I say.

"Spells can be targeted to a person," Alice says. "And I'm guessing to a spirit as well."

I frown. "So then what? All of these things—the dress, the collar, the paintings—were actually sent for *her,* not us?"

"I believe someone hoped you would find her and

potentially helped you to do so by putting all these objects in front of you," Elijah says. "It is possible it would have happened if she had touched any of the other items as well."

I repeat his words to the Descendants.

"And there we were happily doing the research and figuring out how to find her," Susannah says.

"And all along we were being used to trap her," Alice says in disbelief.

CHAPTER THIRTY

I Live in Salem

Mary drops the spell ingredients on the floor of the spare bedroom, and Elijah blinks out.

"Whoever messed with that painting probably knows their spell worked," Alice says.

"Whoever messed with that painting is alive," I say. "Spirits can't do spells. But I also think they might have needed a spirit to help. It's too risky otherwise and too easy to get caught."

"Also, a spirit most likely delivered those packages and left that key on my nightstand," Alice says.

Mary frowns. "Did you ever find out if it was your dad who moved the painting to the attic?"

I shake my head. "So then we agree it's possible a person is doing spells and somehow using a spirit to help?"

"Agreed," Susannah says. "Which makes figuring out who it is a million times harder."

Alice rubs her eye. "Redd was right to warn us. What did we get ourselves into, you guys?"

We're all quiet for a second.

"In that first dream I had, the one that was the warning, there were three objects—the painting, the dress, and a little silver book. We still haven't seen that book," I say.

"No, we haven't," Susannah says.

"And speaking of which, we need to do that memory spell," Alice says.

Mary grabs the spell book off the bed. "I hate the thought of Sam visiting the *Titanic* not knowing who she is, especially after tonight."

"You and me both," I say.

"I think we should stay up," Susannah says. "In case we need to wake you. We can take shifts." She places the black candles on the floor and relights them. "The only time you couldn't be woken up was when you had that dress on, right?"

I sit cross-legged on the floor next to Susannah. "Every other time I've been woken by something normal like an alarm, so I don't think I'm being held there. Even with the dress, once it was off, Elijah could wake me up." I pause. "You don't think I *could* be held there, right?"

Alice turns out the light and joins us around the candles.

"I sure as hell hope not," Mary says, handing me the spell book.

I flip open the worn leather cover and read. "For stronger potency, mix a potion . . ." I skim down the page until I find the section I'm looking for. "If a potion cannot be mixed, a less potent alternative for memory enhancement is possible. Begin by forming a circle."

"Done," Alice says.

"Join hands," I read, and we do. Susannah and Alice lean closer and read along with me.

I close my eyes for a few seconds and focus on my house,

on my dad, on the breakfasts I eat every morning with the Meriwethers. *My name is Samantha Mather. I live in Salem,* I say three times in my head, and reopen my eyes. "Make bright the memories I wish to see, so I may hold them close to me. If they wander, bring them back. Dispel all doubts and clear my path," I say.

Susannah turns to me. "I see you. May you also see." She runs her fingers through the top of the candle flame and lightly touches my forehead between my eyes.

"I hear you. May you also hear," Mary says. She runs her fingertips through the flame and touches my ear.

"I know you. May you also know." Alice runs her fingers through the flame and touches my heart.

"Through my sisters' eyes and my own, the seed of memory is firmly sown." I run my hands over the flame and then over the top of my head.

For a few seconds everyone silently watches the candles burn.

Susannah stands and turns the light back on. "Do you feel anything?"

"No. But I'm not sure I would yet."

Mary blows out the candles.

Elijah blinks in. "I will keep watch over you tonight. I do not require sleep like they do."

I consider arguing with him, but the truth is, it makes way more sense for him to stay up than for the girls. And he's the only one who will see if that object-delivering spirit tries to do anything. I fill the girls in.

"Can he wake us, though, if something happens?" Alice asks, climbing into bed next to Mary. "Break a glass or bang a pot if he has to?"

I nod. I don't need to ask Elijah. I know he can. I pull

the covers up under my arms and avoid looking at him. Jaxon's being a crap friend, Elijah is un-gone, and I'm part of a magic circle? Everything is upside down. Elijah turns off the light and Mary gasps. Something fuzzy pushes against my hand. Broome.

CHAPTER THIRTY-ONE

How Did You Know You Were in Love?

I run my hands down my off-white dress; it's draped in black lace and sparkles in the light. The fabric is covered with intricate patterns of beads.

Mollie smiles at me through my vanity mirror as she repositions my hair on top of my head. "A few more black pearls in yer hair and ye'll sparkle from top to bottom."

I smile, too, but I feel off. "Mollie, do I seem well to you?"

"Always well. Yer one a the happier people I know."

I consider her words. "I just have a strange sensation that I'm supposed to do something or remember something."

"Aye. I hate that feelin'. Makes me all itchy. But besides meetin' yer aunty Myra in the lounge, there is nothin' that I know of that needs doin' or rememberin'."

Aunty Myra. Her name is like a bell in my mind, but I'm not sure why. "What's the date, Mollie?"

Mollie hesitates. "The thirteenth of April. Ya know, I almost wasn't sure." She laughs. "Maybe yer not rememberin' things is rubbin' off on me."

I smile. April feels right.

"All finished," she says, and I stand up.

My corset squeezes me, and the bottom of my dress is so narrow that I can only take small steps. "Will you come with me to meet my aunt?"

Mollie nods and opens the door for me.

She leads me through the hallways and onto an elevator that takes us to an upper deck. We pass men and women in top hats and gowns, talking excitedly about their evening activities, and step into the first-class lounge.

"This way," Mollie says, and I follow her to a table where Aunt Myra and her friend are drinking tea.

"Aunty Myra, sorry I'm late." I stare at her a moment longer than I should. What is it I'm not remembering?

Aunt Myra brightens. "It is perfectly all right. You know Mrs. Brown."

I curtsy to the other woman. Yes, of course I know Margaret Brown. "It's wonderful to see you."

Mrs. Brown pats the cushion next to her on the velvet couch and I sit down. Mollie has taken a seat at a nearby table with a couple of other ladies' maids.

"Mrs. Brown was just telling me how she has been working with a judge to set up a juvenile court to help destitute children. It will be the first in America," Aunt Myra says, and pours me a cup of tea. "Is that not something?"

I feel like I was just studying her. Wait, no, that can't be right. Maybe I was reading a newspaper article about her? "Yes, I believe I read about it somewhere. And about all the amazing work you've done for women."

Mrs. Brown tilts her head slightly and looks surprised. "It seems I have a young fan here, Myra."

I smile and take the cup of tea from my aunt. "You should have a whole group of them, not just me." I pause. "Do you mind if I ask you something?"

Mrs. Brown grins at my compliments. "Ask whatever you like."

"How did you know you were in love?" Even as I say the words, they feel foreign in my mouth. Why am I asking this question?

Mrs. Brown laughs. "Well now, that is certainly not what I was expecting. A great question, though. I have always thought that love is not all feelings and instinct, but is instead a generosity of time. That if you truly love someone or something, you will give them all your hours without a second thought. Ideal moments are exactly what they sound like, ideal and hard not to enjoy. But love has never been about ideal moments for me, but rather every-day ones that are brightened because the other person is there."

"Beautifully put, Margaret," Aunt Myra says. "So you are wondering about love, Samantha? May I ask, is this a philosophical question or a practical one?"

My cheeks redden. "Well, I—"

"Ladies," says a tall man with dark hair, an expensive suit, and a mustache that curls upward at the ends. He bows. "Are you enjoying this fine evening? I hope the refreshments are up to your standards."

"Yes, Mr. Ismay. Everything is just as lovely as it could be," says Mrs. Brown.

Ismay looks at Aunt Myra. "And you, Mrs. Harper? I know you do quite a bit of traveling. I do hope our accommodations are making it easy for you to adjust to sea travel."

What's this guy doing, fishing for compliments? I remember Alexander said Ismay was one of the owners.

"You have really outdone yourself with this ship. She is fit for royalty," Aunt Myra says.

Ismay laughs. "Oh, you are too kind. Too kind. Also, I don't know if you have heard, but I am happy to announce that we are making great time."

"I do hope it's safe to travel this fast," I say, though I'm not sure why. I don't have any fears about sea travel, do I? And I'm verging on impolite. "There is usually ice at this time of year, is there not?" Definitely impolite. What's wrong with me?

He wiggles his nose and looks down at me. "This ship is practically unsinkable, Miss Mather. You have absolutely nothing to worry about."

I nod and pick up my teacup. The nagging sensation that I'm supposed to remember something returns. I suddenly feel like I can't sit still.

"I will leave you ladies to your tea," Ismay says, and bows again.

I straighten my dress. "Aunty Myra, Mrs. Brown, would you mind excusing me? I feel inspired to take a walk and enjoy the night air."

"Of course, dear. Just make sure you get to bed at a reasonable time. I will come and say good night when I return."

I say my goodbyes, and Mollie joins me out on the promenade deck in the cool air.

"Did ya remember what ya wanted to, miss?" Mollie asks.

I shake my head.

"My pa used ta say that if ya sleep, what ya wanted ta remember would be there in the mornin'."

Sleep. Dreams. I fidget with my hands. "Where is your family now?"

"With the rest of the Mullins in Clarinbridge. They own a general store there."

I shiver as we walk toward the railing.

"Oh, miss, I've forgotten yer coat."

"Don't worry. I'll be fine. Let's—"

Mollie raises her eyebrows. "If ya catch a chill, it'll be me fault. I'll just get it quick." She turns around and walks away before I can say another word.

I rest my hand on the wooden railing, which is cold and slick with spray from the ocean. *What is going on with me tonight? I've had nothing but a wonderful time on this ship, and here I am a bundle of nerves.*

I bend slightly and peer over the side of the ship. It almost makes me dizzy. It's a good fifty-foot drop into the black ocean. I walk with my hand resting lightly on the damp glossy wood. The water stretches out endlessly, and there is a dull rumble from the propellers pushing the ship forward.

I stop at the end of the promenade area and lean my elbows on the railing. A breeze whips a few loose pieces of hair onto my cheeks.

All of a sudden, strong hands grab my waist from behind, lifting me up.

"Stop!" I yell, and I try futilely to grip the slippery railing. The person gives me a hard push, and I fall headfirst toward the water.

The side of the ship whizzes past me. My stomach drops, and my dress flaps violently against my free-falling legs. I open my mouth to scream, but it's impossible to get enough air.

And it's loud. No one tells you how loud it is to fall.

Instinctively, I reach my hands out in a dive. They hit the water so hard that it feels like my fingernails have been shoved up into my knuckles. The cold water bludgeons every inch of me, like I dove into concrete instead of liquid. All the heat leaves my body at once. The remaining air pushes out of my chest. I scream, inhaling salt water and—

CHAPTER THIRTY-TWO

It Happened So Fast

I sit straight up, coughing so hard it hurts my ribs. There's a hand patting my back, and voices, worried voices, all talking at once. My lungs burn.

I'm in my black sweats on the floor next to the bed, and Elijah and Susannah are crouched next to me. Mary and Alice stand above us. I'm shaking from shock, or shivering from cold; I'm not sure.

"What happened, Suze?" Alice asks, wide-eyed.

"All I heard was the crash," Susannah says. "And then she was like this, coughing and shivering on the floor."

"Sam, can you talk? Can you tell us what happened?" Mary asks.

I wrap my arms around myself. My fingers are like icicles. "Someone pushed me over the railing. And then I don't know. I must have woken up."

"You dove off the bed without warning," Elijah says. "I only just managed to keep your head from striking the floor."

I repeat his words to the girls from between chattering teeth.

"We need to get you warm," Elijah says. He places my arms around his neck, puts one arm under my knees, and hoists me into the air. The girls take a step back.

Susannah must understand Elijah's intentions, because she throws aside the covers so he can put me under them. "This shouldn't happen, right? Getting hurt there shouldn't mean getting hurt here."

"She shouldn't be able to take spoons, either," Alice says.

Mary pulls at her curls nervously. "Did you get a look at the person who threw you over?"

Elijah tucks the covers over my shoulders, and I curl up.

I rub my hands together for warmth. "No. It happened so fast."

Elijah paces at the end of the bed, looking pissed off.

"Did the memory spell work?" Susannah asks.

"Only kind of. I was questioning myself and asking the other passengers weird things. And I wanted to remember something but I didn't know what."

Susannah sits on the bed next to me. "Do you think your questions somehow angered someone?"

"Maybe? I mean, I did ask Bruce Ismay if it was safe to travel so fast and mentioned all the ice. That could definitely be perceived as a reference to the sinking. Maybe that made someone mad?"

"Hmmm," Alice says. "Let's look into Ismay. And what about Myra? Did you see her? Was anyone talking about her?"

I pull the covers a little tighter. "She was there this time, acting just like the rest of them, the way I usually act when I'm there—as if she's right where she belongs. She was happy and drinking tea with Mrs. Brown like everything was normal in the world."

"What does it mean that she vanished from here and showed up there?" Mary asks.

"I don't know. It's kind of the nature of that place. Everyone's in some happy fog. Also, I spoke to Mollie, whose last name is Mullin. We should look her up, too. Mollie said it was April thirteenth, and it's the ninth here. There's something strange happening there with time."

"So it's still before the sinking?" Susannah asks.

"It seems that way."

"Also, I can't believe you got to drink tea with Margaret Brown," Mary says.

I smile at her and yawn.

Elijah stops pacing. "You cannot go back there after what just happened. We cannot risk it. If you fall asleep, I will wake you up every ten minutes."

"Believe me, I don't want to go back there, but how long can I realistically go without real sleep? A couple of days?" I say.

"Then we will work faster," Elijah says, daring me to argue with him.

CHAPTER THIRTY-THREE

That Is All I Know

Alice and Susannah sit on the couch in my living room. Mary has the armchair and I'm on the floor. We're surrounded by notes, laptops, and research books. Our trunk turned coffee table is brimming with Meriwether snacks.

"Any news from Elijah?" Mary asks.

"Just that he's still looking." I pause. "He's looking, we're looking. It's late Sunday afternoon. You guys are going to have to go home soon. I think we need to do something differently. More direct."

"Like another spell?" Mary asks.

"Our spells have mostly been backfiring on us," Alice says.

I pause. "I think we need to talk to Redd."

Mary looks surprised. "Redd?"

"You guys said she's honest. And she clearly knew something was going to happen before we did. Even if she winds up telling us just some small detail, it would be worth it."

"Interesting," Susannah says.

Alice considers it. "Spirits were never Redd's thing. She was a plant-and-potion type of witch. Buuut you're right—she obviously knows something about this *and* was trying to warn us. I think it's worth a shot."

We make our way into the foyer just as the front door opens. My dad and Mrs. Meriwether come through with bags of groceries.

"You girls going somewhere?" my dad asks.

"Just into town for some fresh air," Susannah says.

"You all deserve it. You've been dedicated to your homework all weekend," Mrs. Meriwether says, nodding approvingly. "If you want to drop by Sugar Spells, write Georgia a note telling her I said you can have anything you want as a reward."

"Thanks," I say. "We might just do that."

The door closes behind us, and we make our way to Mary's Jeep.

"I'm not entirely sure I can handle the cuteness level in your house," Alice says as we get in.

"I'll try to tone it down for you. Cuteness just comes to me so naturally," I say, and Mary giggles.

Alice turns on the engine, and we head toward town.

"Question, why do you always drive Mary's Jeep?" I ask Alice.

"I actually don't like to drive," Mary says from the front seat. "Hate it."

"I wish I had my own car," Susannah says. "But with my little sister's medical expenses these past few years, it just hasn't been possible."

Susannah told us in the fall that her sister's cancer had come back unexpectedly. I always assumed it was Vivian's fault. Guilt grips my stomach. Even now, people are still feeling the ramifications of what she did.

"And even though I do have a car," Alice says, "it's a sports car—"

"You and a sports car are an evil combination," Mary says.

Alice rolls her eyes. "My mother got it for me. It's a two-seater, which obviously is impossible because the three of us—scratch that, the *four* of us—are always together."

Alice jerks to a stop and we all get out. The street that Redd's store is on is bursting with Sunday shoppers. Families are eating at outdoor cafés, and visitors are taking guided tours. A few of the locals watch us, but most of the tourists don't give us a second look. To them our black clothes are just in the spirit of the town.

Susannah stops two stores away from Redd's. "Those are pretty," she says, pointing at black handcrafted candles in a window. We all stop and pretend to be interested.

Alice nudges Mary, and she walks off. We comment on the window display for another thirty seconds, blending in with all the other weekend shoppers. In my peripheral vision I see Mary pull a small vial out of her pocket, drop some liquid in Redd's keyhole, and push the door open.

Alice scans the street like a sharpshooter. "Now."

We walk toward Mary, slip inside the door, and close it behind us. The room's as disorienting and dark as it was before.

"Now what, Sam?" Mary whispers.

"Last time, I found a wall and followed it to a hallway," I whisper back.

"Last time, you were invited," says a voice, and light bursts through a parted curtain.

Redd looks particularly intimidating backlit. The girls tense next to me.

"I'm sorry. We—" I say.

"I don't want to hear 'sorry.' You're not sorry."

We all stand silently. Even ballsy Alice doesn't attempt to talk our way in.

Redd scowls disapprovingly. "Well, are you coming or not?"

I walk toward her. As soon as I reach the curtain, she moves away from it and the cloth hits me in the face. The girls follow me into the round room, with its black velvet curtains, wrought-iron candelabras, and multicolored rugs.

Redd sits on a pillow next to the table and fills five small cups from an old teapot.

"You were expecting us?" Mary asks, looking at the cups.

"Do not confuse the fact that I knew you were coming with the idea that I am happy to see you." Redd looks at me. "I told you I didn't want to be involved. I thought I made it clear."

"I know. I'm . . ." She doesn't want an apology. "There was no one else we could go to and we need help."

"I'm not in the business of helping anymore. I helped this town for years. I'm sure they told you." Redd gestures at the girls.

"You had a store with herbal creams and tonics. My mom always said they were amazing," Susannah says, her hands neatly folded on her black high-waisted skirt.

Redd lifts her chin in the air. "They were the best. People came to me with their sore backs and their headaches, their hair loss and their skin problems. I helped them all." She puts down the teapot and frowns. "But all they did was bicker and complain. Couldn't recognize a good thing when they had it. Drink your tea." She gestures toward the cups like she's swatting a fly. We each take one.

"What if we told you that we didn't need you to get involved, but just wanted you to point us in the right direction?" Mary asks, and lifts her teacup.

"Not a chance. Not since that fiasco in the woods last fall. And not with you four walking around broadcasting your business to the world. You're a freight train headed for a brick wall that I have the good sense not to board."

How much does she know about what happened in the woods?

"I'm *very* careful about my information. I—" Alice's tone is defensive.

Redd raises her hand. "Your protection spells are mediocre at best."

I sip my tea. Honey-lemon-ginger, I think. "Why did you warn me last week?"

Redd sits up a little straighter, and her bracelets clink together. "Because of your general incompetence. Which was very nice of me, if I do say so myself. And more than I should've done."

"No one warns someone because they're incompetent, unless they actually mean to help," Alice says.

Redd looks pointedly at Alice.

"What if we—" Mary starts.

"Don't try to bargain with me. You think you're the first people to show up on my doorstep asking for something?" Redd laughs. "For *years,* people showed up almost every day. I'll tell you what I told them: no. I think you've stayed quite long enough."

I put down my cup. *I'm not leaving until I've said my piece.* "We think someone may have put a spell on the spirits of *Titanic* passengers. And last night we unknowingly *helped* that person trap one of the passengers. What's more, when I sleep, I'm able to go there—to the *Titanic.* It's as if the whole ship has some sort of time amnesia."

Redd's eyes narrow, but she doesn't tell me to shut up.

"You warned us. And that *was* nice of you," I say. "But if you know something we don't and you don't tell us, you will be helping this person get away with whatever it is they're doing. And that means the 'death' you talked about will be partially on you."

"It most certainly will not. . . . How can you . . . You are rotten children for trying to guilt me like this," she says, and drums her fingers on the table. Her jewelry clinks in rhythm. Her expression morphs from one emotion to another, like she's arguing with herself. "Fine." She smacks the table, rattling our cups. Susannah flinches. "I will help you this one time, but after that you don't bother me again. Ever. Agreed?"

We all nod our heads, and I hide my smile. She's cranky and a seriously odd duck, but she isn't a bad person.

"Many years ago, when I was a small girl, there was talk of a warlock who saw spirits like you do." Redd looks at me. "He was a dark sort. There were whispers he was trapping and collecting the spirits for some purpose. But no one knew who the spirits were or why he was doing it."

"Do you remember his name?" Susannah asks.

"Never knew it," Redd says. "And if others knew, they were careful not to say it. They called him the Collector."

"Did anyone try to find out what he was doing?" I ask.

"A few people did." Redd frowns.

"What happened to them?" Mary asks.

"They died," Redd says, and sips her tea.

Alice and I look at each other.

"And where is this guy now?" Alice asks.

"Long dead. He moved away when I was still a girl, and I heard he died shortly after."

"So if he's dead, then why wouldn't you want to help us?" Mary asks. "It's not like he can hurt you anymore."

Redd glares at her. "My tea leaves are never wrong. I've read them every morning for the past forty years. And I'm telling you that they showed him to me again, the Collector, or someone like him. That is all I know."

"Do you think this Collector you're sensing is here in Salem?" Susannah asks.

Redd grunts. "If I knew that, I would tell you and save myself this headache." She gestures toward us. "My leaves tell me what they choose to and nothing more. You cannot force these things."

"There is a dress," Susannah says, "that transported Samantha to the ship the first time. We think there's a spell on it. If we brought it to you, could you help us break it?"

"Not without knowing who the caster is and what kind of magic they're using. Now, it really is time for you to go." Redd stands and we do, too. I can tell by her voice that she's not going to tell us anything else.

"Thanks," I say, but she waves away my words.

"That way." Redd points to one of the chest-high candelabras on my left. "And girls, don't ever try to break into one of my doors again or I will polka-dot your skin for a year. Do we understand each other?"

"Perfectly," Mary says in a higher pitch than normal.

CHAPTER THIRTY-FOUR

I'm Not Leaving

Alice shoves their overnight bags into the back of Mary's Jeep. "Are you absolutely positive that Elijah will wake you up all night?"

I balance on the curb in front of my house, half on, half off. "Yeah."

"Call us if you need us. We'll sneak out," Susannah says.

Susannah gives me a hug goodbye, but her eyes look at something behind me.

I turn in the direction of her gaze. Jaxon and Niki are standing near his truck in his driveway. As I watch, he kisses her. My foot slips off the curb, and I stumble.

Susannah grabs my elbow and pulls me around the Jeep.

Alice slams the tailgate closed. "Now he's just being an ass. He's totally flaunting this Niki thing."

"It's weird, though. It's not like Jaxon," I say as he climbs into his truck and starts the engine.

"He always seemed so nice," Mary says.

"He was," I say.

Jaxon's truck pulls past us, and I watch him drive down our street and away from me. It's been weird not talking to Jaxon these past few days. My life feels emptier without him in it. "I told Jaxon that Elijah was back."

Mary tilts her head. "You think that has something to do with this?"

"Potentially. Jaxon was, well . . ." I can't believe I'm telling them this. "About to kiss me and I blurted it out."

"Just because he got jealous doesn't make it okay," Alice says. "Trying to hurt someone is trying to hurt someone. Period."

Susannah's face scrunches up, like she's concentrating too hard. "I don't know. I never got the feeling that Jaxon was intentionally mean."

Mary leans in. "Okay, I know we're talking about Jaxon. And I want to hear every detail of that story. But *what* is Elijah like?"

"We're in the middle of a crisis and you want to talk about boys? Unbelievable," Alice says.

Mary ignores her. "Just for a minute. Come on, Sam, dish."

I half smile at her. "What do you mean?"

"Details," Mary says. "All of them."

Even though Alice objected, I can tell by her look that she's curious, too. They all wear the same expectant expression.

"Um . . . well . . . he has an accent. A slight one. Kinda British-sounding."

"How old?" Mary asks.

"Eighteen when he died," I say. "He's formal, like in a seventeenth-century way. *Super* stubborn."

"Looks?" Alice asks.

"Tall, about a head taller than me. Dark wavy hair, gray

eyes, high cheekbones. Sometimes when he stands near a fireplace or looks out the window, he looks more like a portrait than real."

Mary squeals. "So basically, he's beautiful."

My face gets hot. Susannah grins at me. They all do.

"You've kissed him, haven't you?" Mary says.

"Uh . . ." I laugh awkwardly. "I . . ."

Alice looks mischievous. "That good, huh?"

I'm sure my cheeks have transcended red and moved on to purple. "You know what? I think I hear my dad calling," I say, and head up my driveway.

"Uh-huh," Mary says, and they all laugh again.

I wave goodbye, but I don't feel like laughing. I shouldn't be talking about Elijah like this. I know better than to get attached to people who leave. I never want to make that mistake again.

"Sam," my dad's voice calls from his office the second I close the door. "Come on in here a minute."

He sits behind his desk, which is covered with papers and books. I take the seat across from him. I always like visiting my dad in his office, getting a glimpse into his business world.

"I got a call back from our Haxtun relative," he says.

I stiffen. "You did?"

"I did . . . and I decided to do a little digging. Funny thing is, she said that no one in our family has been named Myra since Myra Haxtun Harper, who survived the *Titanic,* and who is obviously dead." He stares at me, like he's gauging my reaction.

My heart pounds wildly. "What? That's so weird. Why would someone send us packages that say they're from her, then?"

He continues talking like I didn't ask a question. "And it occurred to me that you thought something strange had happened with the painting in the hallway. So I went and looked through some of Mom's historical ledgers, and wouldn't you know it, that painting is actually of Myra."

I sit perfectly still, nervous that if I even gesture wrong, he'll see right through me. "So what does that mean? Do you think it was a prank or some twisted history fanatic?"

"What I do know is that you already figured out who Myra was, Sam. And what I don't understand is why you didn't tell me."

So much for sitting still. "I didn't. I—"

"Think carefully before you continue that sentence. Every night, you've been poring over *Titanic* history, which I find hard to believe didn't include the Harpers. And I've never known you in your entire life to walk away from an unanswered question. I thought it was strange when you told me not to look into it. Now I'm positive that there's something going on you're not telling me about."

My stomach drops fast and hard. "I . . ." I can't think of a possible out from this situation. "I didn't want to upset you after . . . well, after everything that happened."

"After Vivian, you mean."

I cringe. "Yeah."

"And why would this upset me?" He's not mad, but he's completely serious and focused, like he's searching out a weak spot in one of his business deals.

"You don't like anything like that."

"Anything like what?"

"Magic." The word sticks in my mouth like peanut butter.

He's quiet for a second. "And you think whatever is going on involves magic?"

"Yes."

My dad moves slightly backward, like he's pulling away from my words. "And the other day at breakfast?"

I hesitate. "I saw something."

"And you lied about it?"

This hole is getting perilously deep. "Yes."

"I see," he says matter-of-factly. He rolls a pen on his desk for no apparent reason and frowns at it. "Do you know why I moved away from Salem, Sam?"

"Because of Mom?"

"Yes, but because of magic, too. It brings about bad things, things I've taken a lot of care not to have in my life. Things I don't want in yours."

Maybe I should just explain to him what's going on and why I haven't been telling the truth. "I get it, Dad. I really do. I'm more familiar than you know."

His face shows pain. "Familiar? Do you mean Vivian?"

"Well, yes, but . . ." It's not likely I'll have another opening like this to ask for the potion. I brace the chair I'm sitting on. "I have these . . . Well, see, the thing is, I . . . I've actually done a few spells myself."

"You're telling me *you've* done magic?" His tone has gone from upset to almost frantic. "No, Sam. No. That can't happen. You can't do magic. It's too dangerous."

"But I—"

"No."

I feel like I'm shrinking, like my dad loves me less than he did an hour ago and in the absence of his love I've somehow become physically smaller.

"Don't worry. I'll take care of it." I'm not sure if he's talking to me or himself. I've never seen him this worked up.

"Take care of what?"

"Moving us back to New York City."

"What?" I can't find my words. I can't find my logic. I can't find my breath. "Isn't that a little extreme?"

"Not from where I sit."

"But the Meriwethers . . ."

"They can come visit."

"My friends . . ."

"They can also visit."

"And this house?" *Full of our family history and all my memories of Elijah.*

"We'll rent it or sell it."

I knew he would react badly, but I never expected this. "Wait. I'll stop. I won't do magic."

He shakes his head.

"I just said I'd stop." My voice is getting louder.

"You've been lying to me, Sam. You look like you're barely sleeping. I should have guessed that magic was involved. It always is in Salem. I just thought because you were so happy here . . . I'm sorry, but I think it's best we leave."

"Be mad at me. Fine. But look at all the good things that have come out of living in Salem. Mrs. Meriwether is certifiably one of the best humans on the planet. We have this amazing house. I've made friends. Me, your daughter, the perpetual loner." I'm waving my hands. "And Mom. Mom came from Salem."

His eyes are two iron gates shutting me out. "You'll understand in time that I'm doing this for you."

"I don't *want* you to do this for me!"

If possible, he looks more upset than I feel.

I stand up and my chin trembles. "I'm not leaving." The first tear falls, and I hit it away so violently that my hand smacks against my cheek.

He stands now, too. "Sam . . . ," he says in his consoling voice.

"No." I move away from my chair. "Don't try to convince me this is better. It's not better."

He moves toward me, like he doesn't fully believe I'm pushing him away. I can't really believe it, either.

"You're young still. You don't know what I know about this place."

"What I don't know, or what you think I can't handle? Because I'm the one who got hanged by Vivian, not you." My voice is quavering. "So don't tell me what I know."

He takes a step backward, like I hit him. I walk out of his office, tears on my cheeks.

I run up the stairs, down the hall, and into my room. I slam the door behind me and stop. Elijah stands by my window.

He looks at my wet cheeks. "Samantha." For a brief second his expression softens. "I will return later."

I wipe at my face with my sleeve. "No. Just tell me what you came to tell me."

Elijah frowns. "It does not seem like the time to be discussing research."

"It's the perfect time to discuss research," I say stubbornly, and sniffle.

Elijah raises an eyebrow at me. I can tell he disagrees. He waits for a second, then sighs. "I found a good deal of information on Bruce Ismay."

"Good. That's good," I say, and wipe my eyes.

"Samantha, are you absolutely certain—"

"Yes," I say before he can finish his sentence. I sit down on my bed, which is strewn with *Titanic* note cards and books. "I already know"—I clear my throat—"that the newspapers in his day tore Ismay apart for saving himself, but that's as far as I read about him."

Elijah nods. "There was a great deal of controversy about

his decision. Captain Smith went down with the ship, even though it was his last voyage before retirement. And so did the chief designer, Thomas Andrews, without hesitation. It was discovered that Thomas Andrews's architectural plans had included additional lifeboats, but the owners had declined. This colored the way people viewed Ismay's decision to jump into a lifeboat to save himself; many did not forgive him for it."

"People thought he should have sacrificed himself?"

"People thought he should have taken responsibility for his own ship and not taken a spot on a lifeboat that could have gone to someone else. His reputation never recovered," he says.

"You think he has a reason to want to erase the memory of the ship sinking?" I ask, straightening a stack of note cards about *Titanic* passengers, most of which have "Body not found" written on the back.

"I think it is possible."

I pull my legs up and wrap my arms around them.

"There is also the drowned man you saw in the restaurant to consider," Elijah says. "And the Collector Redd warned you about."

"Man, you really listen to everything the girls and I say, don't you?"

Elijah hesitates. "When something is important, I give it my full attention."

I can't help but think about what Mrs. Brown said about love and time. I swallow. "What about my history teacher, Mr. Wardwell? Did you find any information that might tell us more about him?"

"He has an inexhaustible amount of historical research. His house looks more like a reference room than a home. It will take me some time to go through it all."

"From being a museum director?"

"Yes, certainly. But also from his decade of teaching history and his lifetime of interest in it. I have not found any spell-related items, though."

"What about Mollie Mullin or Ada Mullin? Have you seen anything about them?"

"Not as of yet. I will continue looking." Only, he doesn't blink out like he usually does when our practical conversations are over. He just stands there.

I look up at him, and for a split second I see the old Elijah, the one I used to tell everything to. "My dad wants to move back to New York."

"Move?" He shakes his head. "I just cannot imagine it. You belong here."

My breath catches in my throat. I nod. *I do belong here.* "This is the first place I've ever felt like myself. And I'm scared that if we go back to New York, I'll lose something, you know? That I won't be me anymore. Have you ever felt that way?"

For a fraction of a second he looks so sad. "Yes."

"With Abigail?"

"And with my parents when they were alive."

I know I should stop the conversation, go back to discussing Ismay or Wardwell. That after everything that's happened between us, getting attached to Elijah again is a terrible idea. But right now I don't care. "Were you close to your parents?"

"Very." He looks out the window. "My mother was someone who embodied joy so absolutely that she made everyone around her brighter. We always told her that if she did not have a body, she would burst into the sky like the sun and light the world."

"And your dad?"

"Serious. Quiet. I have often thought my mother was the only person who could make him laugh. Abigail and I used to try, and he loved us, but his face was never as it was when he was watching my mother."

I wait for him to continue, but he stays silent.

"I must go now," he says. "But I will return before you sleep." And he blinks out.

I close my eyes and hug my knees. *Just tonight. This is a one-time deal. No more personal conversations. It will only make things harder.*

CHAPTER THIRTY-FIVE

Has the Whole World Gone Mad?

I sip my coffee and take a small bite of pancake topped with glazed walnuts and whipped cream. My eyes are on my plate. I can't even look at my dad or Jaxon. Mrs. Meriwether tries to start a few conversations, but they mostly consist of polite answers and some mumbling before they peter out. Another minute of silence goes by.

Mrs. Meriwether dabs the corners of her mouth with her napkin. "Okay. Enough. This sulking has to stop. It's Monday, and you're eating hand-whipped cream sprinkled with freshly ground vanilla and cinnamon. I simply will not have it."

The three of us look at her, but no one says a word.

She scans our faces.

"I have to go. I have to pick up Niki—" Jaxon says.

"Well, it will have to wait a minute." Mrs. Meriwether's voice is stern. "We are practically family, the group of us.

And there is clearly something going on, and I want to know what."

Jaxon shrugs like he's totally unconcerned.

We all stare at him.

Mrs. Meriwether tilts her head. "What's the thing here, Jax? You haven't been acting like yourself in days. None of your sweetness or laughter, just endless obsessing over Niki, a girl I've never heard you say particularly nice things about before now. And, Sam, you've got circles the size of Cadillacs under your eyes. I haven't seen you this quiet in ages."

My mouth opens but no sound comes out. My dad frowns.

I put down my fork and study my pancake.

"Sam and I are moving back to New York," my dad says.

"Hold on a second." Mrs. Meriwether's eyes widen, and she waves her hands in the air. "Charlie, you're moving and you didn't tell me? Has the whole world gone mad in the past forty-eight hours?"

My dad flinches, but his expression remains stubborn. "It was only decided last night."

I push my chair away from the table. "Time to go to school."

"Sam," my dad says, clearly upset.

"I'll be late," I say.

Jaxon gets up, too. "Same."

We walk in silence to our bags and exit the house.

Jaxon stops just as he opens his truck door. "Sam?"

I turn around.

"Want a ride?"

I hesitate. "Bad mood" doesn't begin to describe my state of being right now. But I need to talk to him, and this is the first opportunity I've had in days.

I nod and get in his passenger door.

"So you're moving, huh?" Jaxon says. He turns the key in the ignition and backs out of his driveway.

"I really hope not," I say.

"Might not be all bad." His tone is distant.

I glare at him. "Yes. It will."

"If you say so."

How can he be so casual about all of this? Does he not care at all? "I know you're mad at me. And I know you're dating Niki, but you're also acting like we're not even friends."

He watches the road with a calm expression. "We're friends."

"Look, I know you think I've been closed off. And you were right. I was so hell-bent on being normal that I kept pretending certain things didn't exist. I should have told you what was going on with me. Then we had our honesty talk and it ended badly. Can we just call a truce? I really don't want to fight with you."

"We're not fighting."

"But we're also not really talking."

Jaxon shrugs. "So?"

"See, that's what I mean, right there." I point at him.

Jaxon frowns. "What?"

"You're acting like we're not friends." I turn so that I'm facing him. "If you're mad at me, just say so. Yell at me. Or . . . I don't know what, but something other than telling our parents our personal business over breakfast and then pretending like nothing weird is happening."

"But nothing is happening."

I stare at him in disbelief. Did he get swapped out for his evil twin? Where is Jaxon the talker, the one who always wants to get to the bottom of a problem?

The truck slows.

I look out the window. We're not in the school parking lot; we're by a curb in a residential neighborhood.

My pulse quickens as I recognize the brick house. "You brought me to pick up *Niki*?"

He opens his truck door and jumps out.

I jump out, too. He walks right past me and heads for her door. I grab his arm.

"Sam, stop."

"No, you stop. Have you become completely insensitive?"

A door closes, and we both turn to see Niki walking toward us.

She frowns so deeply I wonder if her face will ever recover. "Sam?"

Jaxon pulls away from me.

Niki walks straight to him and wraps her arms around his chest.

"You know what?" I say. "I think I'll walk."

Niki smirks. "Jealous much?"

I tense. "I so don't have the patience for you right now. *Don't* push me."

Whatever Niki sees in my expression must be convincing, because she breaks eye contact and pulls on Jaxon. "Let's go."

Jaxon opens the door for her. For a split second he turns to look at me. Then he goes around his truck and gets in. They pull away without even saying goodbye. The Jaxon I know would never leave me here. Ever.

"Shit." I kick the ground.

I pull out my phone and type in my group text to the Descendants.

Me: *Any chance you could pick me up at Niki's?*

Alice: *Niki's??? We just got to school. Sit tight for a minute. I'm coming.*

CHAPTER THIRTY-SIX

I Never Thought I Would Say This

I push the heavy lunchroom door open. Alice, Mary, and Susannah sit at their usual table near the window, and I head straight for them.

"I heard Sam had a total meltdown this morning about Jaxon dating Niki," Blair says loud enough for me to hear as I pass. I know I shouldn't, but I look at her.

The girls sitting with Blair laugh. I catch Matt watching us from the next table.

Blair soaks up the encouragement. "Apparently, she showed up at Niki's house today all weepy and—"

"You know what's a good story, Blair?" Matt interrupts. "The one from last weekend when you got drunk, broke your high heel, and face-plan'ed right in a pile of—"

"Shut up, Matt!" Blair snaps, turning instantly red.

"Oh, I thought we were tellin' stories? I guess we're not," he says.

I smile my thanks to him, and he nods.

I sit down at the table with the Descendants.

"Dude, if this day gets to be too much, just say the word and we'll cruise out of here and eat donuts in my sound-proofed room until we pop," Alice says.

I laugh. "I have no idea what you're talking about. It's all hearts and rainbows over here." I open up my lunch bag. "How likely do you think it is that Niki and Blair will just drop this whole rivalry?"

"Not very," Mary says. "As far as I can tell, Niki makes it her personal mission to spread gossip."

"You're telling me. There's been an abnormal amount of whispers and looks today. I never thought I would say this, but I actually prefer getting questions about dead people." I unload my enormous Meriwether lunch onto the table.

"So . . . I have a theory about what happened—"

"Suze," Alice warns.

"With Jaxon this morning," Susannah continues.

"Susannah. Seriously?" Alice's voice is rough.

Susannah and Alice stare at each other.

"Mary, what's going on?" I ask.

"Susannah thinks Jaxon's under a spell," Mary says. "But Alice wasn't convinced and wanted to check it out before we said anything to you. She worries that you'll get upset if we're right. Or if we're wrong."

I look at Susannah, my heart beating a little faster. "Wait. Really?"

"She's having one of her feelings, which aren't always right," Alice says pointedly to Susannah.

"I do have a feeling," Susannah says. "And I've had a feeling that something wasn't adding up for *a while now*. I've known Jaxon since we were in kindergarten, and the Jaxon I know would never, under any circumstances, leave you stranded on the sidewalk. It's just not who he is. Plus, something doesn't feel right about him. I talked to him today. He seems . . . cloudy, I guess is the best way to describe it."

Could that really be what's going on with Jaxon? Please let that be it. Wait, that's terrible that I'm hoping he's under a spell.

"You've said a couple of times that Jaxon wasn't acting like himself," Susannah says to me. "I saw him at breakfast that morning at your house. And yeah, he was overly straightforward, but not unbelievably so. But then there was that bracelet thing with Niki. . . ."

My stomach flip-flops. "Spells in objects. You don't think that's how he wound up under a spell, do you?"

"We've gone to school with Jaxon all our lives, and we've seen him date girls before," Susannah says. "He's calm and casual about it. Then all of a sudden, in a matter of a few days, he's head over heels for Niki, buying her a dance bracelet and blowing you off? We've never seen him like this. I spoke to Dillon."

"More like cornered him," Mary says with a smile.

"And even he agreed that Jaxon's Niki obsession is over the top," Susannah says.

"Actually, Mrs. Meriwether said almost the same thing at breakfast this morning," I say.

Susannah nods like I'm confirming what she already knows. "One of these things alone wouldn't be so strange, but all together they paint a really distorted version of Jaxon. And when someone changes their personality overnight like that, I don't see another explanation except for a spell."

"Two things," I say. "First, how do we confirm if he's under a spell or not? Second, what does it mean if he is?"

"If he's under a spell," Mary says, "my two cents is that it's some kind of love spell. And the bracelet gives us a place to start from."

"I'm not following," I say.

"We might need to destroy the bracelet," Mary says. "Preferably burn it."

"So we need to steal it from him?" I ask.

"No," Alice says. "From everything we've read, he'll have to give it to us willingly. For love spells to work well, some part of you has to *want* to participate. And until you choose to *stop* participating, the spell can't be broken. However, if he's under a spell, it's going to be hard to convince him to give us that bracelet."

CHAPTER THIRTY-SEVEN

———————

You Are the Most Important Person in My World

I sit on my bed in a pile of *Titanic* notes. My phone vibrates.

Susannah: *Is Jaxon home?*

Me: *Yeah. I'll text you as soon as I finish eating.*

Alice: *Deal*

Mary: *Hugs* ☺

Alice: *No one needs a hugs text with a smiley face. No one needs a smiley face, period*

Mary: *No one needs a grouch text either*

Alice: *I have no idea how we ever became friends*

Susannah: *Because you're secretly a softie*

Alice: *Um, no*

"Sam!" my dad calls from downstairs. "Dinner."

Me: *Eating now* ☺

Alice: *I want out of this circle*

Susannah: *Who said you were in?* ☺

I make my way down the stairs and toward the kitchen. The smell of melted cheese and tomato sauce greets me.

The small table in the kitchen is set. A pan of steaming stuffed shells, which I know were made from scratch, is sitting in the middle.

My dad walks toward the table. "Cheesy garlic bread and veggie meatballs because I know you love them." He places them down on the table.

"Thanks," I say, but there's no enthusiasm in my voice.

I slide into my chair and he sits across from me. I focus on piling stuffed shells onto my plate.

"Sam, I know you're upset," he says.

I half grunt, half laugh. "I'm not sure 'upset' describes it."

"No, probably not." He hesitates, like he's considering his approach. "I know you really like your friends here."

I look up at him. "I do."

"And I know, believe me I know, how hard it was socially for you in New York."

"Then why do you want to move me away from them?"

"I don't want to move you away from them. I want to move you away from Salem. And I don't, under any circumstances, want you doing magic. I know you can't hear me on this. You think I'm being mean. But it's the furthest thing from my intention. I've always wanted you to experience having best friends, and I can see how much these relationships mean to you. The girls can come and visit on weekends. I'll send a car for them myself, or pay for their gas, or whatever it takes. I'm not trying to hurt you."

"Taking me away from Salem *is* hurting me. It's not just my friends. I mean, it is. But it's also this house with all of our family stuff in it. It's the weird town that treats Halloween like it's the last party before the apocalypse. It's Jaxon and Mrs. Meriwether. It's a lot of things."

My dad almost laughs. "You know, I wanted out of this place from the moment I could drive. But your mom wouldn't hear of it. To her, Salem was the world. It was part of her identity in a way that I'll never fully understand. I've never told you this, but I truly believe that she would still be alive if we hadn't stayed here."

I tense. I know exactly why she died. "You think it was because of magic?"

He nods. "That's why I don't want you to learn it or be anywhere near it. You are the most important person in my world. And I won't risk you, even if you're mad at me for the rest of your life."

I exhale. "Dad, the magic isn't gonna go away if we move back to New York. I see spirits." I pause. "I'll just be that strange girl that everyone thinks is delusional. It's not like that in Salem. People here actually believe that I see them, and they don't think I'm a pariah. They like me for it."

My dad's eyebrows push together. "I'm not sure what to say to that."

"Well, at least you can admit it," I say.

"I guess so. Although, frankly, the idea that you're seeing dead people scares the hell out of me."

"Sometimes it scares me, too."

"We could try hypnosis."

"Dad."

"I'm not allowed to try to help?"

"You're not allowed to try to fix me. I'm not broken."

⌒

I stand on the brick sidewalk outside of my house with my arms wrapped around my chest against the night air. The girls pull up to the curb.

"You ready?" Mary asks, getting out of the Jeep.

"Ready," I say. "Although I still can't figure out what

Jaxon and a love spell could possibly have to do with the *Titanic,* the Collector in Redd's warning, and all the Myra objects."

"Yeah, but if we find out he *is* under a spell, it would be too much of a coincidence for it to be happening right now," Alice says as we walk to Mrs. Meriwether's front door. "And I don't believe in coincidences."

"Agreed," I say. "Plus, if it is the bracelet, then we're talking about another spell in an object."

"But what possible connection would a spell on Jaxon have to a spell on *Titanic* passengers?" Mary asks.

"Not a clue," Alice says, "which is why I'm seriously hoping we find out it's not a spell."

Susannah knocks. It only takes a few seconds for Mrs. Meriwether to answer.

"Girls! What a lovely surprise. Come in." She closes the door behind us. "You're just in time to try my lavender lemonade and my cream puffs filled with white chocolate mousse and crushed raspberries."

Mary's mouth opens. "Can I live with you?"

Mrs. Meriwether laughs.

"Is Jaxon home?" I ask.

"In his room," Mrs. Meriwether says. "Want me to call him down?"

I shake my head. "I'll just pop upstairs for a minute."

The girls follow Mrs. Meriwether to the kitchen.

I take the stairs fast, running my fingers along the driftwood banister, and stop in front of Jaxon's closed bedroom door.

I knock. "Jaxon?"

He opens it, and his familiar woodsy scent billows out. "Sam?"

"Can I come in for a minute?"

He steps aside, and I walk past him into his navy blue bedroom, which is filled with handmade furniture. There are model ships on the walls.

"So what's up?" Jaxon says without any of his usual friendliness.

"Just wanted to see if you had the history homework," I say.

"It's in the packet. Page twenty-seven, I think. Was that it? I'm kinda in the middle of something."

"Also, I saw you got one of those bracelets."

"Huh?"

"The bracelet you were wearing the other day with the anchor on it, the ones the dance committee's selling?"

"Uh-huh," he says, staring at his phone and not looking at me.

Man, is he rude. "I was thinking about getting one myself."

"Cool."

"Do you mind if I take a look at yours?"

"I'd rather not."

"You're saying you're not going to let me see your bracelet?"

"I guess not." He types on his phone, and a small piece of the blue cord peeks out from under his sleeve.

"It's right on your wrist. Is it such a big deal to take it off for a second?"

Jaxon eyes me suspiciously. "Sam, I'm busy." He looks down at his buzzing phone, and the tension leaves his expression. He smiles.

"Dude, you left me stranded in front of Niki's this morning. The least you could do is look at me instead of your phone for the two minutes I'm in your room."

Jaxon answers his phone. "Hold on just a sec, Nik." He looks at me. "Sam, I gotta go."

Well, that settles that. I walk out, because I don't know what else to say. *Jaxon's definitely under a spell. How did I not notice this sooner?*

I quickly head down the stairs and into the kitchen. The girls all look at me with questioning eyes, and I'm pretty sure my face betrays the answer.

"Cream puff?" Mary offers.

"No thanks. I just ate a big dinner," I say.

"Now wait a minute," Mrs. Meriwether says. "You look upset, Sam. Was Jaxon rude? He's been in a mood recently."

"No, not exactly," I say.

"We think Jaxon might be under a love spell," Susannah says.

Did she just tell Mrs. Meriwether that? The world blurs for a second.

"Samantha was checking out the bracelet he's wearing to see if it has a love spell on it, and my guess is that it does," Susannah says, and looks at me.

Mrs. Meriwether places her hand over her heart.

"Samantha, I think you should go home," Susannah says, her voice measured and confident. "Alice, will you go get the spell book? I think between what we brought and what's growing in Mrs. Meriwether's garden, we'll have enough ingredients if we need to do an additional spell."

"A love spell?" Mrs. Meriwether says. "I *knew* something wasn't right about the way he was acting toward Niki, but I wouldn't have guessed this."

"I'm not leaving," I say, incredulous. "If he's under a spell, I want to help break it."

Susannah shakes her head. "Your father already wants you

to move away from Salem. This is only going to further convince him that magic is bad. And breaking the spell or not won't depend on you being here." She pauses. "Also, if you care about your dad and Mrs. Meriwether's friendship, you won't strain it by doing magic in front of her."

I waver. "But it's Jaxon."

Mrs. Meriwether nods, tension pulling at her forehead. "I don't want you to go, either, honey. But Susannah's right. Go on home and we'll keep you updated. And I promise if we need you we'll call."

Alice drags me down the hallway and out the door like a mother pulling her child away from the playground.

I stop when we reach the driveway. "You're not going to tell her everything that's been—"

"Are you insane? Definitely not. We'll tell her it's Niki's fault and that's it. And *you* need to keep yourself calm. You already did your part. Let us take a whack at it. I didn't know Suze was gonna out us like that, either. But she always has her reasons, and as much as I fight her, when everything comes to light . . . she's usually right."

CHAPTER THIRTY-EIGHT

I Just Wanted to Stay

I chew the crap out of my pen cap and stare out the window at the Meriwethers' house.

Elijah blinks in.

I swing my legs down from my window seat and take the cap out of my mouth. "What's the update?"

"Alice took Susannah and Mary home, and now it is just her and Mrs. Meriwether. Jaxon is thoroughly refusing to co-operate. They have tried everything from logic to bargaining to get him to willingly take off the bracelet. Currently, he has locked himself in his room and is talking to Niki."

"And Mrs. Meriwether?"

"Committed to finding a solution and shaking large spoons at whoever did it."

I smile at the visual. "How does this connect to everything else, Elijah? If this is just Niki being infatuated with Jaxon, then I get it. But if it's tied to the *Titanic* and possibly to the Collector, what's the motive?"

"I could not say. It seems more likely that Niki attained a love spell. But the fact that it came in an object is troublesome. When did you notice the change in his behavior?"

I tap the pen against my note cards. "I guess I really noticed a shift the day after the drowned man gave me the dog collar."

"The day after you went on a date with Jaxon."

"It wasn't a date." Who cares if he thinks it was a date?

"Is it possible someone thought Jaxon was distracting you from focusing on Myra?" he says.

I consider his words. "You're saying you think whoever's behind this might have wanted us to find Myra so badly that he or she would actually try to eliminate Jaxon?"

"It is not an entirely good reason, but it is the only one I can think of," he says.

"No, it actually could make sense," I say. "All of those Myra objects showed up in a really short period of time, like someone urgently wanted us to find her. And in that case, maybe Jaxon was a distraction. But what's the rush? Why didn't this person just trap her himself?"

"Perhaps he or she could not locate her," Elijah says. "I did a great deal of searching, you will recall, but it was you who ultimately found her."

"Elijah, do you think Redd could be right? That this person is actually collecting spirits?"

"I think that it is more logical than not, considering what we have observed," Elijah says.

"You are invited back," Ada says, and Elijah and I jump. She stands in the middle of my room. Her hair is in braids again. Only this time there is no joy in her expression, no laughter.

My heart thuds. "Ada?"

"You are invited back," she says again, a little louder.

"Invited where? To the *Titanic*?" I ask.

She nods.

I move toward her, but she takes a step away from me.

"Who told you to tell me that?" I ask.

She studies her hands. "A man."

"What kind of man? Can you describe him?"

She looks around nervously. "He had hair on his face. Not a mustache like my papa, just a little bit."

There is only one spirit I've seen who is unshaven. "Was he about this tall?" I hold my hand up above my head.

She nods.

"Irish accent?"

She nods again.

The drowned man. "What did he tell you?"

"Nothing. Just that I was to say that. I told him I didn't want to come here again. That I saw you on the ship. That I was scared you were a ghost. I just wanted to stay with my mum. But he said I had to. This one last time. To tell you that you were invited back."

"I'm not a spirit. I promise you I'm not."

She eyes me like she's not sure. And I can't blame her. I was scared of her when she first showed up, and she looks more harmless than I do.

"What is your family name, Ada?" Elijah asks.

"Sage. My given name is Elizabeth. Ada is my middle. But my sister Stella always says that Ada is much prettier and that I should be proud I have such a good name."

I freeze. I wrote out a note card for the Sage family last night. "Ada, what's the date? Do you remember?"

She scrunches her face up. "The thirteenth of April?" She blinks out.

"The same date Mollie said it was two days ago? The day hasn't changed for them," I say. I run over to my bed and sift through my pile of passenger note cards.

My fingers tremble slightly as I grab the Sage family card. Elijah moves to my side and reads over my shoulder.

"Mr. and Mrs. Sage boarded the *Titanic* at Southampton with their nine children," I read out loud. "Wow, nine. They had purchased a pecan farm in Florida. That's right, she said something about them going to Florida and how Stella didn't want to. Here she is." I point to the card. "Elizabeth Ada Sage, age ten. And here's Stella, too, age twenty. Stella got in a lifeboat, but when she realized her family couldn't join her, she got back out." My voice catches. "Both parents and all nine Sage children died in the sinking. So much for women and children first."

"Those rules were mainly for the first- and second-class passengers. The third-class passengers were trapped behind gates," Elijah says.

I nod. "I know. They were locked in when the ship sank. It's wrong."

Elijah frowns. "Yes, a system in which value is placed on human lives because of wealth or position or race is an utmost injustice."

I place the Sage family note card back on my bed. And now in death they're back behind those gates. Who would do such a thing? I'm here worrying about having to go to the *Titanic* as a first-class passenger with tea and parasols; meanwhile, some of those passengers have probably been locked in steerage for the better part of a century. Maybe Redd was right. I don't even know how privileged I am.

"Was the man she was referring to the drowned man?" Elijah asks, snapping me out of my thoughts.

"I'm pretty sure. But I have no idea who he is. I mean, he's a spirit. But was he a *Titanic* passenger? Is he *the* Collector? Ada just looked so rattled. Every time I've seen her before, she's been giggly and happy."

"When she thought you were a dream."

"Mmm-hmm. She definitely wasn't coming here intentionally. And what did you make of that invitation? Why invite me back when someone threw me off?"

"She said 'one last time.'"

I look at Elijah. "Yeah, I caught that. Why 'last,' though?"

Elijah's eyebrows furrow.

My phone buzzes. It's Alice in our group text.

Alice: *No luck. I'm staying the night with Mrs. M. I'll be at breakfast tomorrow. Text if you need me.*

CHAPTER THIRTY-NINE

So Tragic and Romantic

Mrs. Powell leans against her desk, holding *The Truth About the Titanic* in her hand. "When you read first-person accounts like this one, you realize how subjective they are and how much is left to interpretation. Gracie made a strong effort to interview people and cross-check stories. But we can also see how his voice, and his understanding of what happened, play a role in his account. We always think that history is fact and literature is fiction. But the truth is, they are all stories. And the people who tell them influence our understanding in various ways."

She places the book on her desk and scans the room. "So tell me, what sort of influence do you notice in this story, good or bad? What did you take away from this one?"

The guy next to me raises his hand. "I think men like Gracie did a brave thing, letting the women and children get into the lifeboats first."

"Yes, certainly," Mrs. Powell says. "It also says something about how women were viewed."

The boy looks confused.

A girl raises her hand, like she's not sure if she wants to.

"Yes, Maya."

"It showed who he thought mattered and who he thought didn't." Her voice is a little shaky, probably just like mine when I speak in class.

"Ah. That's a very interesting point. Elaborate," Mrs. Powell says.

"Ships like the *Titanic* were made for immigrants. They were funded from the money of good, honest workers. Yet there isn't much in the book about minorities or people not in the first class, even in the research he did afterward. And the third-class passengers had the highest death count by far. Even third-class women and children," Maya says.

My chest tightens. *Ada.*

Mrs. Powell smiles. "There is certainly something to be learned by what is omitted—*who* is omitted—from stories, especially historical ones. Very nice."

She scans the room. I direct my eyes to my notebook. *I'm not here and you can't see me.*

"Sam?"

I sit there for a second, trying to think past my exhaustion to what I've learned during my research. "The way Gracie talks about the before moments made an impression on me. Before the ship sank, I mean."

Mrs. Powell waits for me to go on.

"Everything was so luxurious and happy, like everything was okay but not quite. And there were a thousand tiny things that decided the fate of the ship. The completely still water that prevented the lookouts from seeing the iceberg.

The nearest ship's Marconi operator going to bed and turning off the radio system. The lack of lifeboats. The arrogance that stopped the ship's operators from worrying about the iceberg warnings in the first place." *Ada, Nora, Mollie . . . all those people who didn't make it off.* "Why is it that when you're headed for a disaster, some part of you almost always knows?"

"It's a good question," Mrs. Powell says. "There are accounts of passengers who were said to know with certainty that *some*thing was going to happen, even if they didn't know what and couldn't stop it. Esther Hart is said to have stayed up all night every night in her clothes waiting for the unknown disaster, the ship's cat carried all her kittens off board before it left Europe, and people canceled their journeys at the last moment because of a feeling. I suppose it's important to trust yourself. Even Gracie says that if he hadn't gone to bed early that night and hadn't been exercising with some frequency, he would never have had the energy to survive the freezing water."

The bell rings.

"Have a good lunch," Mrs. Powell says over the noise of the chairs moving against the floor. "Only three more days left of *Titanic* curriculum before the much-anticipated Spring Fling. Give it your all."

Her words remind me of Ada's yesterday. *This one last time.* I exit into the hallway and almost collide with Mr. Wardwell.

"Sorry," I say.

Mr. Wardwell straightens his blazer. "Sam. Well, this is a lucky coincidence. I had wanted to talk to you."

"Oh?"

"I tried to get your attention after class, but you were out the door too fast."

I try to hold back my yawn, but fail.

He takes a better look at me. "You seem awfully tired and distracted recently. Is everything okay?"

I eye him suspiciously. He's never asked me if I was okay. In fact, I'm not sure he's ever really liked me at all. "I'm fine. Thanks."

"Also, it's time to decide what to do about those missed exams from last semester. A paper should do it. I'm around for office hours today."

Alice doesn't believe in coincidences. Maybe I don't, either. "I can't today."

Mr. Wardwell frowns. "Tomorrow, then," he says with finality, and walks away.

I rub my eye with the heel of my hand and push through the lunchroom doors. I head straight for the Descendants. Blair and her friends whisper behind their hands as I pass. She looks like she wants to say something to me, but instead she glances at Matt and then goes back to her conversation. I'm sure Niki didn't waste any time telling people about me insisting on seeing Jaxon's bracelet. I take my seat facing the window, my back to the lunchroom.

"I feel terrible for Mrs. M. It took me an hour to convince her this morning that keeping Jaxon home would only agitate him more," Alice says.

Mary scowls at the cafeteria. "And it's not helping that this school is a breeding ground for gossip."

"Yeah, it'd be nice if they all just shut up already," Alice says loudly enough for the tables next to us to hear. The few people looking in our direction immediately busy themselves with their lunches.

I pull a piece of paper out of my pocket. "So I had some time in history today, and I went through my third-class passenger cards looking for Mollie Mullin again. I couldn't find a single passenger with that last name or anything similar.

So I looked for anyone named Mollie. No such luck. There were, however, a lot of passengers named Mary."

Susannah's eyes light up. "That's an old nickname. I had a great-aunt Mollie whose proper name was Mary. I hadn't thought of that."

They all lean toward me.

"This is the thing: I found Denis and Mary Lennon, who boarded in Queenstown," I say. "Originally I thought they were brother and sister because that's how they were listed on the passenger ledger. But when I started looking up each of the Mary passengers, I found a news article that said Mary's last name was really Mullin and that she and Denis were actually eloping to the United States."

"Whoa. The brother-sister act was a cover?" Mary asks.

"Yeah. They were being chased by Mollie's brother, who had a gun. Her family didn't want her to marry Denis because he was the barman in their general store. Her family thought he wasn't a good match. But her brother didn't show up until right after the *Titanic* left port, and the two got away."

"Did they survive?" Susannah asks.

An image of Mollie laughing and telling me stories about her family pops into my thoughts. I sigh and shake my head.

"How did we not learn about that story?" Mary asks. "It's so tragic and romantic."

"So many people were forgotten," I say. "They didn't make the cut for the lifeboats, and they didn't make the cut for historians."

"Change of plans. I'm going to the Spring Fling as Mollie Mullin," Mary announces, and I smile at her.

Alice chews on her thumbnail. "What does it mean that a third-class passenger is now a first-class maid?"

"And why do Henry and Myra believe I was with them in Europe and Asia when I never was?" I ask.

"Someone or multiple someones are intentionally rewriting history," Alice says.

"And keeping the *Titanic* stuck in time before its sinking," Susannah says.

"April thirteenth," I say, remembering Ada's and Mollie's answers.

"And today is the twelfth," Mary says, and we all look at her. "You don't think something is going to happen tomorrow when our time catches up to theirs, do you?"

No one answers, but I can tell by their faces that they are thinking about Redd's warning.

"Wardwell just asked me to come in for office hours," I say.

"Did Elijah find anything in his house?" Susannah asks.

"Lots of *Titanic* info, so much that he hasn't even made it through everything. But nothing magical," I say. "So basically, we have no solid leads on how or if he's involved."

CHAPTER FORTY

However Broken It May Be

I look out my bedroom window at Mrs. Meriwether's house. The lights are out, and the last I heard from Alice, Mrs. Meriwether invited her to stay the night again. I sit down on my bed, then stand right back up.

My phone says it's 11:08 p.m. I make a lap around my bedroom and pull my hair up into a ball on top of my head. We're no closer to finding out who's collecting *Titanic* spirits, tomorrow is April thirteenth, Jaxon's still under a spell, Mrs. Meriwether looks as worn out as I do, and my dad wants to move. I take another lap.

Elijah blinks in with a mug in his hand. I stop pacing.

"Passionflower tea with honey," he says, and offers me the mug. "You need to rest."

I stare at it. "What are you doing?"

"This was used even in my time to quell nervous energy. You have been walking around this room for the better part of an hour." His tone is gentle.

I don't feel like anything could stop me from being nervous right now. And Elijah being nice to me only puts me more on edge. "Just because you're helping to solve this, and we're spending time together, doesn't mean everything's suddenly okay between us."

"Quite the contrary," Elijah says. "The only reason I am here is that everything is far from stable. But it does not change the fact that you must get at least some amount of sleep, however broken it may be."

"You know what I mean, Elijah."

He looks like he wants to respond, but changes his mind. "Take the tea."

I grab the mug from his outstretched hand and blow on the steaming liquid. "Did you find anything?"

"I have started searching Blair's house. Nothing we do not know. Either they are all extremely diligent about not leaving any evidence or we have overlooked something important."

I sip my tea. "Also, I can't come up with one logical reason Niki or Blair would want to help collect the spirits of *Titanic* passengers. It's possible Wardwell does for the historical appeal of it, but that's a weak motive."

"Unless it is not logical," Elijah says.

"What do you mean? That it's emotional or personal or something?"

"Potentially."

I look up from my tea. "Actually, what if it is personal? What if we're not looking at this the right way?"

"How do you mean?" Elijah asks.

"Maybe the Collector has a grudge of some sort—a grudge that directly relates to the *Titanic*."

Elijah considers my words. "The *Titanic* certainly left a wake of financial and personal ruin. It is not unlikely that the motive could be linked. The only issue is that approximately fifteen hundred people died, many of whom we know little about, not to mention the exponential number of extended family members the passengers had in countries all over the world."

"I know. But consider this . . . Redd said the Collector died when she was young and that he recently showed back up in her tea leaves. What if we start there, look at the town records for when she was a child and see if anyone stands out as being connected to the *Titanic?*"

"Clever. I will go to the town hall tomorrow."

"I think we should go now," I say.

"We?"

"I'm coming."

Elijah raises an eyebrow. "You think that is wise?"

"No. But what if Mary's right that there's something significant about the thirteenth? Or worse, what if Redd's warning is right? I don't think we can afford to wait." I slide my feet into my black boots and grab my hoodie.

Elijah and I walk the back way to the city clerk's office. The hood to my sweatshirt is pulled as far over my face as possible.

Elijah turns down a shadowed alley next to a brick building and I follow. The town is uncomfortably silent, so much so that any tiny sound causes my heart to race. He stops in front of a door and reaches his hand through the wood. It clicks open. I step into the dark building. It smells like old paper and wood polish.

"Wait here," he says.

"Elijah . . . ," I say, but he's gone.

I look both directions, even though it's so dark that there's no point. A shiver runs down my back.

Elijah appears with two lit chamberstick candles. I jump backward, scowling at him.

He hands me a candle, and I'm fairly certain there is an amused look in his eyes. "This should be enough light to read, but not enough that anyone outside the building will see us. Just the same, avoid windows."

Elijah leads me into a room of shelves full of files and folders. There are three round tables with chairs. Each table has a computer on it.

"It's a mini-library of paperwork," I say.

"Indeed." Elijah walks to a nearby shelf and holds his candle up. "These are the records and local newspapers for the past hundred years."

It only takes him a minute to pull a stack of binders and place them on a table. We sit down with our candles, and I'm reminded of all the nights we stayed up doing research together in the fall.

"We shall start by looking at local newspapers on or around the *Titanic* anniversary during Redd's childhood," he says. "Every year there is at least one article commemorating the disaster. And if there was a *Titanic* survivor or a survivor's relative in Salem, it is likely that person would have been asked for a quote or an interview."

"That's actually really smart," I say.

"You sound surprised," he says.

"That's because I am."

He tries to hide his smile, but the corners of his mouth betray him.

"Elijah?"

"Samantha."

"Thanks for the tea."

He smiles, and for the first time since he came back, his dimples appear. "You are very welcome."

I look away from him and I'm annoyed all over again. How dare he come back here with his thoughtful gestures and his dimples and make me feel this way. I clear my throat and change the subject. "You pulled those binders like you already knew where they were. How do you know your way around this place so well?"

"I spent many an hour here when you asked me to help you figure out if your family was cursed." He flips through an old newspaper.

"Oh." I remember that day I bargained with him in the secret study to help me. I thought he was the most frustrating person I had ever met. Still do. I laugh.

"Yes?" he asks, and looks up at me.

"Nothing," I say, and open a binder. *Go away, nostalgia!*

For the next half hour we pull *Titanic* articles and flip through pages. The tips of my fingers get stained black from the old newsprint.

"This is so sad," I say. "I just read a story about a woman who checked herself into a sanatarium after the boat sank, never again wanting to talk about what happened that night. People say it was probably the screams from the passengers in the water that haunted her."

Elijah nods. "A great many of the survivors had night-mares about it. It is likely that the passengers in the water were pleading for help for the fifteen minutes before hypo-thermia set in. Many families were split up while evacuating. Can you imagine being in a lifeboat and wondering if that voice in the water belonged to your relative?"

I shudder. "I can't. I really can't. But why didn't they help them?"

"Some wanted to. There were arguments in the lifeboats about whether they would be overturned if they went back. One man finally did. But he was too late."

I pull another binder toward me and try to swallow the lump in my throat. I open the cover and instantly the candles blow out.

"Eli—!"

Before I can finish his name, he's there, his hand on my arm.

I hear him strike a match in the darkness, and a small flame lights up his face. My heart plays a drum solo in my chest.

"What the hell was that?" I whisper.

"You mean 'who,'" Elijah says, and relights our candles. "And I am not certain. The spirit came and went too quickly."

All the hair on my arms stands up, and I shudder. The binder that I just opened is missing. "Is there another way to get those newspaper records? Maybe a digital copy some-where?"

Elijah scans the room. "I will certainly look." He hands me my candle and offers me his arm. "But at present, let me walk you home, Samantha."

CHAPTER FORTY-ONE

Elijah Waits for Me

I rub my eyes as I walk toward homeroom. These nights of Elijah waking me up every ten minutes are catching up with me big-time.

I grab the homeroom door, and someone touches my elbow. I whip around.

Matt smiles. "Whoa. Sorry. I didn't mean ta scare ya."

"No worries. I'm just extra tired this morning. Makes me jumpy," I say.

He scans my face. "I can see that. What'd ya pull an all-nightah?"

"Something like that," I say.

"It's only midweek. You keep goin' like that and you'll never make it to the dance—excuse me, *Spring Fling*," he says, like he finds the whole thing ridiculous.

"Aren't you on the dance committee? Shouldn't you be excited?"

"About plannin' an event with Blair and Niki?" He laughs.

"It's just a means to an end. Accordin' to me parents, I don't have enough extracurriculars to get into a good university. Leadership skills? I don't know."

I attempt a smile, but my face just isn't up to it. I point at the door. "You going in—"

"Actually . . . hold up." He glances over his shoulder and pulls me away from the classroom.

"What's going on?"

"I don't know. I'm 'aving an altruistic blip or somethin'." He lowers his voice. "So 'ere's the deal. Niki's family and Blair's family went out to dinner together last night, and I overheard the two of 'em whisperin' about ya."

My shoulders tense. "How so?"

"Honestly, I didn't hear much. But it sounded like they had some big plan. Niki kept sayin' she couldn't wait for tomorrow. Today, technically. I just felt bad not givin' you a heads-up."

Big plan? My stomach flips. "Thanks for the warning."

"No problem. And get some sleep," he says, and walks past me into homeroom.

I take a breath and push the door open. The girls are already there. I sit down next to Susannah and tell them everything Matt said.

"It's the thirteenth," Mary says.

"Jeez, Mary, you need to stop saying that every two seconds. You're gonna give me a twitch," Alice says. "We don't even know for sure if it means anything other than the typical Niki gossip."

Susannah looks at me. "When Niki goes on the attack, she's usually spreading a rumor—some part of which is true. That's how she gets people to believe it. But then again, we shouldn't be underestimating anyone right now. Especially not her and Blair."

"If it's gossip, that's fine. Gossip, I can handle," I say.

The bell rings.

"Settle down, everyone," Mrs. Hoxley says.

Blair walks past my desk, makes eye contact, and winks.

Not good.

The class quiets, and Mrs. Hoxley launches into her typical morning speech about homework and study habits.

I lean my head on my hand, and my eyelids droop.

"Samantha," Elijah says, and I sit up so fast that I smack my elbow into my desk.

Mrs. Hoxley gives me a warning look.

"I have just come from the records room," Elijah says.

One look at his face tells me I'm not going to like whatever he has to say. He never visits me in school.

"I did, in fact, locate the digital scans of those newspapers. However, the ones we want were missing."

Damn. I pull out my notebook and open it to a fresh page. I write: *Is there a backup?*

"Also missing. What is odd, though, is that the scans were on a machine in a rarely frequented storage room. Everything was covered in a layer of dust, *except* that one hard drive. I believe that is what it is called."

Me: *Someone rushed over there in the middle of the night?*

Elijah waits for me to finish writing. "Someone alive. Spirits do not leave fingerprints."

Me: *Whatever was in those newspapers must have been revealing. Do you think there was a name we know in those articles? Someone we would immediately recognize?*

"Likely. I will also check neighboring towns to see if any of their records might be helpful."

Me: *And I'll ask the girls if there are any other ways to get old Salem newspapers.*

He hesitates. "Be cautious, Samantha. I do not know what we may have triggered with our visit last night."

Me: *I'm always careful.*

He raises an eyebrow and blinks out.

I write down our entire conversation and pass it to Susannah, who reads it and passes it to Alice and then Mary.

The bell rings.

"The town hall is really the only place to get local newspapers. Some of the historical societies around here keep their own records, but mostly on the Witch Trials. I'd be surprised if they had much on the *Titanic*," Mary says, and we all stand up.

"If our grandmothers were still alive, they might know where we could start," Susannah says.

We make our way into the hall.

"The thing that worries me," I say in a hushed voice, "is that if someone went to the town hall in the middle of the night, that person has to be here in Salem."

"I was thinking the same thing," Alice says. "And no one would do that unless they thought we'd recognize their name in the paper. I think we just confirmed that we must know the person who's doing these things." We all look around the hall suspiciously. "Everyone be extra careful today. And as soon as we're out of here, we'll figure out how to help Elijah get more information."

The girls and I nod and share a worried look. We turn our separate ways down the hall.

I open the door to Wardwell's AP History class.

"Ah, Miss Mather. I will see you during my office hours after school today," Mr. Wardwell says.

"Actually, I can't today. I have—"

"That's what you said yesterday. But unfortunately, I'm

going to need you to make time today. Thursday and Friday are impossible for me because of Spring Fling preparations."

"Is there any way we can do it next week?" I ask.

"Not if you plan on passing this class," he says.

CHAPTER FORTY-TWO

I Do Belong in Salem

The last bell rings, and I make my way through the hallway. Two girls ahead of me whisper behind their hands and look in my direction. The weird thing is, they don't laugh. They frown.

I unload my books into my locker. Please let Elijah have made some headway. His not coming back to school is a good sign. I click my locker shut and turn around. Mary, Alice, and Susannah are standing right behind me.

"Whoa," I say. "Way to creepily sneak up on someone."

"I'm so glad you think so," Alice says. "I worked long and hard on that technique."

Mary bounces slightly and grins at me. "Give it to her, Suze."

Susannah pulls a small black velvet box from her Victorian jacket. She holds it out to me in her palm. "From us."

I look at each of them. "What's this for?"

"Just open it," Mary says, clasping her hands together with all the enthusiasm of a kid at a birthday party.

I flip the lid. Inside is a delicate silver broom necklace. It looks handmade.

Alice pulls her own broom necklace out of her blouse.

"It's our personal symbol for our circle. It binds us. Alice chose it when we were kids. We all wear one," Susannah says.

"It's silly," Alice says. "But at eight, I thought it was super cool."

I open my mouth to say thanks, but my voice catches. Elijah was right. I do belong in Salem. And all of a sudden, I want to cry.

"Well, it's not *that* bad," Alice says, but she's smiling.

"It's not bad at all," I manage, smiling too.

"Consider yourself official," Susannah says, and links her arm through mine as we head down the hallway toward Wardwell's.

I slip the necklace over my head just as we pass a couple holding hands. They look from the Descendants to me and frown.

"I think we can definitively conclude that whatever gossip Niki and Blair spread today was related to me," I say.

"Agreed," Susannah says. "Normally, I would be annoyed. But I'm actually relieved."

I nod. "The only strange part is that whatever they said isn't getting me judgy looks but sad ones. Have you guys heard anything about it?"

"No," Alice says. "But people wouldn't tell us rumors about you. They know better."

"Let's be honest, Alice," Mary says. "People don't usually talk to us at all about anything. Not if they have to meet that death stare of yours. And I don't know what you saw today, but we got just as many looks as Sam."

They got looks, too? I stop in front of my history classroom. "I'll be fast."

"We'll wait here," Susannah says.

I push open the door, and Wardwell looks up from a stack of papers. "Please sit."

I plop down in a chair next to his desk.

He clears his throat. "I'd like you to complete the remainder of the work you missed by writing a five-page paper."

"Sounds good. I can do that," I say quickly.

"I want you to use the research you've done these past weeks on the *Titanic* to create a fictional narrative," he continues.

The last thing I want to write is a paper on the *Titanic*, but I know him well enough to not even attempt to ask for a different subject.

"For fun I will give you an object that is similar to objects recovered in the wreckage. You will examine it, determining what kind of a passenger might have carried it and what their story was from the moment they boarded until the moment they arrived home—or didn't arrive home, as the case may be."

Object. I glance at the door and catch a glimpse of Alice's face in the small window.

Wardwell opens his desk drawer. "Be careful with it and do not lose it." He places a silver book the size of a playing card on the desk in front of me. It twinkles in the bright classroom lighting.

I stand up so fast that my chair almost topples over. *The silver book from my dream.*

"Is there a problem?" he asks me, examining my face like he's looking for something specific.

"What? No. Charley horse," I say, and rub the back of my calf. Damn it. I can't believe I reacted like that. This lack of sleep has me all jumpy.

Alice comes through the door, with Mary and Susannah behind her. "Want a ride home, Sam?" She feigns surprise. "Oh, sorry, Mr. Wardwell. I didn't realize you guys were having a meeting."

"I'd ask you ladies to wait outside, but we are technically finished here." Mr. Wardwell points at the silver book. "Make sure you take that with you, Sam."

I don't move. There is no way I'm touching that thing.

Think. I scan his desk. "Is it old?"

"Fairly."

"Oh, well, I don't want to just shove it in my bag, then," I say. I grab two tissues from his tissue box.

"It's not that delicate," he says, but I've already got it wrapped up.

I make my way out of the classroom with the girls. We put a good hundred feet between us and his door before we start talking.

"You know this is the silver book from my dream, right?" I say, pointing at my shoulder bag.

"Why do you think we came in, Sherlock?" says Alice, and pushes open the door leading to the back field. "You seriously need to work on hiding your emotions. You looked ten kinds of flustered in there. If Wardwell is in on this *Titanic* spell, you just set off warning bells."

"Did he say anything we should know about?" Susannah asks.

"Possibly. He did use the word 'object' to describe it," I say. "If he knew anything about our conversations, he could have chosen that word to mess with me."

"He also looked really adamant about you taking it,"

Mary says as we walk across the grass. "He didn't take his eyes off you."

The guys' lacrosse team jogs past us.

"Sam," Dillon says, and stops. His usual happy tone is missing. "Hey, can I talk to you for a minute?" He glances at the girls. "Alone, if that's cool?"

"Uh, sure. What's up?" I say. *Did something happen with Jaxon?*

He leads me away from the girls. "You're not getting in a car with them, are you?"

"Huh?"

His breathing is slightly labored from his run. "The Descendants. Don't you think you should steer clear of them, at least until you know if it's true?"

"Hold on, what are you talking about?"

He looks at me like I'm the one saying shocking things. "Everyone is saying that it was your stepmother who tried to hang you in the woods. And the reason the Descendants haven't told anyone is because they're planning their revenge or something. Everyone's saying they've bewitched you. I mean, it *is* super weird that you guys haven't hung out for six months and now all of a sudden you're inseparable."

My stepmother. My stomach clenches so hard I grab it. "*What?*" I walk two feet away from him and then back. What is he saying? People know it was Vivian? But how would they even . . . Jaxon. The conversation we had in his truck. Holy shit. I press the heel of my hand into my forehead. Jaxon must have told Niki. It's as if someone sucker-punched me. I know Jaxon's under a spell and that it's not his fault, but the betrayal is so big that I can't swallow my upset. Tears prick my eyes.

I jog back to the girls.

"Sam, wait!" Dillon calls after me, but I don't stop.

I speed-walk right past them.

"What the hell happened back there?" Alice asks, keeping pace with me.

I get in the Jeep and they follow. "They know about Vivian. Niki knows. Which means Jaxon told her." My voice catches on his name.

"Shit!" Alice says, and hits the wheel with the palm of her hand.

"How could he do that?" Mary says. "That's horrible. Even under a spell, that's horrible."

"And people are saying that the reason you guys didn't tell anyone is that you're planning your revenge. People think we're suddenly hanging out because you bewitched me."

"This is Niki's lie, but it's not typical. Someone is setting us up," Susannah says.

"The only thing to do is try to ride it out," Mary says. "Not acknowledge it. There's no evidence it was your stepmother. The police would have questioned you about it way earlier. It's actually good you heard it from Dillon now instead of being surprised in class. Everyone would take your reaction as a confirmation that it's true."

"Riding it out isn't the issue. What if something does happen to me?" I say.

"That was my thought, too," Alice says. "Now, there's a story. A reason for us to have conflict."

"Redd's warning," Susannah says. "Maybe you are the target, Sam. And maybe we're the ones supposed to take the fall for it."

"It's the thirteenth," Mary says.

No one responds.

"The book," I say. I cover my hand with my sleeve and pull the tissue-wrapped package out onto the seat between me and Susannah.

"Here," Susannah says, and hands me two pens.

I pull back the tissues with them. The small silver book is engraved with a lacy pattern, and there's a ship in the center. "You guys? Am I wrong, or is this the same ship drawing that was on those raffle tickets that put the seasickness spell on Susannah? The tickets *Blair* gave us."

"You're not wrong," Susannah says before anyone else can respond.

We all look at each other.

I push open the front cover with the pens. The off-white first page reads:

𝔑ame:	
𝔇ances:	𝔈ngagements:
1.	*1.*
2.	*2.*
3.	*3.*

"That's not a silver book, that's a silver dance card," Mary says with surprise. "My aunt has some in her antique shop. Women used to carry them at balls and things and write their dance partners down in them." She leans over the center console to get a better look. "That one looks legitimately old."

I flip to the next page, but it's the same as the first, and so are all the ones after it. "A blank dance card, though? What does it mean? It's the third object in my dream. It has to be significant."

"Maybe there was an actual dance card on the *Titanic* that has a real story?" Susannah suggests.

I pull out my phone and search. "Nothing pops up. And all the *Titanic* artifacts are cataloged in museums. If this was a real one, or a replica of a real one, it would be easy to find."

My phone vibrates in my hand.

Dad: *Where are you?*

Me: *With the girls.*

Dad: *I need you to come home now.*

I stare at my phone. Something must have happened. He never talks like that.

CHAPTER FORTY-THREE

You and Me Both

I jump out of the Jeep and sprint up to my house, the girls on my heels.

I push open the door. "Dad!"

He's standing in the foyer.

"I need you to go pack your things," he says.

"Wait, is that why you called me home?"

"We're leaving bright and early. Take whatever you need for a few days, and the rest we'll have shipped." I can tell by his tone that he's dead serious. He looks at the girls. "I'm sorry to do this, but I'm going to have to ask you girls to head home. I need to talk to my daughter."

"But—" Alice starts.

"I really must insist," my dad says. The girls walk out the door reluctantly.

"Dad, what happened? You're scaring me."

He waits for the door to close. "First, I got a call from one of your teachers, a Mr. Wardwell, telling me that he was worried about you. That you were all jumpy in his office this afternoon and that you look like you haven't been sleeping for the past week. Only to be followed by Jaxon coming over saying all kinds of wild things about you and the girls and how they're potentially bad people? At which point Mae tells me Jaxon doesn't mean it because he's under a spell?" He pauses. "Which, I can see by your lack of shock right now, you knew about."

"Dad—"

"No, Sam. I told you what my fear was about Salem. I don't know if Mae is right about Jaxon or not, but if so, I'm not taking the chance. If someone is using magic at your school against Jaxon, of all people, then it's no longer safe for you to be there. I told Mae that she and Jaxon could come with us."

I take a deep breath, trying not to panic. *I can't leave Salem right now. I just can't.* "Did she accept?"

"Not yet," he says. "But I have her in the ballroom right now, and I'm trying to convince her. You'll want to get started on that packing. We're leaving right after breakfast tomorrow."

"You're in the ballroom and not the living room or the kitchen?" I ask, peering down the hall. *Is it because they're fighting and don't want me to overhear?*

"Time to pack, Sam," my dad says, pointing toward my room.

I walk past him and up the stairs. I can't argue with him when he's in this kind of mood. If I push now, he might put me in the car and drive to New York this very moment. And there is definitely no explaining the *Titanic* at this point. Not only would he make me leave immediately, but he'd probably burn the house down just to make sure nothing with magic in it ever comes near me again.

I close my bedroom door.

"Elijah?" There is fear in my voice.

He blinks in.

"I went—" I start.

"I saw."

"My dad—"

"I know."

"We have to fix this—solve this, whatever—tonight or I have no possibility of convincing him to stay." I dump the tissue-wrapped dance card onto my bed. "What do you make of this thing?"

He furrows his brow and his posture is tense. "It is reminiscent of the objects you have been receiving all along—seemingly random, but not. If it in any way relates to Myra and Henry, there is no information telling us so. We have already researched them ad nauseam."

"Maybe it's more literal than we think? Maybe it's about the school dance?" I crack my knuckles. "It does have the same image as those raffle tickets Blair handed out."

"I have checked Niki's and Blair's houses," he says.

"But what about the room where the dance committee meets? Maybe there's something there?" I say.

"Potentially. Or the venue where they are holding the dance? I will go now."

There is a tapping on my window, and I whip around. Elijah already stands by the glass. Did he blink across the room to get there that fast? I can just make out Alice, Mary, and Susannah through my lace curtain. Elijah unlatches the window and opens it.

"Jeez, you scared the crap out of me," I say as the girls climb in.

"You and me both," Alice says. "These bozos forced me to climb the latticework on the side of your house. An experience I hope to never repeat."

"It took ten minutes to convince you and two minutes to actually do it," Mary says.

"I will check the school," Elijah says, and disappears.

"We have no time for you two to bicker," Susannah says to Mary and Alice. "Sam is leaving in the morning."

For a second the room gets unnaturally quiet.

I clear my throat. "I was just talking to Elijah, and we were thinking this dance card might have something to do with the Spring Fling. Or with Niki and Blair's dance committee? Elijah went to check out the committee room."

"Not a bad call," Alice says.

"Let's think this through—the connection with the Spring Fling, I mean—and see if there are any other meanings or associations we can come up with," Susannah says.

We all look at her.

"Weeell, the first thing you need for a dance is a date," Mary says.

"Says you," Alice says, and Susannah gives her a warning look.

I pace. "Jaxon asked me to go with him. And now he's under a love spell because of that bracelet sold to him by the *dance committee*. So there's one connection. What else?"

"You would need a costume," Susannah says, and we all look at the white box that the emerald gown came in like it might come alive.

"We thought that specifically had to do with Myra," Alice says. "But maybe not entirely?"

I rub my forehead. "Music? There needs to be music to dance to," I say. "But there hasn't been any music that . . ." I freeze.

"What?" Mary asks. "You just figured something out, didn't you?"

"I don't know why I didn't think of this before," I say.

"The very first time you guys came over . . . Mary, you turned on the record player in my ballroom with that old-timey music. We were talking about taking pictures here before the *dance*." My voice is fast and nervous. "And then I left the room because . . . Holy hell, that was also the day I got the dress."

"Okay. This is good. This makes sense. We need to go look at that record player," Alice says.

"We can't yet. My dad and Mrs. Meriwether are in the ballroom right now."

Susannah's eyebrows push together. "What are they doing in there? Will they be long?"

"You know, I don't know. They're almost never in there. I just assumed they . . ." My voice trails off and I look at Alice. "Wardwell called my house. Jaxon came over ranting about you guys. And for unknown reasons my dad is now in the room with that record player? No such thing as coincidences."

I dart out of my room, the girls at my heels, and toward the ballroom. The second we enter the downstairs hallway, there is a scratching noise, followed by the low hum of orchestral music. My heart jumps into my throat, and I break into a sprint.

We barrel into the room full speed only to stop dead in our tracks. The record player is on, and my dad and Mrs. Meriwether are slow-dancing. The whole scene has a displaced eerie quality to it, like a dead animal in the middle of a vibrant garden.

"Dad?" I say, running up to them, but he doesn't answer.

"Mrs. Meriwether?" Susannah says at the same time.

Silence.

I pull on my dad's arm, but they just keep turning, slowly and methodically, like they can't hear me or see me.

"Dad!" I yell, my voice cracking.

Alice claps her hands by their faces, but it's as though we don't exist. I can't help but think of that time I went to the *Titanic* and managed to take the spoon—I was there and not there at the same time.

I yank my sleeves down over my hands and grab the record from the old gramophone. I break it over my knee. But it makes no difference; even without the music, they continue to slow-dance.

"Dad, please. It's Sam. Just look at me." My voice is verging on desperate.

"You guys need to see this," Mary says from the floor, next to the record I just broke.

"Elijah!" I yell as I bend down.

We crowd around Mary. The record title is "Nearer, My God, to Thee." My heart beats wildly.

"Samantha?" Elijah says, looking from the record to my dad and Mrs. Meriwether.

"We learned about that song in history class," Susannah says. "It's—"

"The one that's famous for playing while the *Titanic* sank," I say, finishing Susannah's thought.

"Where is the jacket? The record jacket," Elijah says with urgency.

I open the cabinet with my cloth-covered hands and grab at all the records, spilling them onto the floor. I push through the messy stack and land on the empty cover for "Nearer, My God, to Thee." I flip it over.

The girls lean closer to read the lyrics on the back.

> *Though like the wanderer, the sun gone down,*
> *Darkness be over me, my rest a stone;*
> *Yet in my dreams I'd be nearer, my God, to Thee.*

"The message from my bones," Alice says in disbelief.

"The whispers from that spell we did," Mary says.

"We need the spell book and the dance card," Susannah says, and Elijah blinks out.

I pick up the record jacket, turning it over again. Something shifts inside. "Hang on, there's something else in here." I pry the jacket open and shake it. A heavy piece of stationery falls to the floor.

Alice hovers over my shoulder, and Elijah blinks back in with the spell book and the dance card, placing them on the floor next to us. I carefully unfold the stationery.

Dear Miss Samantha Mather,

Your presence is requested at the clock on the Grand Staircase within the hour. Sign your name to the dance card and I will take care of the rest. If you have doubts as to the urgency of this invitation, I suggest you consult Redd, as you are wont to do. Kindly appear within the hour, or I fear I will not be the only one who is disappointed.

I search Elijah's face for an answer. He looks as panicked as I feel.

"It's a threat," Susannah says.

My stomach clenches, and I look at my dad and Mrs. Meriwether. *Who exactly is threatening me? And with what?* "An hour. We only have an hour."

"Why Redd?" Mary asks. "Does this have something to do with what she told us?"

"I don't know, but between this letter and the trance, we need her," I say. "She knows way more about magic than we do. I don't see any other way with the time we have."

"I agree with Sam on this one," Alice says. "This letter suggests Redd might know something we don't."

I stare at my dad's vacant expression. "I'll go get her."

"I'll drive—" Alice says.

"No," I say. "The letter was for me. Stay with Susannah and Mary and the spell book. Try to figure out how to break the spell on my dad and Mrs. Meriwether. I'll bring the dance card. Redd's place is only a few blocks away. I'll get there just as fast if I run."

"You shouldn't go alone," Mary says.

"Elijah will be with me." My voice is stubborn. "Please, just figure out how to help them."

I run toward town the back way, Elijah by my side. We head up a narrow alley behind Redd's building.

Elijah stops in the shadows.

I turn around. "What are you doing? We don't—"

"I cannot follow you," he says.

"You mean into Redd's protected room? I—"

"Samantha, you must ask her to allow me in, to adjust her spell," Elijah says. "Or bring her out of that room so that I can hear what she says."

"I'll do what I can. It all depends on time." I turn, but he touches my arm.

"Promise me you will not sign that dance card while you are in there."

I look at him. "I'll do everything I can not to."

He takes a step toward me. "Promise me."

"Elijah . . ."

"Samantha, you know as well as I do that if you sign that dance card, you will be putting yourself under another spell."

"Believe me, I have no desire to sign it. But I also have no idea what I'm being threatened with. You remember Redd's warning. You saw my dad and Mrs. Meriwether."

"Still, you must not sign it," Elijah says.

My mouth opens in disbelief. "What are you even saying right now?"

"If there is danger, we will find a different solution," he says.

"With what time?" I say much louder than necessary.

"If you sign that card and go to that ship, I cannot protect you. What if whoever threw you overboard succeeds this time? What if Redd's warning was about you?" His intense eyes hold mine. "If you die there, Samantha, you could get trapped just like all the other souls."

Suddenly it's hard to breathe. I know he's right.

"If you sign that card, I might never see you again. There are many things I can endure. But that is not one of them." For the first time since he came back, he feels like the old Elijah. And it hurts.

I step backward. "Don't you dare say something like that to me right now."

He doesn't flinch. "I am saying it."

"You've been here for months without a word. You gave me no explanation. And now you . . . you just can't."

"I am aware how unfair it is to say these things to you. But this is more important than being fair," he says.

I shake my head. "I don't buy it. You're suddenly worried about being around me after months of . . ."

Elijah moves close to me, his gaze focused and insistent. "You asked me if I had the opportunity to pass on with my sister. I did. But I did not take it. There was never a question of my leaving, knowing you were still here."

I'm at a total loss for words. It feels like someone is tearing my heart in two.

My phone buzzes. I break eye contact with him.

Alice: *Update?*

"Time is running out," I say, and force myself to turn toward Redd's door and away from his demanding eyes. "I need to go." My voice is barely a whisper.

I grab the handle. It immediately twists in my palm. Redd would never leave her door open, would she? I slip inside, closing the door behind me and closing Elijah out.

"Redd!" I yell, and my voice cracks.

There's no answer. I follow the zigzagging wall to the curtain and push it open.

Redd is on the floor, blood leaking from what looks like a knife wound in her chest.

"No!"

I press two fingers into her neck. No pulse. She holds a silver pen in her hand. The room spins. The words of the invitation come rushing back to me: *Sign your name to the dance card. . . . I fear I will not be the only one who is disappointed.*

Panic throbs in my temples. Redd told me not to come back here. She said she was serious. Did she know this would happen? Is this my fault?

I look down at Redd's still face. I can't let this happen to someone else. What if my dad and Mrs. Meriwether are next?

Me: *Get me out of here and call 911*

I grab the dance card out of my hoodie pocket, not bothering to cover my hands with my sleeves this time. The blood on my fingers tints the cream pages. There is a pull to it, like the dress but stronger. I scan the room, but there's nothing to write with other than the blood-soaked pen in Redd's hand.

I take it from her and sign my name on the top line.

CHAPTER FORTY-FOUR

Follow Me

I smile at the bronze cherub statue and start up the Grand Staircase. I take each step slowly so that I don't trip on the hem of my green silk dress. The main landing is directly ahead. Above it is a huge wrought-iron-and-glass dome, from which a chandelier hangs.

I stop on the platform next to the elaborately carved clock. It depicts two angels. *Honour and Glory Crowning Time. Someone told me it was called that. Or maybe I read it somewhere?*

I scan the stairs above and below me. I'm meeting someone, but for the life of me I can't remember the details.

"Twelve steps, just as I said!" Uncle Harry says to Mr. Stead and the two generations of Jessups as they approach the bottom of the staircase. His voice is bright, and he holds an amber-colored drink. I smile down at the group of men, but they are too caught up in their conversation to notice me.

"But I ask you, my dear fellow, does the Grand Staircase

not include *all* the levels?" Alexander's father asks, sweeping his hand up and down dramatically.

My uncle turns to Mr. Stead. "What say you? Is the Grand Staircase the entirety of the stairs, or is it this, the dome, clock, and cherub? Symbolism or literalism? This should be an easy answer for a writer."

Mr. Stead scratches his white beard.

"Come now, think carefully. Can you take the legs from a horse and still call it a horse?" prods Alexander's father. He holds a wad of money in one hand and a drink in another.

I laugh. They're gambling, no doubt. Aunty Myra would be furious if she knew. But I'm not going to tell her. They look so happy. And it's a wonderful, sparkling night. Who am I to spoil their fun?

Alexander looks up and sees me grinning down at them. I immediately look away. I don't want him to think I'm staring. But when I look back, he's walking up the stairs toward me.

Alexander bows, his blue eyes twinkling. "How is it that you are all alone this evening, Miss Mather?"

"I'm meeting someone," I say, although I'm not sure why since I can't remember who it is.

"Would that someone mind if I borrowed you for a stroll?"

I scan the people at the bottom of the staircase again, where Uncle Harry, Mr. Stead, and Alexander's father still argue.

Alexander smiles. "They won't even notice if you and I wander off. They have been at it all night. Holed up in the smoking room, where the women will not reprimand them." He laughs. "Next they will be betting how many portholes there are."

"Do you want to go outside?" I look up at the railing above us. "I would love to get . . ."

Bruce Ismay approaches the balcony and leans over it, scanning the people below. By his side is someone who looks familiar. He wears a butler's uniform and is strangely unshaven. Young, maybe early twenties. *How do I know him?*

The unshaven man and I make eye contact, and my heart beats a little faster. *Why am I nervous? Everything is wonderful.* He looks from me to Alexander. He says something to Ismay, and they turn around and walk away.

"Wait," I say. I lift my dress in one hand and run up the stairs.

When I reach the higher landing, they're gone.

Alexander rushes up the stairs behind me. "What happened? Are you well?"

"I know that man," I say, not sure how to explain the odd feeling that I need to talk to him.

I walk to the nearest door and open it. It leads out onto the boat deck. The air is only lightly chilled, and there's a warm breeze. The water laps in the distance. No Ismay. No unshaven butler.

Alexander steps in front of me. "I must insist that you tell me what is going on here. You are acting as if something is wrong, of which I can see no cause."

I look at him. "You're right. I don't know why I did that. I just felt this strange urge to talk to that man."

"I am that boring, eh?"

I smile at him. "You're not boring at all and you know it. How many other passengers bribed their way onto the ship to get away from their horrible aunts?"

"Well, when you say it like that . . ." He grins. "So, Miss Mather. Shall we take that stroll? Or would you like to continue to chase unknown men around the ship?"

I laugh. "You make me sound like a lunatic."

"Your words, not mine."

I push him playfully. "I do want to take that stroll, but . . . You know Bruce Ismay, right?"

He laughs loudly. "Of course. Everyone does. You want to *stroll* with Bruce Ismay?"

"Obviously not. I just want to talk to him or, well, someone he's with. Do you know where he'd be?"

"Most likely the lounge or smoking room. Unless he retired for the evening." Alexander sighs. "Come, I will take you to look for him. But if he is not there, you owe me not one stroll, but two."

I smile. "Agreed."

He offers me his arm and I take it.

A crew butler opens the lounge door for us and we walk inside. I scan the happy socializing people.

"There, Samantha," Alexander says, and nods toward a group near the large fireplace. Aunt Myra, Mrs. Brown, and someone I'm pretty sure is the Countess of Rothes sit on plush couches. Standing by their table are Bruce Ismay and the unshaven butler.

I stop short. Seeing them with my aunt feels wrong, uncomfortable.

Alexander stops with me. "Now that we have found him, you look positively glum."

"I don't know. I just have this bad feeling."

He squeezes my hand. "Nothing bad is going to happen to you while I am here."

I nod at him and start walking again. *Why am I acting so strangely? Alexander probably thinks I'm neurotic.*

Aunty Myra spots me and waves me over. "Samantha, come join us. Mr. Ismay was just telling us some fascinating facts about this ship."

I approach the group with Alexander at my side. "Oh?"

Aunty Myra smiles.

Alexander bows to them. "Ladies. Ismay."

Ismay wears a smug grin. "If you lovely ladies are interested, I can surely convince Captain Smith to give us a tour of the bridge. I saw him not twenty minutes ago in the smoking room."

I look from him to his unshaven butler. What's going on here? He's taking them on a tour? I don't want him to. I really don't want my aunt going anywhere with that butler. I can't even pinpoint why. It's just an instinct, a powerful one.

"This very moment?" asks the Countess of Rothes.

"I always say there is no time like the here and now." Ismay sounds like he's showing off.

Mrs. Brown puts down her sherry. "Why not? It might be good fun."

"No." My voice is too loud and too fast. They all turn to look at me.

Alexander steps forward. "I think what Samantha is trying to say is that it is late."

My aunt smiles. "You are both sweet to worry, but really, a little exploring never hurt anyone. Besides, we will get a good view of the stars."

"Excellent," Ismay encourages.

My aunt, Mrs. Brown, and the Countess of Rothes all stand.

Anxiety rises in my chest. *No, no, no.* I push Ismay with both hands. "You will *not* be taking my aunt anywhere, especially not with him!" I point at the butler.

The women gasp.

Ismay brushes off his suit where I pushed him and frowns. "Miss Mather, I cannot imagine what I have done to upset you so. I was just offering to show them the bridge because they expressed interest in how the ship runs."

"Samantha, that was unquestionably rude," my aunt says. "You owe Mr. Ismay an apology."

I look at their shocked faces, and embarrassment flames my cheeks. I don't have a reason—nothing other than a feeling. They were all having a nice night, and I came along and caused a scene. *There's something seriously wrong with me.* "I'm terribly sorry, Mr. Ismay. I don't know what came over me."

"It is my fault," Alexander says quickly, and everyone shifts their focus to him. "You see, we were reading a book earlier with a scene quite like this one. A comedy, you know. And we were laughing about what it would be like if people actually did things like that in proper society. I said that if I ever met a girl with that much nerve, I wouldn't waste a second. I would propose to her then and there."

Did I just hear him correctly? My already-red cheeks deepen their blush.

The women's shocked faces soften. The angry group is suddenly alive with oohing and aahing.

"How romantic," says the Countess of Rothes.

Aunty Myra brings her hand up to her mouth. "Of all the curious surprises. And to shock us all like that."

"The creativity of the young," Mrs. Brown says.

I look anywhere but at Alexander. Did he just propose? Or did he just save me from my worst social blunder ever?

Alexander laughs. "You will have to forgive us for the abrupt exit, but I would like to speak to Samantha alone—with your permission, Mrs. Harper."

"Of course!" she says.

"Follow me," he whispers in my ear.

CHAPTER FORTY-FIVE

Somewhere Between
Excitement and Fear

Alexander unlocks a cabin door.

"You want to talk in your bedroom?" I ask, my voice somewhere between excitement and fear.

He turns to me, slightly startled. "It is a suite, the largest on the ship, with a sitting room and a private promenade. I would never presume to take you into my bedroom. But if you are uncomfortable, we can surely go somewhere else. I just thought a private moment might be nice."

"Of course. I'm sorry. I didn't mean . . . I guess I'm just nervous."

He opens the door. "Nervous good or nervous bad?"

I step into a beautiful sitting room with elaborate dark wood paneling, a fireplace, and a plush seating area. "That depends on what you say next."

He smiles at me with his clear blue eyes, and my stomach drops. He gestures toward the couch. "Can I get you anything to drink?"

"Sherry would be lovely," I say as I take a seat. I'm not entirely sure why I said that. Do I even like sherry?

Alexander walks over to a set of crystal decanters and pours a reddish brown liquid into a crystal glass. He hands it to me and takes a seat next to me on the couch.

"What did you want to talk about?" I sip my drink; it's sweet and strong and tastes slightly of cherries.

"What do you want, Samantha?"

"Want?"

"In the whole world, I mean. If you could have anything, what would it be?"

I meet his eyes. It's a strange question, but somehow it feels relevant right now, like I was just thinking about this very topic. "Well, I would like for things to be less complicated . . . simple and happy. Yes, I want to be happy. But I think that's what everyone wants."

"Do you think you could be happy with me?"

I sip my sherry. "What you said in the lounge. The story you told them. Why did you say it?"

"To get you out of your situation, of course."

"Oh." My chest deflates, like when you make eye contact with someone and then realize they're actually looking at the person behind you. "You embarrassed me in front of my aunt and Mrs. Brown. They all thought . . ."

He grins. "No. You embarrassed yourself in front of those women. I saved you."

I stand up, more humiliated than I've ever been. "Thank you for the sherry. I have to go."

He stands up, too, blocking my exit to the door. "You said I was too young to get married."

"I know what I said."

"And you are younger than I."

"Also known by me." I put my sherry on the mantel and push past him.

He grabs my hand. "But maybe we are not too young."

"What?" I turn to look at him.

"Maybe there is a reason that I left my aunt's, that I didn't like any of the girls she introduced me to. That I am on the *Titanic* and so are you."

My heart pounds, and I wonder if he can feel it through my hand. "Are you saying you want to marry me?"

"Would you say yes if I am?"

I warm from his words, from the pull of them. "Yes," I breathe.

He places my hand on his chest and wraps his arms around my waist. He looks down at me. "Then I am asking."

My body presses into his. "And I am accepting."

He leans his head down and gently places his lips on mine. They're warm and strong.

He releases his hands from my waist. "I have something for you."

Alexander turns on a record player, and soft orchestral music fills the room. But instead of being soothing, the song grates on my nerves, like it's associated with a bad memory.

He opens a velvet box with a beautiful diamond ring inside. "Will you have me as your husband, Samantha Mather?"

My heart flutters. "Yes, Alexander Jessup, I will."

He takes the ring out of the box and slides it onto my finger. It sparkles in the candlelight. The anxiety from the music melts away, like an echo in the back of my mind.

He smiles so big I get lost in it. He places my arms around his neck, and slowly we turn. "I told you that you would dance with me before we reached New York. I believe you lost the bet."

I laugh. "What'll you do with your victory?"

"Claim my prize."

"Oh yeah?"

His smile is mischievous.

"What?"

He pulls me over to the record player and hands me a silver dance card with lacy engraving and a ship on the front. *I was just talking about a dance card, wasn't I?* I look from the record player to the dance card. It all feels familiar, and not good familiar.

He frowns. "You don't like it? I'm sorry. I thought you would find it romantic. It's silly." He reaches for the dance card.

"Wait." I stop his hand. "It *is* romantic." I smile at the insecure look on his face. "I want this dance card, and under no circumstances will I give it back to you." I pause. "In fact, if you don't sign it, I'll be severely disappointed."

He grabs a silver quill-tipped pen off the desk, beaming. I open the dance card to the first blank page.

He takes a small pocketknife from the table, flips it open, and pricks the end of his finger. A bead of red appears. He dips the pen in it and writes his name largely over the entire "Engagements" section.

"Alexander! Blood? Really?" I watch him. *Blood? Knife, dance card, record player, pen.*

He frowns. "I want to be with you forever. Do you not want the same thing?"

I touch my forehead. "I just . . . There is something I can't remember. Something right at the edge of my thoughts. Does that ever happen to you?"

He takes a step forward and runs his hand along the side of my neck. He kisses where his fingers just were. "Do you want to be with me?"

"I do."

He pulls my sleeve off my shoulder and kisses my bare skin. "Do you love me?"

"Yes."

He kisses me right under my chin. "Then sign your name," he whispers in my ear.

My collarbone tingles and my hand goes to it. My fingers find something small and metallic. I look down at it. *A broom necklace?*

Alexander holds my other hand in his and pricks the tip of my finger with the knife.

"Couldn't I just write my name in ink?" I ask.

He puts the knife down on the table. "Blood means more. Blood cannot be broken."

I look at my finger with the droplet of blood on it, and he hands me the pen. An image of blood on my hands flashes before my eyes. *Music. Record player. Dance card. A broom necklace. A pen. Blood. Blood-red . . . red . . .*

"Redd," I say, and the second her name leaves my lips, I feel different. Strange, like my mind is a cloudy sky starting to clear.

Something odd flickers in his eyes, and Alexander pushes the pen closer to me. "Sign, Samantha."

Another cloud moves. "Alice," I say.

"Who?"

"Alice. She gave me this necklace." I look at him, with his perfectly combed hair and his shining hypnotic eyes. I hope he can explain what I'm saying to him. I don't quite understand it myself.

For a brief second he appears worried. "I'm afraid I do not know her."

I look down at my necklace. "Alice is close to me. A friend maybe. A friend from New York?" I roll the necklace between my fingers. "Not New York. That's not right. I know her from somewhere else."

"Samantha, please, this night should be about us, not about friends and the past," Alexander insists.

I hear the agitation in his voice, and I want to agree with him. But I can't let it go. Something about the necklace is pulling at me. "Salem?" The moment the word leaves my lips, thunder rattles my cloudy memory. "Salem," I say more definitely. "I live in Salem."

"Your family is from New York," he says, taking a step closer. His gaze is focused and intense.

I'm ruining this moment, aren't I? "Yes," I say. "Of course." I pause. "What's wrong with me, Alexander? I feel like my mind is being pulled in two directions. Half is here with you and half is somewhere else."

He takes my hand in his. "There is only a small divide between excitement and fear. You just need to focus on what makes you happy. You are happy here with me."

"I am happy. Very happy."

He gently lifts my hand and dips the pen in the blood on my fingertip.

I lay the dance card against the edge of the record player. He hovers next to me.

The song fades, and the record slowly spins to a stop. I examine it for a moment. "Nearer, My God, to Thee," I read out loud.

Alexander guides my hand to the paper.

"The song that played when the *Titanic* sank?" I say. And suddenly there's a flash of a beautiful room with a record player on a cabinet. Two people dancing. A note.

"Do not say that, Samantha," Alexander says, his eyes tensing. "We are on the *Titanic*. Do not say that."

More images appear in my mind—a stack of note cards with the words "Body not found," a little girl in braids, a painting of my aunt, a small box with a broom necklace, my dad hugging me. *My dad.* I take a step away from Alexander.

"My name is Samantha Mather," I say. "I live in *Salem*." As clear as day I remember sitting in a circle on the floor of my spare bedroom doing a memory spell. *Through my sisters' eyes and my own, the seed of memory is firmly sown.* And with that moment the rest of my memories come rushing back. "Alice *is* my friend. And the *Titanic did* sink."

Alexander's jaw tenses. "I told you to *stop* saying that."

I stare at Alexander. His once shining eyes look a normal blue.

He stares back at me, the tension between us thick.

I blink at him. Am I seeing this correctly? How could this be right?

"Matt?"

He flinches ever so slightly. "Alexander. I am Alexander here."

"Your accent . . . you're . . . American?"

He smirks. "You should take it as a compliment really, that I went through all that trouble to sound British. I put on my best show for you."

My mouth opens and I hesitate. "But . . . I didn't recognize you. I mean, I saw you so many times."

"The dress," he says, his words clipped.

"Wait, I don't understand. *You* put the spell on the dress?"

He nods like this should be obvious to me.

"Hold on, you're not saying . . . *you're* the one responsible for all this?"

He stands a little straighter.

Oh holy hell. What have I done? I said I would marry

him? I *kissed* him. I scan the room. The door is behind me. "How did no one know you could do magic? How did the Descendants not know?"

He scoffs. "That's the thing about the Descendants. They don't want to believe that anyone besides themselves *can* do magic. Hence the accent."

Well, that's true. "So you *pretended* to be an exchange student to come to Salem."

"I knew you were related to Myra. I had been looking for her for a long time."

Elijah was right; he couldn't find her himself. "You sent Ada, didn't you?"

"And you liked her."

I do. I do like Ada. "She's a person."

"You think I don't know that?"

"Well, you keep her here like a prisoner."

Annoyance flashes in his eyes. "I give her and all the rest of them the most beautiful ship in the world. Everyone here is *happy.* That's what everyone wants—you said it yourself."

My shoulders tense. "Fake happy. Entitlement and luxury are *not* the same thing. Just because you're alive and they're dead gives you no right to take away their choice. You're like the people who loaded the wealthy passengers first, as if they were more deserving of those lifeboats."

"Frame it however you want. Happiness is happiness. Tell me this isn't better than your world of Nikis and Blairs, where your father won't let you do magic, where your stepmother tried to hang you."

My mouth opens. I will punch him in his neatly combed head. "You don't get to judge the value of my life—or anyone else's, for that matter!"

"Oh yeah? I was with you the first time you came to the

ship. You barely even tried to remember your life in Salem. And how long did it take before you gave up on trying at all? One night, maybe two?"

My cheeks burn. "Because you put me under a *spell*."

"Admit what we both know, Samantha."

"How do you explain this, then? How do you explain me remembering myself in the midst of your proposal?" I almost choke on the word.

"I suspect the Descendants had something to do with that, although I don't know what. You wouldn't have done it by yourself," he says.

I study him. Could he be right that I wanted to be happy so badly that I didn't resist? "But Blair and Niki? Mr. Wardwell?"

He shrugs. "If I could put a spell on you, do you really think it was much trouble manipulating *them*?"

He had access to everyone. He lives with Blair. He's on the dance committee. He's been pulling the strings right in front of us. Susannah was right when she likened him to a serial killer who sends letters to the police. "You put Jaxon under a spell."

"You weren't focusing," he says.

"But you were working with spirits. . . . How did you . . ." It dawns on me. I'm as bad as the girls, thinking I'm the only one with special abilities. "You see spirits, don't you? You're *the* Collector that Redd was sensing?"

His prideful look returns.

The image of Redd bleeding on the floor fills my mind. "And now Redd's dead. . . . How could you!"

He breaks eye contact for a split second. "You know that is as much your fault as it is mine. You wouldn't let it go. *You* got Redd involved, not me—"

"Bullshit!" The word explodes from me. "Own what you did, Matt! You killed an old woman. You're trapping spirits against their will—"

"I said my name is Alexander here. I won't tell you again." He takes a fast step toward me.

I stand my ground. "My dad. My dad and Mrs. Meriwether. What did you *do*?"

At the mention of them the tension leaves his eyes, like he knows he's in control. "It doesn't matter now. Or it won't very soon. Your aunt was the last passenger we needed."

My mind spins. "You have all of them?"

"Every single one," he says with pride. "And everyone inside will remain inside."

Elijah's warning rings in my head. He plans on keeping me here? With all these spirits for the rest of time? No. I'm not doing that. I can't do that. "We? You said Myra was the last passenger 'we' needed."

"I thought you would have pieced that together by now." He laughs. "Maybe you're not as smart as I give you credit for. I'm not the first Collector, just one of them. I'm actually Alexander the Fifth. Building this spell and collecting these people took five generations of Jessups the better part of a century. Most people couldn't do something like this."

Redd's story about the Collector when she was a girl. My eyes widen. "It was your family's last name I would have found in the old Salem newspapers, wasn't it?"

He looks at me like he is trying to decide something. "You remember that story I told you about buying tickets off of someone to get on the *Titanic*?" He doesn't wait for me to confirm that I do. "That was Alexander the First. Only, he couldn't afford to barter his way to first or second class. He had carried his family's entire fortune with him to start a business in America. As you may have guessed, he never made it onto a lifeboat. And his family was financially ruined. His daughter died when his wife couldn't afford a doctor. His wife died shortly after of a fever. His son was adopted by the Wilder family and moved to America. He lost *everything,* including his name. But his son was old enough to remember, and he was determined to right the wrongs. He did his part, as did his son, and his grandson. And now it's my turn. I am going to give Alexander the pleasant journey he deserved."

For a second I just stare at him. Alice was right. They're trying to rewrite history. "So one family gets privilege and power"—I gesture at the lavish suite—"at the expense of everyone else? Don't pretend for a second that this isn't selfish. You say your ancestor *deserves* this? What about all those third-class passengers locked in the bottom of the ship? What do they deserve? What about free will? You're not—"

"Oh, come on. I see spirits, Samantha, like you do. You know how awful it is for them to be stuck throughout the ages, never passing on. This place is like a retreat."

"Do you even hear yourself right now? A ship that sank and killed fifteen hundred people is *not* a retreat. It's been more than a hundred years—this place is nothing more than a distorted time loop, a tomb. You want to do something? Help them all pass on, don't trap them here!"

Anger flashes in his eyes. "I'm not going to warn you again about talking about the *Titanic* like that."

"That's how you talk to someone you just proposed to? How confused are you?"

"You should jump the hell off your high horse, Samantha, and be *thanking* me right now." By the look in his eyes and the tone of his voice, I know he believes what he's saying. "You pulled that stunt in the lounge, questioning Bruce Ismay about the speed of the ship. It was Alexander who threw you over that night. Do you know how long it took me to convince him that I didn't need to kill you right away? To let me do things this way instead?"

A chill runs through my body. *Right away? This way instead? Please, Alice, Elijah, someone get me out of here.*

"Where are the other Jessups? Why have I only seen you and Alexander the First?"

Matt smirks like he's been waiting for me to ask this question. "They each maintained the spell until their deaths, and they passed on. The only way to stay here if you weren't originally a passenger . . . is to *die* here."

I look down at the silver dance card he wanted me to sign in blood.

Matt follows my line of sight. "That would have been the gentle way to go."

Three more seconds under his spell and I would have signed my life away. I glance over my shoulder at the door.

"Don't bother. Even if you get out of this room, you would never make it off the ship."

"That's what you think."

"That's what I *know*. Do you really think I could let you leave after you figured out what this place is? Who I am? You should have left it alone."

"So seal me out." Although the moment the words leave my mouth, I regret them. I can't leave these spirits trapped here for the rest of time and do nothing. I'd be as bad as him, assuming my life counts for more.

"It doesn't work that way."

I take a step backward. The room suddenly feels claustrophobic. "So your solution is to kill me?"

"I just want to help you transition," he says, like I've got it all wrong.

"Like hell you do. If it's so great here, *you* die and transition here."

"I maintain the spell, Samantha, and will for my entire life. I can't die until there's someone else to take my place. It was passed on to me when my father died in a car crash last year."

I grip the engraved dance card in my hand, my pulse impossibly fast.

"I'm trying to do this the nice way." The threat is clear in Matt's voice.

"Well, I'm not." I yank at the dance card, tearing the page.

He reaches for me, but I grab the knife he pricked my finger with. "Don't you even *think* about touching me again. I'm not under your spell anymore."

"You can't do magic here, Samantha, not without your physical body. And besides, you're part of the *Titanic*'s story now. You helped make this happen. You belong here and you belong with me." He's so confident that for a second I almost doubt myself.

Almost. I slowly back up toward the door with the knife held out in front of me. "No, I'm not part of the story. I never was. I don't belong with you, and I *definitely* don't belong to you. This ship isn't real!" I feel the doorknob against my back.

"I told you not to say things like that," he says angrily, his cool demeanor broken. "Unless you want to go headfirst into the ocean! I'm the best choice you have. You go out there, and it won't be only me. Alexander the First will hunt you down."

"I'll take my chances."

"But will you take a chance with your father and your neighbor?"

My heart skips a beat. What was that trance he put them under? "You wouldn't—"

"Like I didn't with Redd?"

I clench the doorknob so hard I'm surprised it doesn't crumble in my hand.

"Stay, and I will give you everything. Walk out that door and you will lose your entire world."

"My world isn't yours to take." I twist the knob and swing the door fully open. A breeze blows in. The air is noticeably colder than it was a half hour ago.

Matt lifts his hand, feeling the cold air that's blowing into the room, doubt shimmering in his eyes. "What did you do? Samantha, stop!"

He lunges at me, and I jab with the knife. It sticks an inch into his upper thigh. His eyes widen.

I don't hesitate. I run.

CHAPTER FORTY-SIX

I Would Go Headfirst into the Ocean

I make a sharp left, running as fast as I can away from Matt. My legs strain, and I hold both hands in front of me, pushing open the door to the staircase.

That last moment I spent with Matt loops in my mind. The look in his eyes when he asked me what I had done, the knife lodging in his leg. What did he mean, though? What *did* I do?

I run the short distance from the stairs to my room and burst through the door. "Mollie!"

She stands up from where she was mending a dress. "Miss, what happened? Yer in a state."

I grab her arm and pull. "We need to go somewhere that's not here."

She resists. "But the mendin' . . ."

"Mollie, please. We need to leave *now*. This is the first place he'll look. I'm in danger."

She drops her needle.

"Do you know of a place, an out-of-the-way place that no one goes?" I try to picture what I know about the *Titanic* layout. "Anything close by? A storage room, a pantry even?"

"Aye. There's a maid's pantry. It's only used durin' the day."

"Perfect."

I grab Mollie's hand, and we run. Luckily, we don't have far to go and none of the passengers are in the hallway to see us.

Mollie pushes through the door to the maid's pantry. I lock it from the inside.

"Miss, yer scarin' me. What happened?"

I grab Mollie by the shoulders. "Can I trust you?"

Mollie looks like I just kicked her. "How could ya ask me that? Ya know me better than most."

"That's the thing. I don't."

Mollie's eyes widen. "You do, Miss Samantha. I have been workin' with yer family fer a long time."

"No, you haven't."

She gasps. "I don't know what's got ya all fired up, but I think we should go see yer aunt. Ya don't sound well."

I look her square in the eye. "I just need to know if I can trust you."

"A course ya can!" she practically yells.

I assess her. "Good. Because I need your help. You know this ship better than I do. You know the back passages."

Mollie narrows her eyes suspiciously. "Miss, I do know the back passages. But I am not takin' ya anywhere until ya start tellin' me how yer in danger." She puts her hands on her hips.

"Matt . . . Alexander Jessup is trying to kill me."

She opens her mouth and closes it again. For a few seconds she's quiet.

"You don't believe me, do you?"

Mollie presses her lips together. "I'm not sayin' that. I'm just sayin' that it sounds a little odd, is all."

How can I possibly explain this to her with no time? Or convince her of who she really is? It breaks my heart that she doesn't even remember the fiancé she died trying to be with. I push my fingers into my temples. "You say we've known each other for a long time, right?"

She nods.

"Have I ever lied to you or sounded an alarm for no reason?"

Her eyebrows push together. "Well . . . no."

"Good. Then you have no reason to mistrust me now," I say. "Just give me a minute to think, Mollie. And then I promise I'll try to explain."

She crosses her arms. "I suppose a minute couldn't hurt."

I rub my forehead. *Think, Sam. What are you missing here?* Matt said that he couldn't die before he passed the spell off to someone else. Does that mean if he does die, the spell falls apart? I bite my lip. No, I'm hardly going to murder the person trying to murder me. And the chance of the Descendants or Elijah figuring out how to wake me up is pretty slim if they haven't done it by now. There's always the hope that they figure out who he is, but he wasn't even on our radar.

I pace. Okay, what else did Matt say? He got angry at me a few times. The first was when I said the *Titanic* sank. Actually, *all* the times he got mad at me, I was talking about the ship sinking or about the past. What if he wasn't getting angry that I was questioning the realness of his spell? I mean, he knows it's a spell. What if he was actually worried that my words could *affect* the spell?

I stop pacing. *He said "What did you do?" after he felt the cold air. He told me to stop saying what I was saying or I would go headfirst into the ocean.* I look up at Mollie. "Did you notice the temperature drop in the past hour?"

"I did. Why?"

"Has it ever been cold on this ship before, any other day you can remember?"

She considers my question. "A little cooler in the evenings, but never cold. The weather is consistently pleasant."

"What if the cold air isn't random?"

"Pardon?"

"What if I changed something?"

"I'm not followin'."

What if I challenge this place more? Could it tear the fabric of the spell? Maybe even break it? "Mollie, we need to go outside, somewhere that's secluded. I want to tell you a few things and see if . . . Actually, no. Where's my aunt?"

"In the lounge."

"Perfect," I say, and grab the lock on the door. I pause. "Before we go, can you promise me something?"

"What?"

"Can you promise me you won't let anyone, especially the Alexander Jessups on this ship, drag me off against my will, no matter how reasonable they seem?"

Her eyes widen. "What an incredible thing ta say. Like I would allow anyone ta drag ya off fer any reason."

"No matter how conflicted you feel."

She waves her hand at me, like I'm getting more ridiculous by the minute.

Good.

CHAPTER FORTY-SEVEN

To Follow Your Heart

I pull Mollie up the stairs as fast as she'll go and out onto the deck. There are people dressed in heavy coats milling about, enjoying the night. I speed-walk toward the lounge. Twenty feet from the door I stop and grab Mollie's arm.

"Mollie, I need you to think about what happened on the night of April fourteenth, 1912. It was something important. Something sad."

She blinks at me. "Miss? The fourteenth?"

"Do you remember?"

Her brows furrow.

"The *Titanic* sank," I say.

"Miss! What an awful thing ta say!"

Did I imagine it or did the temperature drop a tiny bit more?

"Your name is Mollie Mullin. You're from Ireland. Your family owns a general store in Clarinbridge. You told me that." I scan my surroundings, looking for Matt.

"Aye."

"But you didn't leave them to become a maid. You ran away with the guy you loved, a barman in your family's store. Your parents didn't approve, and so you planned to elope to America. Your brother chased you. But you and your fiancé got on the *Titanic*. You listed yourselves as brother and sister. Denis and Mary Lennon."

"Denis Lennon," she says. "Denis Lennon." Something in her face shifts. "Why do I know that name?"

Mollie shivers. The temperature definitely dropped that time.

I take her hand and push open the lounge door before the crew butler can do it. He raises an eyebrow at me.

"Miss, why do I know the name Denis Lennon?"

I pause. How long has she been separated from him, forced to play some role the Jessups designed for her? I soften my voice. "Think about what I said about how you ran away. Do you remember running? Do you remember getting on the *Titanic*? How it struck an iceberg? You were in steerage, Mollie. You weren't my maid." I take a breath. "You and Denis . . . died together."

Mollie looks startled. I know the fog of Matt's spell, how disorienting it is and hard it is to fight through. *Damn you, Matt. You can't do this to people.*

In the lounge, Henry, Hammad, and Mr. Stead are with my aunt and the other women near the fireplace. They laugh and smile and drink. The Jessups, though, are noticeably absent.

"Samantha!" Aunt Myra beams and beckons me to join them. The whole group turns to acknowledge me as we approach. "That ring! Henry, do you see that ring? Tell us the whole story. Do not spare a detail."

I look at my hand. I forgot all about that charade of a

proposal. *Shit.* I turn to my uncle and steady my voice. "How are you feeling, Uncle Harry?"

He smiles. "Exceptionally well, dear niece."

They all watch me, waiting for the story of my engagement.

"But I thought you had the grippe." The word sticks in my mouth with its foreignness. I look over my shoulder.

"Well, I . . . I am quite well." His eyebrows furrow.

"Do you remember when you got married?" I ask my aunt. "After you bought your first home near Gramercy Park? How you had that painting commissioned of the two of you?"

Aunt Myra puts her sherry down. "Yes, of course."

"Do you remember talking to me about it in the *attic*? My attic in Salem?" *Please, Myra. Remember.*

"The attic, dear?" Her confusion deepens.

"It was just a couple of days ago," I say quickly. "You were looking for Uncle Harry."

"Well, that does seem a little familiar." She hesitates. "No, it could not have been a couple of days ago. We were in Europe. I am not sure I know what you are trying to ask me. Does this have to do with your proposal?"

"I'm not engaged!" I say too forcefully. They all stare at me uncomfortably.

"She was just waiting for me to tell the story," Matt says behind me.

My legs tense.

He stops next to me and smiles, big and bright. Alexander Jessup I is with him. I take a small step backward.

"Alexander, you're limping," Mr. Stead says to Matt, and they all rattle off their concerns.

He holds up his hands. "I am quite well." Matt turns his smile to me. There is something else in his eyes, anger smoldering right under the surface. "It is an incredible story, actually. You would not *believe* how sweet Samantha is. When I got down on my knee and asked her, she said yes and fainted straight off. She fell right onto me with her glass of sherry. I sustained a small cut, but nothing to be concerned over."

They gasp.

"Of course, I caught her before she hit the floor. And she was not hurt, which is all that matters."

There are approving murmurs from the group.

"She wept when she came to, seeing me bleeding like that."

What is he doing? "I did *nothing* like that." My voice is barely controlled.

"Do not be embarrassed by romance, Samantha. It is one of the best things about human nature," Mrs. Brown says with kindness in her voice.

My hands clench into fists. How dare he manipulate me.

"And I will *not* tell you what happened after that," Matt says with twinkling eyes. "Because if Samantha feels shy about the fainting, she will absolutely feel shy about this."

Everyone makes agreeing sounds like it's all just so perfect.

"But I'm afraid the whole evening gave her quite a shock. She has not been herself since. I think she is in much need of rest," Matt says with fake concern. "You lovely people don't mind if I steal her once more?"

They look at me like I'm some poor frail girl and Matt's so wonderful. Even Mollie examines me more closely, like what Matt said might be true.

My heart beats a mile a minute. *You filled my world with the Titanic, Matt. Now watch me use it against you.*

I focus on Mrs. Brown. "You wondered how I knew so much about you the other night; you called me your fan. I am. The world is. At least, they are now, in the twenty-first century." She opens her mouth to say something, but I keep talking before she can get a word out. "You were born in a cottage near the Mississippi River. You didn't want to marry your husband, J.J., at first because he wasn't rich, and you wanted to be able to give your father a better life. But you changed your mind and decided to follow your heart. And it all worked out. J.J. was smart and ambitious. And when you *did* have money, you did the most amazing things for women and children. You made your life count by always giving to and doing for others. And when the *Titanic* started sinking, you helped passengers into lifeboats. You helped row your own lifeboat, and you were one of the ones who fought to go back and save the drowning passengers who were screaming for help. Much later, the newspapers nicknamed you the Unsinkable Molly Brown. But they were wrong. No one ever called you Molly; your nickname *was* and *is* Maggie."

Matt's hand wraps around my arm. I try to pull it back, but I can't without making a scene. And I need to look rational right now. Alexander I takes a step toward me.

Mrs. Brown's eyebrows rise, and the color drains from her face. "How could you possibly know those personal things about me?"

"The *Titanic* sinking?" Uncle Harry says. "Come now, niece. Maybe you have had a bit too much excitement tonight."

"It's my fault. We were drinking sherry to celebrate," Matt says. "The *Titanic* would not and could not sink. But do not fault my fiancée; if you cannot drink on your engagement night, then—"

"And you, Countess," I continue before he can turn the conversation. His fingers dig into my arm. "You are much the same kind of woman. Strong, kind. You raise money for people in need, especially for schools, hospitals, and women. You got your nursing training so you could better assist the Red Cross. And when the ship went down, you rowed your lifeboat, too. And encouraged everyone, to keep their spirits up. After it was all over, when people called you a heroine, you responded by saying, 'I hope not. I have done nothing.'"

The Countess of Rothes tilts her head, like she's considering my words.

"Maybe we have all had a bit too much to drink, eh?" Alexander I says.

"Guilty," Matt says.

"No." My voice is more insistent. "Mr. Stead. I took your spoon."

"My spoon?"

"My apologies, everyone," Matt says. "I should have insisted Samantha take rest. She was just so excited to tell you all."

"We understand completely how alcohol and a shock could upset someone," Alexander I says.

I talk over him. "In the café, Mr. Stead, that day you were having lunch and discussing President Taft's invitation. I took your spoon." My voice is edging on frantic, and now I do try to yank my arm out of Matt's grasp. "You published a story in the 1892 *Review of Reviews* called 'From the Old World to the New.' It was about an accident involving a White Star Line vessel and an iceberg. Everyone was saved. But that doesn't happen here. This is not that story. And when it really happens to you, and the *Titanic* sinks, you don't chase down a lifeboat. You sit quietly reading a book in the smoking room."

"I think this poor child is hysterical," Alexander I says. "She is clearly not well. She must be hallucinating."

Matt nods, like it's all very sad that I'm delusional.

Alexander I steps toward me. "I think we should take her directly. This is a most serious case." He secures my arms. The whole lounge has stopped to watch.

I try to pull away from Alexander I, but he's stronger and bigger. The women all look horrified, and my aunt has her hand over her mouth.

"Let go!" I shriek, but he drags me away. "Your dog!" I yell at my aunt and uncle. "Where is your Pekingese? Where is he? He was on board with you! He survived!"

Matt follows as Alexander I pulls me.

I dig my heels in, but that makes no difference. "The *Titanic* struck an iceberg at eleven-forty p.m. on April the fourteenth!" I scream to the entire room.

Alexander I clamps his hand over my mouth. "You put us in danger, all our years of hard work. Careless!" he says to Matt. "I will handle this from here."

Matt flinches. "She is unwell," Matt says loudly to the room. "She does not know what she is saying. Forgive her."

The ship lurches, and for a moment we're still. Still and quiet, like the engines stopped. Two crewmen throw open the lounge door, and bitterly cold air billows into the room.

Ismay comes through. "Everyone just keep calm now! We need you all to make your way out onto the boat deck."

The cold air . . . but I didn't think . . . the boat lurching, the engines stopping. I did affect his spell. I just never thought it would be like this. I make eye contact with Matt. His expression is panicked.

The next second stretches like everything is in slow motion.

Between the cold air, Ismay's announcement, and my words, the lounge passengers panic.

I yank and twist. Alexander I's eyes are threatening. He pulls a small knife out of his coat pocket. Fear blurs my vision.

Matt steps forward to block me from people's view. "Your father will suffer for—"

I lift both of my legs and kick Matt straight in the chest. He flies backward into a table.

"Mollie!" I scream. And she's there, swinging a crystal decanter at Alexander I's head. He falls.

Mollie grabs my hand, and we run through the crowd as fast as we can.

CHAPTER FORTY-EIGHT

No Matter What Happens, No Matter How Scary Everything Is

Mollie yanks me through a door and down a hall. We take so many twists and turns that I'm not clear where we are. Although I'm pretty sure we're a couple of decks down. I suck in air. She pushes through another door into a small staircase.

I pull her to a stop. "We need—"

"I remember Denis Lennon." Her eyes are fierce and her breath is heavy.

"When did you remember him? When exactly?"

"While ya were talkin' in the lounge. It came slowly. Yer words felt right. I began ta agree with 'em. And then suddenly I saw Denis in me mind. I remembered. I'm *dead*, miss." She glances nervously at the door. "And I remember the Jessups. I remember the young'un puttin' a spell on me and Denis. And how we both flickered and disappeared."

Mollie remembered, the ship is sinking, and yet we're all still trapped here? How is the spell still holding? *Oh no!*

"I might have made a mistake." I press the heel of my

hand into my forehead. Matt said that if I didn't stop talking about the sinking, I would go headfirst into the ocean. What if he meant this, that I wouldn't break the spell at all, just disrupt it enough to sink the ship and everyone on it? "We need to go to steerage, Mollie. We need help."

Her eyes widen. "The ship is goin' down. Steerage will only trap us. We'll wind up underwater in that metal cage again."

"Do you remember that little girl Ada? She's managed to blink off this ship a few times recently. She's the only one I know of who has. Well, the only one who would help us, anyway."

Mollie hesitates for a second, fear in her eyes. She looks at the door. "Nora will know which cabin is hers. We need ta hurry." And we're moving again. Fast.

My whole body strains forward, charged with adrenaline. Mollie winds us in and out of hallways and tiny passageways. We keep our heads down and our mouths shut. Crewmen are everywhere we go, handing out life jackets and knocking on doors. With each turn I scan every face, expecting to find one of the Jessups.

Mollie lifts a hatch, and we climb down a ladder into the ship's belly, emerging into a part of steerage I've never seen.

It's too quiet. The halls are practically empty.

"They're still sleepin'." Mollie's voice rings. "No one woke 'em!" She picks up her dress and runs down the hall.

There are no hordes of stewards handing out life vests here. These people weren't given a chance in life, and they're not being given a chance in death.

Mollie pounds on Nora's door, and I pound with her.

The door opens, and a squinting Nora stands on the other side. "What's all yer drummin' about? I was dreamin' of . . ." Her eyes focus on us and she frowns. "Sweet Jaysus. Ya two look like ya seen the devil."

"The ship's flounderin'," Mollie says.

Nora takes a step backward, like we physically hit her. "How long?"

Mollie exhales. "Soon."

"Nora, I need Ada," I say. "Do you know where her cabin is?"

"Aye. Down that way. Take yer first left, 'bout three doors farther on yer right."

And just like that, the girls in Nora's cabin are all moving at once.

I turn to Mollie. "Don't wait for me."

"But—"

"Get as many people as you can above deck!" I say as I run into the hallway. Groggy confused passengers are starting to wander out of their rooms.

"The ship is going down!" I yell as I pass the waking people. I'm met with surprised eyes.

One, two, three doors. I pound. No answer. I pound more.

A sleepy middle-aged man with a mustache and neatly parted hair opens the door and blinks at me.

Ada's father? "Is Ada here?"

He frowns. "Yes, miss. But it is the middle of the night."

"You need to get your family up and dressed. We struck an iceberg."

"Papa?" I hear from inside.

I walk past him. Ada slips out of the bed she shares with her sister. Her hair is in disheveled braids over her shoulders, and she rubs her eyes.

I steady my voice. "Ada, how did you get to me in that other place? You said when you took a nap, right? Through your dreams?"

She nods.

Ada's mother sits up. "Miss, we already checked, and the

man at the gate said the noise was nothing. That there was no need to be concerned."

"He did say just that," Ada's father confirms.

"He was wrong," I say. "I'm telling you. You need to get your family dressed and above deck. The *Titanic* is going down." I would never forgive myself if I not only sank this ship a second time, but sank it with Ada locked in steerage underwater for who knows how long.

I kneel down so that I'm at eye level with Ada. "How did you get to that other place, the one where you visited me, Ada?"

She frowns. "I do not know. It just happened."

"Do you think you could do it again? If you thought about that place, could you go there?"

Ada shakes her head. "I don't know."

"Ada, please . . ."

"They would have told us if there was a possibility of floundering," Ada's father says to me.

"They didn't. And there aren't enough lifeboats." My tone is forceful. "If you stay down here, you'll be flooded."

Ada's mother stands up and looks at her children. "Coats. Now!" They jump into motion at her words.

I hear Mollie's voice from the hallway, screaming for the passengers at the gate to break it down.

I grab Ada's shoulders. "Listen, Ada. This is important. Do you remember the guy you saw in my bedroom the last time you visited?"

She nods.

"His name is Elijah. No matter what happens, no matter how scary everything is, Elijah can help. The second you can figure out how to go to that other place, I need you to go to him. And I need you to tell him that the Collector is Matt Wilder. He'll understand."

Ada's mother slips a coat onto her.

Mollie appears in the doorway with wild eyes. "He's here. The oldest Jessup. I caught sight a him through the gate. He told the guard ta unlock it. He's comin' through."

"Go, Mollie! Take the ladder. Get to the boat deck. I'll be right behind you."

"Samantha—"

"Go!" And she does.

"Did you hear me, Ada?" My voice is fast.

"The Collector is . . ."

"Matt Wilder," I say.

"Matt Wilder," she repeats.

"Don't forget. Please, Ada, please don't forget."

I run out of the room. At the end of the hallway is Alexander I. And he's not alone. The drowned man is with him. They look right at me, and I sprint toward the ladder.

CHAPTER FORTY-NINE

I Need You to Remember

I grab the ladder rungs. My dress gets tangled around my feet. I scoop up the skirt and hold it between my teeth, looking over my shoulder. The drowned man and Alexander I run down the hall toward me. I climb faster, my heart in my throat.

A hand wraps around my ankle and yanks. I brace against the ladder and kick at the drowned man with my free leg. He loses his grip momentarily, trying to avoid my swinging foot. I hoist myself up to the final rung and scramble onto the upper deck.

I run through the narrow passageway and into a hall. The floors are starting to slant, and I'm headed downhill. I steal a glance behind me. The drowned man's right on my heels, but Alexander I is lagging. I bound up a staircase, taking the steps two at a time, and into another hall. The drowned man's shoes drum on the stairs behind me. *There's no chance of losing him when he's this close.*

I push through the door into the first-class dining room and sprint past the once-beautiful tables. I hear the door open behind me. I don't look back. The floor is strewn with broken plates that slid off the tablecloths. It takes all my concentration to maneuver around the fallen chairs.

I reach the Grand Staircase, my adrenaline raging, pushing me up and up and up. The drowned man keeps pace, step for step.

I run for the door to the boat deck and bang it open, hurting my hands. The icy air cuts like frozen razors. My legs strain against the incline, screaming from the exertion.

There are crowds on the deck. The band plays cheery tunes that compete with the fearful yelling from the passengers. There is only one lifeboat left that I can see. Mollie is by the edge of the crowd waiting for it.

"Mollie!" I scream. "Get help!"

She turns, and I run toward her. We make eye contact, and she looks past me at the drowned man. Her eyes widen. She doesn't move a muscle. His footsteps close in on my own.

"Mollie!" I scream again, pleading with her to do something, anything. But she just stands there, staring.

I sprint right past her.

Something crashes behind me loud and hard. I look over my shoulder, and the drowned man is lying on top of Mollie on the floor. I slide to a stop. *No!* She must have stepped between us and he knocked her over.

"Don't you touch her!" I yell, running back to them.

He pushes up off of her, his eyes locked on me. Mollie gets up, too. I spot an oar leaning against the wall. I grab for it, but his hand wraps around my wrist, pulling me back.

"Stop, Denis!" Mollie screams.

For a split second I freeze and so does he. *Denis? Not Mollie's Denis? How can that be?*

Mollie steps between us, yanking on his arm with all her might to get him away from me.

"Move!" he yells at her, pushing her away.

I try to pry his fingers off my arm, but he's too strong.

"Look at me, Denis! Look at me and tell me you don't know me!" Mollie yells.

His eyes flicker with uncertainty.

"You're *my* Denis," she says with so much emotion that he does look at her. "I ran away from me family and everyone I loved ta be with ya! They said we couldn't be married. Me brother chased us all the way ta the harbor. Do ya remember? I need you to remember me. Please!"

His eyebrows push together like he's struggling to concentrate. His grip loosens ever so slightly, and I pull my arm away, taking a few steps backward.

His eyes move from Mollie to me.

She grabs his face, forcing his focus back to her. "Ya couldn't even stop ta shave," Mollie says. "We got on this ship by sheer Irish luck. I chose *you*. I chose ya over all me family and everythin' I've ever known."

The hardness in his expression melts away. "Mollie?"

And she starts crying, big heaving sobs.

He wraps his arms around her. "Don't cry, me love. Don't cry," he says. But he's crying, too. And hugging her so tightly it's a wonder she can breathe.

The floor beneath us tilts more and we all stumble.

"We need to get to higher—" An arm wraps around my waist and cold metal presses against my neck. *Knife!*

"Time to go," Matt says in my ear.

No!

Mollie turns to me, fear seizing her expression. Matt pulls me backward and away from them.

"What've I done?" Denis says, and walks toward us. "Miss!"

"Stay where you are, Denis," Matt warns. "You already did what you needed to do. You brought her up here."

"No . . . I . . . Ya took Mollie from me!" Denis's eyes are wild. "Ya made me scare this girl." He points at me. "I didn't know what I was doin', who I was!"

Mollie inches her way over to the oar.

Matt steadily backs us away from them and toward the railing. I open my mouth to respond, but the knife pushes into my skin and I shut it again.

Mollie wraps her hands around the oar. Alexander I runs up the deck toward us.

"Mollie, take one more step and I will slit her throat," Matt warns.

Alexander I grabs Mollie, throwing her to the ground. Denis hits him. The floor tilts again and we slide. Matt grabs the railing, pressing my stomach into it and securing his hands on either side of me. The knife is still in his hand and precariously close to my side. The black water lies quiet and unaffected fifty feet below.

"Kill her!" Alexander I yells.

Mollie screams and Denis loses his balance. She, Denis, and Alexander I slide, grabbing at the slippery deck to no avail.

"Mollie!" *No no no!* I push against Matt, fighting him to release me. I grab on to the railing, turning my body around so that I can see him. "Stop this! The ship is going down! You need to let them go! Let them pass on!"

"And who made it sink?" he says accusingly.

People below us scream as they slide off the ship into the water. The deck slants even more now, and I clutch the railing. "Stop hurting them!"

"Is that what you want, Samantha?"

"Yes! That's what I want." My voice is heavy and angry.

"You want me to die?"

His words catch me off guard. "No. I want you to break the spell."

He shakes his head. "I can't let all these spirits go. My grandfathers spent decades collecting them, my father did, I did." His hand tightens around the knife and his voice is resolute.

I scan the deck near my feet for anything I can use to get away from him. There's nothing except slanted ship floor. My heart beats fast in my freezing body.

"So you're going to let these souls fall into this icy pitch-black water all over again? Can't you see how terrified they all are? They don't know they're dead—they think this is all really happening. And how long will you keep them there while you repair your spell? Months? Years? You and your family are so concerned with your own selfish needs that you took away their right to remember, to choose, to pass on. This ship isn't for these spirits, it's for a handful of egomaniacal warlocks!"

The deck tilts more drastically below our feet. Any minute now this ship is going to lift in the air.

Matt's eyes harden.

I try to move away from him, but there is nowhere to go.

The deck shifts again. Matt slides against me, shoving my back into the railing. The water is moving steadily up the deck, reaching for us. I look down at the panicked people, clinging to anything they can. There's nothing on the floor but some rope where the lifeboats were tied. My frozen hands strain to hold on to the railing.

He stares at me intently. My eyes flit to the rope and the water below. He lifts the knife.

I grab his wrist, but he twists his hand and the knife slices through my skin. I scream. Blood drips down my arm.

The lights flicker.

I hook my leg behind his and fling all my weight into his chest, throwing him off balance.

The force knocks the both of us loose from the railing, and we crash onto the slanted floor. And we're sliding quickly down the deck. I manage to roll off his chest and pull away, but he clings to my bloody wrist.

The sound of metal tearing comes from the bow of the ship. The lights go out. Screaming, there's so much screaming. A funnel breaks off and falls into the water with a huge splash, crushing the people below it.

I reach out as we slide past the rope, and I grab it with my uncut hand. We come to an abrupt halt, him hanging from my bloody wrist.

"Sam," he says, his eyes pleading with me.

I hold on to his wrist. "Break the spell, Matt! Stop all this!"

"No." His voice sounds smaller.

He's losing his grip on my slippery blood-soaked arm. His fingers slide down inch by inch. Even in the dark, I can make out the fear in his eyes. He falls.

"Saman—" he yells as the ship becomes vertical. But before he completes my name, he ricochets off a wall and slams into a pointed corner of railing. The sound of his bones cracking on metal fills my awareness.

I press my forehead into the rope and clench my body tightly around it. The loss of blood and the chase have robbed me of my strength. I slip down, bit by bit. Pain radiates through my icy skin. As the ship sinks faster and faster, the water rises steadily to meet me. Matt has disappeared beneath its bubbling surface.

The black water grabs at my legs like a million frozen teeth. I suck in air and down I go, still holding my rope. The water swirls around me in a whirlpool of suction. There is pressure on my ears. Down and down into a cold muffled world.

I let go and kick with everything I have. My blood mixes with the water, pulling heat from me faster than before. And everything is quiet—the screaming on the deck gone, the sounds of the dying blotted out. My lungs ache with desperation. *Dad.* I kick harder. *Elijah.* The darkness continues.

I want to take a breath. I have to. *Please.* Above me the darkness fades to gray. My lungs burn. From dark gray to medium gray. *Is that light?*

Each second rings out in pain.

I catapult into the lighter water, my body screaming at me to give in and stop struggling. A face appears, murky and getting closer. *Matt!* His arms reach out for me. His eyes are huge, and his mouth is open as he sucks in water. His fingers grab at me and he inhales. I push his hands away. His fingers go limp and his wide eyes stare—

My dad leans over me. "She's awake! Sam? Can you hear me?"

It smells like freshly baked cookies, and the ground is hard beneath my back. I stare up at the stone counters of Mrs. Meriwether's kitchen. Someone is crying in the background. Mary?

"Sam? Sam? Can you talk?" my dad pleads.

"Dad?" My voice is desperate. And there's pain. My limbs feel like blocks of ice.

Alice holds a cloth over my arm and is pressing down on it with both hands. There is blood all over her fingers.

Mrs. Meriwether kneels down next to me. "It's sterilized," she says, holding a needle. Alice lifts up the cloth, and as the needle heads for my skin, my vision blurs.

CHAPTER FIFTY

My Heart Beat

I squint in the dim light, trying to make sense of the furniture shapes. *My bedroom?* My temples pound like I have the worst hangover in the universe. And everything aches.

"Sam?" my dad says. He sits on my vanity chair right next to my bed.

"Dad?" My voice is scratchy and low.

Tension releases his shoulders. I rub my eyes and wince. My left arm hurts like hell. There's a big bandage wrapped around it. I sit straight up.

He catches my shoulders. "Whoa, take it easy."

"Dad, are you okay? Are you hurt?"

"Me? You barely make it out of some spell ship alive and you want to know how I am?" He shakes his head. "Sam—"

"Dad, I didn't use magic. I—"

"Wait." He holds up his hand. "Let me finish."

I close my mouth.

"I don't know if you realized, but I was conscious while I

was in that trance. I couldn't speak or react, but I could hear everything."

So he heard us discussing the spell, heard me speaking to Elijah, heard the girls doing who knows what type of magic?

"At first I was furious and kicking myself. I thought that if I had just taken you back to New York sooner, none of this would have happened."

I don't say anything. I wouldn't even know where to start.

"But, Sam, you should have seen the girls. Alice was barking orders. Mary was mixing some kind of memory spell."

My eyes widen. "They used a memory potion on me?"

"Practically doused you in it."

"It helped. I remembered who I was. I don't know if I would have otherwise," I say.

My dad nods. "Susannah was talking—or rather, writing messages—to someone named Elijah, trying to figure out how signature spells worked and how to break them. They dripped potion on that green dress and on the broken record."

"It must have been so weird for you," I say.

"No. It was heartbreaking. I realized that they were using a potion you asked Mae for days ago. That you and the girls wanted to mix the memory potion, and that you didn't because of me. I actually robbed you of the tools you needed to stay safe."

I pull at my fluffy comforter.

"You were right when you said that I didn't know what you knew," he says, an unusual heaviness in his voice.

"You were trying to protect me."

"But not in the right way."

I look up at him. "What are you saying?"

"I'm saying . . . I'm still not comfortable with magic. But Mae was right; you need to learn how to control it more than you need to run away from it. If you want to live in Salem, we can stay. I don't ever want to realize again that it was my own stubbornness that put my child in danger. I've learned this lesson twice. There won't be a third time."

Tears form in my eyes. "We can stay?"

"We can stay."

My door creaks open, and Mrs. Meriwether comes in, bringing the scent of warm sugar with her.

"I heard voices and I thought . . . My girl!" Mrs. Meriwether puts her hand over her mouth. "What can I get you? Are you hurting? Are you hungry?" She crosses my room in no time and cups my face in her hands. "Let me look at you."

I soak up her smile. "Jaxon . . . is he okay? Acting like himself, I mean?"

She nods. "And he's here. Jaxon and the girls. If you thought we wouldn't be keeping vigil until you woke up, then you thought wrong."

My dad squeezes my hand.

"How long was I out?"

"More than twenty-four hours," my dad says.

I guess all those nights of broken sleep finally caught up to me.

Mrs. Meriwether walks to my bedroom door. "She's awake!" she yells. "Come on up!"

Their feet are fast on the stairs and down the hall.

Mary is the first one in, with Alice and Susannah right behind her. Mary has traces of Meriwether crumbs on her face and starts crying immediately. "Sam, I was so scared. I didn't know what to do. A cut appeared. And your body temperature started to drop. You wouldn't stop bleeding. I just . . . You don't know . . . I was so scared. I'm just so happy you're okay."

I look at Alice. "Matt?"

"Dead," she says quietly.

"They found him in Salem Harbor with a broken back and crushed bones. The cause of death was drowning," Susannah says. "They can't figure out how it happened. It's all over town."

I shiver, remembering his knife and the look on his face when he dropped from my hand. I nod, pushing the image away.

"Redd?"

Susannah shakes her head, and everyone falls silent.

Jaxon appears in my doorway, and his face lights up when he sees me. "Sam." He smiles, and it's a real Jaxon smile.

"Okay, okay. Let's not overwhelm Samantha," Mrs. Meriwether says. "Do you want me to bring you food, honey?"

"Not yet."

They all exit my room, all but Jaxon, who looks anything but comfortable. He sits down in the chair my dad was using.

"That spell," I say.

"Yeah . . . Sam, I didn't know who I was, what I was doing. I just—"

"Believe me, I know. It's an awful, gross feeling."

Jaxon nods. "A nightmare."

We're both quiet.

Jaxon breaks eye contact with me. "I just don't even know how to begin to—"

"Jaxon, don't. You don't need to say anything."

Jaxon studies his hands. "Yeah, well . . . How do you feel about opening your get-well gift?" He looks behind him.

I follow his line of sight to a box on my vanity. "I feel great about that."

Jaxon reaches behind him and picks up a present wrapped in blue tissue paper. He places it on the bed next to me.

I pull back the paper, revealing a wooden box with a boat carved on the lid. The boat is a perfect replica of the one down by the wharf where we had our first real conversation. "The *Friendship*?"

"I made it."

I look up at Jaxon. "Stop. You did not."

"I did. Take it as a peace offering. I should never have gotten mad at you that night after the restaurant. That was totally unfair. And, well, everything after that sucked, too. There are a lot of things I wish I could take back."

I lift the lid, and inside the wood grain is smooth and beautiful. "Can we still have our trust arrangement?"

He smiles and it almost looks like his eyes glisten. "I'd really like that."

"Jaxon!" Mrs. Meriwether calls from downstairs. "Sam needs rest."

Jaxon stands up. "I guess that's my cue."

I lie back on my pillows and look at my present. Broome stretches his paws out from the blankets near my feet. He blinks at me and curls up.

I put the wooden box on my bedside table. There is a single lilac in the vase.

I sit bolt upright. "Elijah?" No response.

I pull my sore body out of bed, our last conversation, the one when I pushed him away, playing in my mind.

"Elijah?" I breathe.

"Samantha."

I whip around.

His expression is unreadable. "Ada gave me your message."
"She did?"

"Shortly after the spell was broken. And she gave me one for you in return. She insisted I memorize it and repeat it to her . . . three times." His eyes smile. "She said that her mother always told her that if you come across someone sad and you do not try to make them smile, then you have disgraced your own humanity. And that even though they did not know it, the passengers on that ship were sad. But you made everyone smile again. She said you would know what she meant."

I soak up his words.

He hands me a small stack of letters. "Some of the other spirits came as well before they passed on. They left these for you."

I peek inside the first envelope and see Mollie's name. I hug it to my chest.

"Also . . . Ada asked me if I was your boy."

"My what?"

"Your boy . . . like the one in Stella's diary, she said. And then she laughed at me."

My cheeks warm. "She found me sulking after you and I talked again for the first time and you apologized for kissing me."

He looks conflicted. "I was trying to—"

"I know. But I don't need you to protect me."

He raises an eyebrow.

"Besides, I'm not going to believe you if you say you're leaving this time."

"Indeed."

"So what now?"

He moves toward me, stopping so close that I'm sure he can hear my heart beat. He smiles, dimples and all. "Now . . . here we are."

"Indeed," I say, imitating his old-world accent.

"And I am not apologizing." He leans toward me, hovering over my mouth like a question. He gently presses his lips into mine.

I reach out and grab on to his shirt, ignoring my arm. His lips part mine, and our kiss graduates from gentle to insistent. He puts one hand on my lower back. My legs vibrate. He runs his other hand down my ear and over my neck. I press into him, melding my body with his.

CHAPTER FIFTY-ONE

This Is Who I Am

I sip sparkling pear cider and stand next to Alice, watching Susannah, Mary, and Susannah's girlfriend dance. The venue my school rented for the Spring Fling is decked out in luxurious *Titanic* decor. Green velvet chairs surround antique tables strewn with nautical napkins and flower displays in the shape of anchors. The walls are dark wood with bookshelves, and there is an enormous, blazing fireplace. The ceiling is covered with tiny lights that look like twinkling stars. A string band plays everything from modern to classical. Almost everyone is on the dance floor, with a few groups hanging around the food tables.

Everyone is dressed in *Titanic*-inspired evening gowns and suits. We, of course, are in all black. When people ask us who we're dressed up as and Alice tells them that "we're in mourning for all the passengers who were locked behind gates and never given a chance," there is an awkward silence, and then they walk away.

Jaxon catches my eye from the drink table. He's with Dillon, and they're both laughing so hard that Dillon is wiping at his eyes. I smile at Jaxon and he nods at me.

"Are you positive you're okay with all this *Titanic* stuff?" Alice asks, studying my face.

I must look a little emotional. It's hard to be here and not miss Ada and Mollie, my aunt and uncle, and all the others. To know the fate so many of the passengers suffered, how little chance most of them had of surviving. And yet, I know how lucky I am to have met them at all. "Yeah. I really am okay with it."

"If you say so," Alice says, but her tone is doubtful. She's been by my side all evening. I half think she's guarding me.

I turn to her. "Are you?"

"Am I what?"

"Okay?" There is something quieter about her since this whole thing happened.

She exhales. "Truth? I don't know. It was a close call, Sam. I didn't see what you guys saw about Niki and Blair. And I missed Matt entirely."

"I missed him, too."

"Yeah, but you had a spell on you not to recognize him. What's my excuse?"

I shake my head. "Alice, don't do that."

"It's hard not to."

"I'm serious. Don't do it. I did that with Vivian. Twisted it through my mind over and over. I hated myself."

Alice's eyes are strained, like she wants to believe me but can't quite.

"And when I couldn't come to terms with it, I tried to push it away. Bury the whole thing. Vivian, magic, you guys . . . everything." I pause. "You were actually the one who helped me stop. Did you know that?"

She lifts a surprised eyebrow. "When I yelled at you?"

"When you told me that I had the opportunity to do something and that I was being selfish."

"You were."

I smile. Leave it to Alice to insult me while I'm trying to cheer her up. "I've been thinking a lot about what you said these past couple of days."

"About teaching me how to see spirits?" Her icy blue eyes brighten.

"About getting over myself and *doing* something. When you got that message from your bones, you knew something horrible was coming. You came to me. But I was too stuck in my own head, worrying about my own problems."

Alice nods in agreement, but not in a judgmental way.

"There I was, watching Matt repeat the injustice of what had happened to all those spirits. Noticing how the accounts we were reading left out Ada and Mollie and so many others. And yet I didn't understand my role in it. I couldn't see what you and Redd could see, that something had to be done. And what wound up happening? Matt manipulated me and those spirits for his own agenda. Vivian, Matt. I'm not gonna let that happen again. It's time for me to make my own decisions about what I do with my magic, about who I want to be."

"Like helping dead people pass on?"

"Exactly." I take a good look at Alice. "It's up to us, isn't it? That's what you were trying to tell me that day you yelled at me. It's up to us to make sure this doesn't keep happening."

She smiles. A rare occurrence for her.

Mary bounces up to us, her curls in an elegant updo. "Oh no. Alice is smiling. What's going on?"

Alice looks happier than I've seen her in days. "I think we're starting a detective agency for the dead."

Mary's mouth opens. "I love it! We'll be like Sherlock Holmes. The hats, the capes, the whole nine."

I laugh. *What did I get myself into?*

"And Sam's going to teach us how to see spirits," Alice says.

Mary shivers dramatically. "No way. That's your deal. I'm good *not* seeing them."

Across the room an old woman with long salt-and-pepper hair sips tea and stares at me. *Redd?*

I put down my pear cider. "I'll be right back."

I weave through the dancing people, catching glimpses of her as I go. Just as I reach the edge of the crowd, she raises her eyebrows at me and blinks out.

I do a three-sixty, but she's gone. Maybe I'll start with Redd. Help her finish what she needs to so she can move on. That's the least I owe her for what she did for me.

I turn back around. Elijah is standing in a shadowed corner watching me.

"You know, I found a lilac on my bedside table this morning," I say, moving closer to him.

He's in a suit with his hair combed. It's unfair how attractive he is. "There is no scent in all the world more alluring." He offers me his hand. "May I have the pleasure?"

I slip my hand into his. "You may."

He wraps his arm around my body. I move slowly in rhythm with him, my face tilted up toward his.

"Elijah, do you ever think about the spell Vivian did that almost brought you back to life?"

"Every day," he says, and pulls me closer.

In my peripheral vision I can see people stopping to watch me dance with thin air. And I couldn't care less. This is who I am.

The *Titanic* letter that appears in *Haunting the Deep* has a fascinating story of its own, involving a long line of remarkable women from my family tree. It starts way back with my great-great-great-grandmother Maria (pronounced muh-RYE-uh) DeLong Haxtun, to whom the letter was written.

I've been able to track so many of my ancestors' adventures through Maria's robust and frequent correspondence—as far as I understand, she was quite the favorite in my family. (And I've got to say, reading all that gorgeous cursive makes me a little weepy that no one writes longhand anymore.) Maria received the letter recounting the fate of Myra Haxtun Harper and Henry Sleeper Harper—her cousins—shortly after the *Titanic* sank and the Harpers returned home safely. In addition to the *Titanic* letter, Maria also had a picture of Henry Harper in her possession.

Maria's granddaughter—my great-grandmother—Adrianna Storm Haxtun Mather (I am proud to be named after her!) preserved Henry's picture, the *Titanic* letter, and many newspaper clippings from 1912 related to the sinking. Adrianna was a teacher and an amateur historian, and labeled all the family heirlooms she collected over the years with notecards (hence the mention of notecards in this book and in *How to Hang a Witch*). The handwriting on the envelope containing the *Titanic* letter is hers, and so are the notes below Henry Harper's picture.

This personal slice of *Titanic* history might have lingered in a box somewhere collecting dust, except that my grandmother Claire Mather had the foresight to pass on all the family stories. When I was a little girl, she held my hand and talked me through the many heirlooms that had fallen into her care, breathing life into old portraits and Victorian wedding dresses stashed in trunks. Romance, intrigue, and grandiose apology presents were all well represented.

The funny thing is, there is so much history in my grandparents' home that you are just as likely to find a curious diary from the 1700s in the back of a button drawer as anywhere else. In fact, the *Titanic* letter was nestled among a stack of other old letters and newspapers in a desk. There was nothing to indicate that it was special besides the word "Titanic" written on a manila envelope. When I first stumbled across it, I thought, "No, not *that Titanic*. Couldn't be."

Also odd (or maybe kismet!) was that I discovered the letter right after Random House acquired *How to Hang a Witch*. Here I was with my first book deal *and* a letter about Henry

Sleeper Harper's brush with the *Titanic*—the same Henry who was the director of Harper & Brothers publishing house before it became HarperCollins. It seemed obvious to me that the next book I wrote should be about this letter and the incredible women who preserved it and handed it down through the generations.

Myra and Henry didn't do interviews after the *Titanic* sank, and as far as I know, this is one of the only written records of what happened to them that night in 1912. They were unbelievably lucky in that they both survived, along with Hammad Hassab, who was in their employ, and their dog. Their survival was likely only possible because Myra saw the iceberg scrape past her porthole and realized the danger. She quickly woke her husband, and their entire party was able to board one of the first lifeboats.

As it turns out, in the moments after the ship struck the iceberg, many passengers were nervous about getting into the lifeboats. They were being told to trade an enormous, luxurious steamer that they believed was unsinkable for a tiny boat that would be lowered by rickety ropes fifty feet into icy black water. Even when the threat of sinking became more obvious, there were a number of people who needed to be coaxed or pushed into those lifeboats. Perhaps because of this reluctance early on in the boarding process, the crew allowed a few men to accompany their wives. Henry was ill at the time, and it's possible that his weakened state, combined with the aforementioned hesitancy, played a role in his and Hammad's survival.

The more I thought about Myra and Henry's personal story and how they narrowly survived, the more I thought about people's survival in general. The passengers and crew on the *Titanic* came from all over the world and were from vastly different backgrounds. When Captain Smith realized the boat would likely sink in little more than two hours, he ordered the sixteen lifeboats filled with passengers and lowered into the ocean. The crew and company men knew that fewer than half of the people on board would fit into those boats. They had to make choices about whom to save, which resulted in the "women and children first" rule and was ultimately focused on those in first and second class. The passengers also made decisions, some supposedly fighting for spots, and others giving up their seats.

Manuel Uruchurtu, a lawyer from Mexico who made an appearance in this book, has one such story. He was seated in Lifeboat Eleven when a woman he didn't know pleaded to be let in because her husband and child were awaiting her in New York. He gave up his seat, only asking that she visit his wife and seven children in Xalapa, Veracruz. Manuel died, but she lived because of his generosity, and twelve years later, she visited his wife in Veracruz and recounted the tale.

Another group that made a huge sacrifice were the ship's coal workers. The on-duty men in the boiler rooms were the reason the lights stayed on until the *Titanic's* final moments; they shoveled coal into the boilers with little or no hope for their own survival. It's also likely that the off-duty coal workers and engineers assisted the pump operations, selflessly giving others more time to board the lifeboats.

There are so many heartbreaking stories of loss and kindness that it's impossible to tell them all in a fictional narrative. Not to mention the crew and passengers whose stories weren't recorded and are lost to us forever. This was something I really struggled with when I first started this book. I knew I couldn't do justice to all the people I wanted to mention with the space I had. And the more research I did, the more I discovered how many people weren't given the chance even to fight to survive. Nora, Mollie, and Ada are only a few of these. So in lieu of being able to honor them all, I aimed to highlight the mechanism of social privilege that played a part in who was given priority in the evacuation, and who was not. The working class, the immigrants, those whose cries for help went unanswered, make up the vast majority of the *Titanic*'s victims. And it's a social construct that still exists around the world—the privileged receive opportunities that the marginalized do not. While I can't go back in time and be a voice for the people who were lost the night the *Titanic* sank, we can all speak up now.

ACKNOWLEDGMENTS

In the beginning, there was My Pirate, James Bird, who stamped around, shaking his hands in the air and yelling, "That's not a plot! Get a plot and we'll talk." And then patiently encouraged me to revise it as many times as necessary. He makes me better, he listens, and he never stops believing in me.

Then came my wonderful mama, Sandra Mather, who supplied me with cookies and whose pride overfloweth at all my ideas, even the cockamamie ones. As long as she is in the world, I know that I have a safe place filled with love, fluffy pillows, and hot chocolate.

My grandparents Frank and Claire Mather taught me my history, and encouraged me when I decided to write wild stories about it. They are my inspiration and my heart. I couldn't do this without them. I only wish my father, Frank Haxtun Mather Jr., who loved our family history as much as I do, were here to see these books.

My agent, Rosemary Stimola, gently guided me toward skilled editors (yes, plural), who she knew, after many hours of labor and many pots of coffee, would be able to help. I am grateful every day that I get to spend with this fierce, loving, honest woman.

My editor Nancy Hinkel eased me, with great finesse, into paring down my prittle-prattle and replacing it with common sense. Her kindness and wisdom were a light in a storm.

And my editor Melanie Nolan, or rather my editor-detective, beautifully cracked the mystery of my plot and made it shine. She is artful with clues and such a joy. I'm her biggest fan.

My critique partners—Kerry Kletter, Kali Wallace, Jeff Zentner, and Audrey Coulthurst. They didn't stop talking to me after they read my first draft, they pushed me forward when I needed a push, and they are just the absolute best writing friends anyone could have. And Anya Remizova, who listened to me babble on endlessly about my stories and was always there for me.

My large and wonderful family—you all are so incredibly special to me and you never hesitate when I need you. You encourage my ideas and my chocolate habit, and boost my spirit. I could not and would not want to do any of this without you.

Alison Impey and Regina Flath hit a home run with the cover design. I am in awe of you both.

In fact, the entire team at Random House, who support my books in the most remarkable ways, never cease to bring a huge smile to my face. Barbara Marcus, you should have your own superhero character. Mary McCue, you deserve a tropical vacation for all the hours you've spent getting me in front of a microphone (which you also know needs to be pried from my sticky fingers once I get ahold of it). Kim Lauber and Hannah Black, without your brilliance in dressing up every bit of me, I'm sure I would be the emperor without clothes. Kate Keating and Cayla Rasi, you make me squeal like a schoolgirl with your awesome ideas. Adrienne Waintraub, Laura Antonacci, and Lisa Nadel, you represent the message and meaning of my stories, and I will always be grateful for that. Artie Bennett, Alison Kolani, and Iris Broudy, your amazing, detail-oriented minds are the finishing bow that makes all the difference. John Adamo, Dominique Cimina, Judith Haut, Trish Parcell, Aaron Blank, Rebecca Waugh, Katherine Punia, Jodie Cohen, and Emily Parliman, thank you for all the wonderful you bring to each of my books.

Clementine Gaisman, every time you pop into my inbox you bring a little piece of magic with you.

In all seriousness, every single person mentioned here and so many more are the beating heart of my stories. You mean the world to me, and I'm thankful every morning I wake up and realize that it's not all a dream. You make it possible for me to do what I love and have therefore given me one of the greatest gifts of my life . . . to freely be who I am. Thank you. THANK YOU.